CORAL COVE

BOOKS 5-8

CORAL COVE

JAX WILDER

CONTENTS

LOVE REWOUND

THE PERFECT LOVER SPELL

RED, WHITE, AND RAVISHED

HAUNTED BY HER

Published by Rainbow Quartz Publishing

RQPublishing.com

RainbowQuartzPublishing@gmail.com

Edmonds, WA 98026

This is a work of fiction. Names, characters, places, and incidents are either the product of the author's imagination or used fictitiously. Any resemblance to actual events, locales, or persons, living or dead, is entirely coincidental.

Cover design by Miranda Townsend

Edited by Miranda Townsend

First Edition: October, 2025

LOVE REWOUND

A BBF, SMALL TOWN, SLOW BURN,
SECOND CHANCE ROMANCE

LOVE REWOUND

Coral Cove Series

Jax Wilder

For Pattie

Jax Wilder

REWIND RENTALS WAS the last beacon of a bygone era in a world dominated by streaming services. The smell of aged vinyl and old VHS tapes greeted me as I stepped inside, a comforting reminder of the countless hours I'd spent here. This store was the place where the past wasn't just preserved—it was celebrated. We were one of the last video rental stores left, and I'd done everything I could to keep the doors open.

"Good morning, Amelia," Mia Jenkins called, the bell above the door jingling merrily as she entered. She came like clockwork, swapping her returns for fresh titles. She was always ready to chat about her favorite old movies and her love of monster movies in particular. The girl was a sucker for anything wolf-like.

"Good morning, Mia. Looking for anything special today?" I asked, sliding behind the counter.

"Just browsing," she said with a smile. "But you know I always welcome a recommendation if you have one."

"Well, that's good because I have two for you." I held up the first film. "*Wolves* came out in 2014 and is a lesser-known Jason Momoa film. He plays a werewolf wandering the Canadian countryside. It's sexy AF."

"Sold," Mia said, snagging the film from me and appraising the back cover. "It sounds good, right up my alley."

"The other is *The Howling Two: Your Sister is a Werewolf*." I beamed at her.

"They made a part two? Oh my gosh, that's amazing. Yes, to both, please!" Mia said with a toothy grin.

Posters of classic films lined the walls, and shelves were filled with VHS tapes, DVDs, vinyl records, and rare movie memorabilia. It was a place out of time, a haven for those who, like me, clung to the tangible magic of physical media. Sure, it was a little outdated, but it was home.

The door chimed again, and this time it was Mr. Gorman, another regular. "Amelia, do you have that new shipment of 80s horror flicks?"

"Right over here," I said, leading him to a display I'd set up yesterday. "We have classics like *The Shining*, *Nightmare on Elm Street*, and *Child's Play*. But we also have some more eclectic titles like *Popcorn*, *From Beyond*, and *Pieces*. I'm sure you'll find a few in there you might like."

He grinned, eyes lighting up. "You always know just what I need."

Moments like these reminded me why I fought so hard to keep this place open. My parents thought I was crazy, holding onto this relic from the past when everything was going digital. They wanted to sell the store and retire, but I couldn't let that happen. Rewind Rentals was more than a business. It was a piece of our family's legacy.

My phone buzzed.

> Jake: Hey, can we talk? Got someone I want you to meet.

I frowned, wondering what he wanted. He only seemed to show up when there was a crisis because he wrecked his car or apartment or whatever accident he'd found himself in that day. But he was my brother, and I owed him at least a conversation.

> Me: Sure, come by the store.

Jake: Groovy, I'll see you in an hour.

Four hours later than he said he'd be by, the door chimed, and I looked up to see Jake walking in with a tall, dark-haired man.

My heart skipped a beat as Flynn Callahan walked through the door. His presence filled the room, and made my pulse quicken. I tried to focus on the stack of tapes in front of me, but the heat rising in my cheeks betrayed me. As he approached, the familiar scent of him—earthy, masculine—wrapped around me, weaving through me, stirring memories I thought I had long buried.

"Amelia," he greeted me, his voice lower than I remembered. It was the kind of voice that made my stomach flip. I looked up, meeting his gaze, and for a moment, the air between us seemed to thicken, charged with something unspoken. His eyes lingered on my lips before flicking back to meet mine, making me acutely aware of every inch of space between us.

I hadn't seen Flynn in literal years, not since he graduated and moved away. Not since he and... I pushed the thought away. The past was the past, and it could stay that way. I didn't need Sexy-Mc-Look-At-Me-I'm-Flynn-And-I-Do-What-I-Want coming back and messing up my life again.

I got over him, dammit.

"Amelia, you remember Flynn," Jake said with a mischievous glint in his eyes.

"Of course," I said, trying to keep my voice steady. Flynn looked different somehow—more mature, confident. And annoyingly handsome. Fuck. "How could I forget?"

"Hey, Ams," Flynn said, offering a smile that could melt ice in Antarctica.

My knees threatened to buckle. "How long have you been back in town?" I asked, not entirely sure if I wanted to hear the answer.

"A few days ago," he said casually.

I had overheard someone mention a Callahan was back in town, but I didn't allow myself to believe, even for a moment, that it could be Flynn. "I didn't realize you'd made plans to move back."

"It was a recent decision. Life's funny like that sometimes. You know?"

No, I didn't know. And I wasn't about to let him charm his way back into my life. He had broken my heart once, and he didn't get to just walk in here and act like nothing had changed. Things that shouldn't matter right now: the way Flynn smells like home; the sudden, irrational urge to jump over the counter, run my fingers through his hair, and close the distance between us.

I tilted my head, forcing a calmness I didn't feel. "No, I don't. Please, enlighten me."

Flynn looked at Jake, who only shrugged his shoulders and silently exchanged an entire conversation between them. I could only guess at what.

"Jake told me that your parents were thinking of retiring and that you wanted to keep the store open. He mentioned you might need some help around this place," Flynn said, taking in the state of the store. "It looks exactly the same as the day I left town."

Flashes of that painful day attempted to claw their way out of the dark hole I'd buried them in. Like the queen I was, I kicked them back down.

He left, and I stayed. That's all there was to it.

"I wanted to lend my services, for old time's sake," Flynn said.

I forced a smile, my mind racing. The last thing I needed was Flynn swooping in and offering his unsolicited advice. But the look on Jake's face told me he was serious about the request.

"Help would be great," I started, more to Jake than Flynn. "But I can manage just fine."

Jake rolled his eyes. "Come on, Ams. I know you could use the extra pair of hands, or you wouldn't be begging me for help."

"I'm not begging you for help. I wanted you to

have an opinion about the future of Rewind Rentals. Not for you to pawn your friends off on me to get out of having an opinion. Those are two different things, Jake."

Flynn cleared his throat. "In my current line of work, I specialize in assisting struggling small businesses like yours in transforming their financial statements from losses to profits."

I shot daggers at Jake. "That's family business. Jake had no business—"

Jake cut me off. "Can we just have a quick chat? Alone."

I let out a sigh and gave him a curt nod. We walked out of earshot of Flynn.

"Look," Jake said, his voice tinged with frustration, "I know exactly what you asked, but I'm afraid I don't have the answers. When I don't know the answers, I trust the people who do. I prefer to stay in my lane. Flynn is good at this stuff. If you want to save Rewind Rentals, this is the best way I know how."

I shot a quick glance at Flynn. "He's never worked here. Am I supposed to just divulge private information to this guy?"

"He's not just some guy, Amelia, and you know it. Flynn is practically my brother. Besides, it's not like we have a lot of other options right now. If we don't make some changes, we're going to lose this place. We can't live in the red forever."

"It's not that bad yet," I said, but I didn't believe my own words.

"Can you please give it a shot?"

"We can't afford the help."

Jake spun on his heels. "She can't afford a consultant, Flynn."

"No worries. When I turn this place around," Flynn said with a wink. "Not if, but when I turn this place around, the local acknowledgment alone will garner me the respect and word of mouth I'll need to start my firm right here, based in Coral Cove."

"Seems to me he's as cheap as they get." Jake grinned.

My eyes narrowed at Flynn. "Unless you have practical experience in a rental business of this kind, I won't consider your advice on how to change my business. If we can turn a profit, I'll pay you for your services."

"When you turn a profit," Flynn corrected with a grin that could only be described as immoral.

I rolled my eyes. "Fine. When?"

"How about now?"

In such close proximity to Flynn, I could feel the

tension between us intensifying. There was history with Flynn. He wasn't just my brother's best friend. He was a mistake, and I needed to stay focused on saving the store. I couldn't afford to get distracted by someone like Flynn, no matter how charming he was.

CHAPTER 2
FLYNN

MOVING BACK to Coral Cove was the last thing I thought I'd be doing. But there I was, standing in the middle of Rewind Rentals—a time capsule of my childhood. The familiar scent of old popcorn butter and a subtle plastic funk wafted through the air, triggering a rush of forgotten memories. I could almost hear the laughter and feel the excitement as Jake, Amelia, and I perused the shelves, searching for the perfect movie.

Oh, Amelia.

It was a physical blow seeing her again after all these years. She always had this aura about her, the warmth of a wildfire spirit and a drive that drew people in and refused to be put out. But today, the weariness in her eyes and the heaviness in her voice betrayed the immense pressure of trying to keep this place running. I wanted to help. Not just because Jake asked, but because I could see how much this meant to her. After all this time, it was still Amelia.

"Okay, buddy," Jake said, breaking my reverie. "You ready to get to work?"

"Absolutely," I said, rolling up my sleeves. "What's first on the agenda?"

Amelia gave me a wary look, as if she was still deciding whether she could trust me. She bit her lip while she thought. I wanted to bite that lip.

"We need to reorganize the inventory," she said. "Customers have been complaining that they can't find what they're looking for."

"Got it," I said, moving toward the shelves to assess the situation. "So, you're currently organized by…" I trailed off, unsure of exactly what the organization system was.

"By year first and then by genre," Amelia said proudly. "Unfortunately, the previous part-time assistant could not successfully understand and use the filing system. The folks didn't notice right away, which resulted in this. Nothing is where it should be."

My eyes narrowed, trying to find the right way not to insult her in the first five minutes of my first shift. "Okay, we can do that. But could I offer a suggestion first?"

Amelia sighed. "I thought you were going to work first."

"I've always been a strong advocate for the 'work smarter, not harder' approach to life. If organizing movies by year makes it easier for people to locate them, that's excellent. If, however, it's not the best organizational method, we'd save time and the business a good chunk of change by only organizing them once instead of organizing them once now and once later if you decide there's a better method."

Amelia clenched her jaw. "We've been here, in this location since 1978. And for nearly fifty years, we've been organized by release date. It's one of those things that keeps us who we are."

I let out a breath. "I don't want to overstep—"

"Then don't," Amelia said, cutting me off.

I nodded. "Okay."

Too soon.

While we were busy re-shelving tapes, I found myself unable to resist stealing glances at Amelia. With great enthusiasm, she animatedly conversed with a customer, her face brightening as she recommended a movie. It was clear she had a passion for this place, and I respected that. But passion alone wouldn't keep the doors open.

Jake joined me, grabbing a stack of tapes. "Thanks for doing this, man," he hissed. "Amelia has been under a lot of pressure. There's a communication gap between the town's desire to preserve its traditions and the store's attempts to appeal to the younger generations. We have to find a way to stay current while still respecting the essence of this place. Amelia's been through it, and this place means everything to her."

"I can see that," I said.

"When she found out the folks were going to sell, she tried to stay positive. When she found out that they couldn't find a buyer, she lost it."

"I only want to help."

Jake smiled, clapping me on the shoulder. "I know. I know that you're the one person I can count on. If anyone can turn this place around, it's you."

As we continued working, I couldn't help but notice how Amelia's eyes lingered on the old photographs and vintage trinkets, lost in the nostalgia of the store. I just hoped she wasn't clinging to the past, meticulously preserving every aspect, and that instead, she'd be ready to embrace change and let go. From what Jake had shared with me, the business model was no longer sustainable. In order to survive, they would have to make significant adjustments and adapt.

Then there was Jake's overprotectiveness. It was like Amelia was in a bubble that no one was allowed to penetrate. Before we even got to Rewind Rentals, Jake had pulled me aside.

"Look, man, I appreciate you coming out here to talk to Amelia. There's just one little thing." He'd straightened, cleared his throat, and narrowed his eyes. "I don't know what happened between you two in the past. But let's leave it there. Keep your dick out of my sister, and we're golden. Okay?"

I'd only nodded, surprised by his words. I'd assumed for all these years that Amelia had told her brother what happened between us. Either she hadn't, or this was Jake's way of putting his foot down.

"We good?" I asked.

"Yep."

We'd gone to Rewind after, and he hadn't brought it up again. I had a feeling he wouldn't, unless Amelia did. I sighed.

The day went on, and I slipped into a rhythm. Organizing the inventory, chatting with customers, and even handling the ancient cash register—all of it felt familiar. Now and then, I caught Amelia watching me, a mix of curiosity and skepticism in her eyes. With one glance, I realized she still held power over me.

She was still Amelia.

My best friend's sister.

By the time we closed the shop up for the night, we'd made significant progress. The store looked cleaner, more organized, and I could tell Amelia was pleased, even if she was trying to hide it.

"Thanks for your help today," she said, locking the doors. "I have to admit, you did a good job."

As I leaned against the doorframe, a warm smile played on my lips. "Glad to hear it. I meant what I said earlier—I'm here to help. Whatever you need."

She nodded, a small smile playing at the corners of her lips. "We'll see. Tomorrow, we tackle the inventory records."

"Looking forward to it," I said, watching her walk away. There was a determination in her step that I couldn't help admiring.

I headed to my car with Amelia on my mind. She was so passionate about film and preserving history. It was all she talked about today with her customers. In nearly every conversation I overheard, the customer asked about an obscure movie, and she had a story to go with every title. It wasn't just her extensive movie knowledge but also her ability to truly grasp and appreciate films that garnered admiration from everyone, including myself.

Her passion shone brightly, illuminating the world around her like a campfire on a summer night. It was contagious. The reason her organizational system worked so well was that Amelia knew every movie in that store. The reason it was a struggle for other folks was that they didn't want to ask. Not everyone would share her enthusiasm for talking about film.

At least, not yet. And if it meant spending more time with Amelia, well, that was a bonus I was more than willing to accept.

The next morning, I arrived at the store early, armed with two coffees and two cinnamon rolls from the local bakery, Knead the Dough.

"Good morning, Ams," I said, holding out a cup of coffee. "Thought you might need a pick-me-up."

She took the coffee, her expression softening. "Thanks. I could really use it today."

"Early morning or late night?"

Amelia's eyes narrowed. "I came back after grabbing some takeout and worked in the back room until two."

"You should have called me. I would have come over and helped," I said with a light chuckle.

Her eyebrows shot to the sky. "I just needed some time to clear my head."

I nodded, not really wanting to step on that minefield. "What's on the agenda for this morning?"

"I've pulled out the inventory records. It's a tedious task, but my parents never upgraded their digital inventory system," she said, passing a file to me. "The one we have works, but when you have to go through the store item by item, it can feel monotonous."

"I can have a list of inventory systems to you this afternoon, with links to play-test the software," I said, pivoting my strategy at her crinkled nose. "I love this old register so much. As a kid, I was in awe of how cool it looked to play with. These giant gold buttons here." I ran a finger over a few. "It's a privilege to finally get to press them."

"I don't know."

"We could pop this piece out here and run a power cord through that hole there," I said, walking her through my plan. "Then we put a tablet here, where the new display would have your point of sale, and on the customer's side, it would still be the old register."

Amelia's mouth twisted to the side, the gears in her brain ticking away. "Could you set it up in a way so that we could have multiple tablets that could access the same information for inventory?"

"Uh, yeah," I said, shocked she didn't shut me down. "I can definitely do that."

"Okay, email me the information, and I'll look at it tonight."

"I will do that."

"Thanks," Amelia said before grabbing a stack of papers and heading to the back room.

We spent the morning going through the inventory records, a tedious but necessary task. Understanding the scope of things was important. As we worked, we fell into a comfortable silence, interrupted only by the occasional question or comment. It was surprisingly easy, this partnership, and I found myself enjoying the work more than I expected.

By lunchtime, we'd made a significant dent in the records, and I suggested taking a break. "How about we grab some lunch?" I asked. "My treat."

Amelia hesitated before nodding. "Sure. Let's go to Golden Chopsticks. It's just over there," she said, pointing.

"I half expected you to say no," I said, only kind of joking.

"Why?" Amelia asked with a curious smile.

We walked together across the street. "I guess, given everything, I wasn't sure how comfortable you were with having me around."

She sighed. "I'm still not sure."

"I get that."

"But I know I'm glad you're here."

My heart skipped a beat. "Me too."

It felt good to be here, back home, with Amelia.

We were seated right away and placed our orders after the server delivered our drinks.

"I know it sounds crazy," Amelia said, stirring her coffee. "But Rewind Rentals is more than just a store to me. It's part of my family's history. My grandparents started that place because of a deep love for film. My parents met there. I grew up there. I can't let it go. Not without a fight."

"It doesn't sound crazy at all," I said. "I get it. I want to help you keep Rewind. You know, I also grew up there. Maybe not in the same way, but it's part of my history. I can empathize with that."

Her eyes searched mine. "Why are you doing this, Flynn? You could be anywhere, doing anything. Why would you come back here when getting out of this town was the only thing you could talk about?"

I took a deep breath, choosing my words carefully. "Because I believe in this place. And I believe in you."

"That's not what I meant." Amelia crossed her arms.

"Because sometimes in life, you can be so sure you want certain things only to realize later you couldn't have been more wrong."

"Do you really think we can save her?"

"I wouldn't be here if I didn't."

Amelia cocked her head to the side. "Yes, you would. Don't lie."

I chuckled. "You're right; I would. But I'm not lying, Ams. I think that if we act as a team, we could save Rewind Rentals."

A genuine, warm grin spread across her face, illuminating her entire being. "Okay," she whispered. "Let's do it."

We finished eating and headed back to the store. I felt a sense of hope. It wasn't going to be easy saving this old place, but for the first time in a long time, I was excited about something.

CHAPTER 3
AMELIA

THE UNUSUAL SENSE of optimism I felt this morning as I arrived at Rewind Rentals was unexpected. Flynn's presence was sudden, but his help was undeniably making a difference. My parents couldn't keep up anymore, and my teenage part-time help could only do so much. I looked forward to the day ahead, which was a strange feeling considering how overwhelming things had been lately.

I'd been coming and going from these front doors for nearly thirty years. From the creak of the door to the click of the light switch, everything about this place was familiar to me. It smelled like home. It was a comforting reminder of why I was fighting so hard to keep this place alive.

Growing up in this small town could feel limiting. There wasn't always a lot to do unless it was festival season. The nearest large shopping center was an hour away. Rewind Rentals was the highlight of so many youthful Friday nights.

I knew that things had changed and that, with the internet and streaming services, this shop was a dinosaur. I wasn't stupid; I knew what people said. The snide comments from the younger generations echoed in my heart with fear. I knew it was the right decision for Jake to ask for Flynn's help, especially considering Flynn's expertise in the matter.

The doorbell jingled, and the Devil walked in, carrying two coffees and a bag from Knead the Dough.

"Morning," Flynn said with a warm smile, passing me a coffee cup.

"Good morning, Flynn," I replied, accepting the coffee. "You don't have to keep doing this." I took a sip. "Mmm, thank you." I licked my lips.

He shrugged. "I figured if I'm getting myself one, I might as well get you one too. It'll help push us through another day of inventory records."

I chuckled and took another sip. "You might be right. Dorothea's has the most delicious treats."

Flynn passed me a bag, and I pulled out a slice of Inspiration Cake. It was lemon. "Oh, my favorite!"

We spent the morning diving into the inventory records. It was tedious work, but having Flynn there made it more bearable. He had a way of making even the most mundane tasks feel like they had a purpose.

"So, tell me," Flynn said, scanning through a stack of old rental forms. "What's your favorite movie?"

"That's a tough one. Here I thought you were going to ask why we've kept all these," I said, glancing up from my notebook. "But if I had to be honest and choose, I'd say *Before Sunrise* or *Before Sunset*. It's kind of a toss-up between the two."

"Really? I would have guessed you'd say *Casablanca* or something."

I laughed. "I mean, it's a classic and arguably a good choice. But I can't help it. The *Before* series is my favorite. It's like comfort food. It always feels good."

"Mine's *Clue*," Flynn said.

"Weird, I'd have pegged you for *The Godfather*." We both burst into a fit of laughter.

The conversation was natural, comfortable even. Two old friends falling back into an easy rhythm. We continued working, sharing our favorite movie moments and laughing over the ridiculous plots of some of the films in the inventory. It was easy, and for a moment, I forgot about the financial strain and the uncertainty of the future.

We'd made significant progress, and Flynn suggested we take a break. "How about another trip to Golden Chopsticks?" he asked, his eyes twinkling with mischief.

I smiled. "Sure, why not?"

We walked to the restaurant, and the conversation turned to our plans for the store. "I've been thinking," Flynn said as we took our seats. "We need to attract new customers. I have a few ideas for improvements that we can implement, but we should also think creatively."

"Okay, I'm listening," I said, unease settling into my belly. Change was never easy for me.

"So, we talked about the software update, and I sent you an email before we left the store."

"You did?"

Flynn smiled a toothy grin. "Sure did. I'm just that good."

"Thanks."

"I have some big ideas and some smaller ones. But all of them shape around the work we're doing now," he said. "The core problem with Rewind is that technology has evolved, and if we don't adapt, it will be left behind. For better or worse. We're not debating that point, right?"

I sighed. "No, we aren't." I wanted to, but I knew it was a pointless debate. Change was inevitable.

Under the table, Flynn's foot brushed against mine, the contact sending a spark of electricity through me. My breath caught in my throat. Was it an accident, or something more? I couldn't tell, but the thought of his foot resting so casually against mine made my pulse quicken.

Flynn leaned in, his voice low and intimate. "You've grown even more beautiful, Amelia," he said, his eyes holding mine. It was hard to look away. "I missed seeing that smile."

I swallowed hard, my throat suddenly dry. I tried to muster a response, something casual, but all I could manage was a soft, "Thank you." My mind was too focused on the warmth of his foot against mine, and the way his gaze seemed to strip away every defense I had.

"What do you think about expanding your services?" Flynn asked, breaking my thoughts.

"Uh, what do you mean? We have a lot of movies that could go out, but there's only so much shelf space."

"Stay with me on this one. If we clean out the storage room behind the desk, remove the door, paint it bright sunshine yellow, line the walls with shelves, and turn it into an equipment inventory space for rentals. I know this might cost more than you antici- pated as far as changes go, but I think there's really something here. If you expand to offer VHS players, record players, DVD and laserdisc players, and even retro video games, I think you could expand your offers to appeal to a much larger crowd."

"I'm listening."

"Most of the stores here in Coral Cove survive on the tourist industry. You need to tap into that deep well of growth," Flynn took a sip of his water.

"By renting out equipment?" I asked, more than a bit skeptical.

He nodded. "Yeah. There are lots of ways that we can really make this place a destination, and I have ideas for that too. We start with sprucing things up. Yes, we've been doing that. I'm thinking bigger."

"Like what?" I played with my napkin, hoping he wasn't about to go off the rails.

"I've been watching you."

This stopped me short. "Stalker much?"

Flynn chuckled. "You're so passionate about the films and their history, tidbits of knowledge about the way something was filmed, why, or how. You light up every time a customer comes in asking about a film." Flynn found my eyes and seemed to see into my soul. "I'm suggesting that we use your love of film to guide these changes."

The waiter brought by our lunch and refilled our drinks.

"Okay, I'm still listening," I said.

Flynn smiled. "I have connections in the independent film industry, and they are currently working on a documentary about outdated technology. I would like to reach out to them and inquire about the possibility of trading interviews and store access for their film, in exchange for doing some small filming and voice-over work for Rewind. I'd like to record you talking about the films you love. My goal is to enhance the engagement and historical aspect of Rewind Rentals."

"Could we shoot video, or would it be more like a song?" I asked.

"I'm considering capturing videos of collectibles, films, and even the filming sites of that movie that was made here in the early 2000s." Flynn shoved a bite of sweet and sour chicken into his mouth. "Mmm. I forgot how good this was."

"Okay."

"Okay?" he asked.

"Okay, call your friend and see if they're interested in using Rewind Rentals for their movie," I said.

"Alrighty then, I'll make the call today."

"What other ideas did you have?"

"What are your thoughts on hosting events, like a movie night or film trivia?"

I nodded, intrigued by the idea. "That could work. We used to have movie nights years ago, but we stopped them because attendance dropped off. We have a giant room upstairs, and my grandparents set up an old projector. I always thought it would be great to bring in a bunch of couches and chairs. Really comfy stuff and serve popcorn, candy, you know? Maybe it's time to bring them back?"

"Exactly," Flynn said, leaning forward. "We can market it on social media, get the word out. Create some buzz. Bring in a popcorn machine and candy. I think it would have a lot of potential. I have a furniture guy as well."

"Of course you do," I laughed and took a bite of my rice. I hesitated, the familiar doubt creeping in. "But what if it doesn't work? What if we put in all this effort and still don't make enough to keep the store open?"

Flynn reached across the table, his hand covering mine. "We won't know unless we try, Amelia."

His touch was warm, reassuring, and I believed him. For better or worse, what was a few thousand dollars and a failed try? The store would close if we didn't do something.

"Okay," I breathed. "Let's do it."

After lunch, we headed back to the store with a renewed sense of purpose. Flynn set up a makeshift office in the back of the room, and we started brainstorming ideas for movie nights. We created a list of potential themes, from classic film noir to 80s nostalgia, and began drafting a marketing plan.

As the afternoon wore on, the store filled with customers, and I found myself feeling more and more excited. Organizing the inventory, chatting with regulars, and even handling the ancient cash register —it all felt familiar.

Flynn was right there beside me, effortlessly chatting with customers and making them feel welcome. His presence brought a new energy to the store, one I hadn't realized was missing until now. Maybe it was his casual demeanor, the way he treated every stranger off the street like they were an old friend. It was disarming, and I could see how people were drawn to him.

By closing time, we were both exhausted but filled with a renewed exhilaration, the kind that comes from a day well spent.

"Thanks for today," I said, turning the key in the lock. When I glanced up, Flynn was leaning against the doorway, looking far more attractive than he had any right to. The musky, woodsy scent of him filled the air between us, intoxicating and impossible to ignore.

"Glad to hear it. I meant what I said earlier—I'm here to help. Whatever it takes," Flynn said, nodding, a small smile tugging at the corners of his lips.

"I'll see you tomorrow," I replied, waving goodbye.

"Looking forward to it," he added, his voice low and smooth, almost a purr.

I watched him walk away, his confident stride making it hard to look away. As much as I was starting to recognize the value he brought, a nagging voice in the back of my mind reminded me that letting him in was a risk. He left me once before, and the fear that he could do it again lingered. I needed to stay focused on saving the store, not on someone who might bail on me when I needed them most.

CLEANING out the back room proved to be more of a workout than I'd anticipated. Dust swirled in the air, catching the light streaming through the small window, and my muscles ached from moving boxes and old equipment. Amelia was just as dedicated, sorting through piles of old VHS tapes, DVDs, and even film canisters. She moved with an intensity that only she could muster.

"Hey, Amelia," I called out, pulling a large, dusty projector from a corner. "Look at this. I didn't know your grandparents had one of these."

Amelia glanced up, her eyes widening. "Wow, that's ancient. I think they used it for movie nights way back in the day."

"We should clean it up and see if it still works," I

suggested, already feeling a surge of excitement at the idea.

"Good idea," she said, smiling. "It could be a great addition to our movie nights."

"Do you have any reels for it?"

"Yeah, those film canisters over there," she pointed to a shelf stacked with giant round metal containers.

"Wicked."

We spent the next hour cleaning and setting up the projector, our hands brushing occasionally as we worked side by side. Each touch sent a jolt through me. I shook it away, reminding myself why I was here. Amelia needed help saving the store, not a complicated romantic entanglement.

"Okay, moment of truth," I said as I loaded an old film reel labeled 'Opening Day' onto the projector. "Let's see if this thing still works."

The projector whirred to life, casting a flickering image on the wall. We watched in amazement as the scenes from the store's opening day played out before us. The footage was grainy, but it was charming, showing Amelia's grandparents welcoming their first customer.

"This is incredible," Amelia whispered, her eyes glistening with nostalgia.

As the film continued to play, I couldn't help but

feel a deep connection to this place. It wasn't just about saving a store. It was about preserving a piece of history, a legacy that meant so much to Amelia and her family. I glanced at her, noticing the soft smile on her lips as she watched the old footage. Her passion for Rewind Rentals was palpable, and I admired her more for it.

"Flynn, look at this," she said, her voice filled with excitement. She pointed to a scene in the film where her grandparents were standing. "They used to host all kinds of educational movies with the local kids and the library. They were really into giving back to the community."

"That's amazing," I said. "We could bring something like that back. Make it part of our community outreach."

Amelia nodded, her eyes shining. "Yeah, I think that would be wonderful. It's a way to honor their legacy and also bring more people in."

As we watched the footage, a peculiar energy seemed to vibrate through the room, making the hairs on my arms stand on end. Suddenly, a bright flash of light erupted from the projector, illuminating the room with a brilliance that seemed to pause time for a moment. Amelia and I both jumped back, shielding our eyes.

When the light faded, we turned to look at the

wall. The film continued to play. But something wasn't right. Hanging on the dusty wall was a faded movie poster, one neither of us remembered seeing before.

"What the heck is that?" Amelia asked.

I stepped closer, examining the poster. "It's that old classic by Hitchcock, *The Birds*." I couldn't shake the feeling that it hadn't been there before.

"Was that always there?" I asked, glancing at Amelia, who shook her head slowly.

"I'm not sure. How odd..." she murmured, touching the edge of the poster gingerly.

We didn't make a big deal of it, chalking it up to a trick of the light or an overlooked relic from the past. But as we returned to our work, the poster remained, its presence a silent testament to the magic that lingered in the air of Rewind Rentals.

We spent the next hour lost in the memories captured on the film. It was a beautiful reminder of what Rewind Rentals stood for and why it was worth fighting for. When the reel ended, we sat in silence for a moment, letting the nostalgia wash over us.

"I'm glad you're here, Flynn," Amelia said. A smile played at her lips. "I don't think I could do this without you."

Her words took me by surprise, and I felt a

warmth spread through my chest. "I'm glad to be here too, Amelia."

AS WE CONTINUED WORKING over the next week, I started implementing some of my ideas. I brought in a team to update the store's electronic filing system. At first, Amelia resisted, clinging to the old ways, but as my guy highlighted the advantages, her perspective shifted. It made managing the inventory easier and allowed us to focus more on the customer experience.

The more time we spent together, the more our shared history and unresolved feelings surfaced. One evening, as we were wrapping up for the night, Amelia turned to me, her expression serious. "Flynn, I need to ask you something."

"Sure, what is it?" I asked, a knot suddenly forming in my stomach.

"Why did you come back?" Her voice was barely above a whisper. "I mean, really come back. Was it just because Jake begged you for the sake of the store? Or was it something else?"

I took a deep breath, choosing my words carefully. "It started with the store, Amelia. But being here, working with you, it's made me realize that being here has always meant more. I missed Coral Cove, but more than that… I missed you."

She looked at me, her eyes searching mine for the truth. "I missed you too, Flynn," she admitted. "But I don't know if I can go back. A lot has changed in six years."

"You were counting?" I asked.

She shrugged.

"I'm not going anywhere, Amelia."

There was a moment before she replied. In that moment, it felt as though a weight had been lifted, and a sense of lightness washed over me. We stood there, surrounded by the history we were fighting to preserve. She reached for my hand. "I've heard that one before."

"Ouch. I guess I deserved that."

Amelia laced her fingers in mine. Maybe all wasn't lost.

CHAPTER 5
AMELIA

AS I DRIFTED off to sleep, a feeling of hope washed over me, something I hadn't experienced in quite some time. The following morning, I arrived at the store with a sense of purpose. Today was the day we would begin its beautification transformation, and this old storage space was getting a remodel.

"Morning, Ams," Flynn called out, pushing the door open with his shoulder as he balanced two coffees and a bag of pastries from Knead the Dough.

"Morning," I replied, looking up from the counter where I was cleaning up some paperwork I'd left out the night before. My eyes brightened when I saw the coffee. "You're spoiling me at this point. I hope you understand you'll never be able to stop bringing the coffee. You will forever be required to bring treats after I appoint you the King of the Bakery. It's a rule. I didn't make it. I'm just the enforcer."

From a deep guttural place, Flynn chuckled. "Just trying to keep us both motivated," he said, handing me a cup. "Today's going to be busy."

The first part of the morning was spent finalizing our plans for the back room. Just like he promised, Flynn had called a buddy making a film about technology, and they were super excited to come out and see the shop. They were eager to start filming.

Flynn and I worked side by side, clearing out the last of the old equipment and setting up the new shelving units. The back room was slowly transforming into a bright, inviting space. Per his suggestion, we painted the walls a cheerful sunflower yellow. We didn't have all the new products in the mail yet, but true to his word, Flynn had connections. We got a good deal on vintage systems.

Around noon, Flynn's friend Rory arrived with her film crew. She was a tall, dark-haired, strikingly beautiful woman with an air of confidence about her. Rory's approach sent a wave of unease through me.

"Flynn, it's so good to see you," Rory said, pulling him into a quick hug. "I've been looking forward to this since you mentioned it weeks ago."

Weeks ago? It's only been… I tried to do the math, but everything felt like a blur. Had Flynn been planning from day one? Maybe before he was back in town?

"Same. I really appreciate you doing me a solid." Flynn returned her hug. "This is Amelia, the heart and soul of Rewind Rentals."

Rory turned to me with a warm smile. "It's truly a pleasure to meet you, Amelia. Flynn's told me so much about you and this amazing little store."

"Nice to meet you too," I said.

There, I was polite. I didn't shoot her daggers or make a snide comment.

Rory didn't seem to notice my hesitation. She immediately started discussing the plans for the video, gesturing animatedly and outlining her vision for us.

As Flynn and Rory talked, I couldn't help but feel a bubble of jealousy grow inside me.

I had zero reason to be jealous. We weren't officially anything. Flynn said he wasn't going anywhere. And that sounded great, but it was overshadowed by the past. He left once before, and just because he said he wasn't going anywhere didn't mean he was staying for me.

Love for Flynn had consumed me for years. Ever since a barbecue at the neighbor's house in the sixth grade. Back when my mom and his mom were friends, before his parents split. Before he and

Jake became inseparable. Flynn Callahan was my world.

And then he left, and my world shattered.

We spent the next few hours filming different segments of the store. I felt awkward at first, but Flynn's encouragement helped, and I found my rhythm. Rory was professional and efficient, directing her crew with ease.

During a break, I went outside looking for some air. Flynn found me a couple of minutes later.

"You okay?" he asked.

"Yeah, I'm fine," I said, but my voice lacked conviction. "Rory seems really...friendly." That was as much kindness as I could muster. The green monster inside of me was rearing her ugly head.

Flynn glanced through the window at Rory, who was chatting with one of her crew members. "Rory? She's just enthusiastic. We've known each other our whole lives."

My eyes narrowed. "How well do you know her?"

Flynn seemed to understand what was bothering me. "Amelia, Rory is my cousin. She lived in another state, so we didn't see much of each other until six years ago." He rubbed the back of his head uncomfortably. "That's when she moved to the area for school. She stayed with me for a while. She loved it so much, she stuck around. There's nothing between us but family."

Relief flooded through me. "I didn't know. I thought…" I trailed off, too embarrassed to finish the thought.

"I get it," Flynn said gently. "But you don't have to worry about her or anyone else."

Everything in me wanted to believe him.

We stood close, so close that I could feel the warmth radiating from his body. The air between us crackled with tension, every breath I took filled with his scent, his presence. Flynn's hand reached up slowly, his fingers brushing against my cheek as he tucked a strand of hair behind my ear. The touch was gentle, almost hesitant, but it sent a shockwave through me, making my heart pound.

"I've spent years regretting my choices. Whatever this is, I'm not going to mess it up. Not again." He leaned in ninety percent of the way. His eyes full of heat.

Our eyes met, and for a moment, time seemed to stand still. I could see the conflict in Flynn's eyes, the same war raging within me. I wanted to step back, to put some distance between us, but my body betrayed me, leaning into his touch instead. I was drawn to him, like a moth to a flame, and I knew I was about to get burned.

When Flynn finally closed the distance and kissed me, it was slow, deliberate, as if he were savoring every second. His lips were soft, warm, and the kiss was filled with years of unspoken words, pent-up desires. I melted into him, my hands finding their way to his chest, clutching at the fabric of his shirt as if he were the only thing keeping me grounded. The kiss deepened, becoming more urgent, more needy, until we were both breathless, the world around us forgotten.

I thought about all the things that had passed between us. All the firsts we shared. All of my most important firsts were with Flynn. Did I want my others to be with him, too?

I inhaled him. Longing and passion intertwined as our tongues danced in harmony. Flynn ran a hand through my hair, pulling me closer.

Someone cleared their throat loudly.

We pulled apart to find Rory standing there. "I don't mean to interrupt but—"

"Oh my stars, I'm so sorry. Yes, let's, um," I brushed my shirt and hair down.

Flynn was as composed as ever, completely unbothered by the fact that we were caught in the act.

"I'm so sorry," I said again.

Rory laughed. "No worries at all. Really, it's totally fine."

We went inside and continued working. The atmosphere in the room lightened considerably. Rory's crew captured some fantastic footage of the memorabilia we had in the original spaces upstairs and down.

Rory approached me with a request. "Amelia, would you mind sitting down for an interview? I really think your story and passion for the store would add a lot to the documentary."

I hesitated for a moment, but Flynn's reassuring nod gave me the confidence I needed. "Sure, I'd be happy to."

Rory set up a chair in front of the camera and adjusted the lighting. "Just relax and speak from your heart," she said with a smile. "We want to capture your genuine love for this place."

I took a deep breath and sat down, feeling a mix of nervous excitement.

Rory started with a soft, encouraging tone. "Amelia, can you tell us about your earliest memory of Rewind Rentals?"

I smiled, letting the nostalgia wash over me. "It's the buttery smell of popcorn and watching *The Little Princess* on the old projector. I must have been around five years old. My grandparents ran the store back then. Every Friday night, my grandma and I would cuddle up on one of the couches. It was my favorite weekly ritual. This place has always felt like home."

Rory nodded, her eyes bright with interest. "What inspired you to take over the store and keep it running after all these years?"

"My parents wanted to sell the store and retire," I said, my voice growing more passionate. "But I couldn't let that happen. This store is more than just a business to me. It's a piece of our family's history and a vital part of the community. People come here not just to rent movies, but to relive memories, to connect with something tangible in a world that's gone digital."

Rory leaned forward slightly, encouraging me to continue. "How has Flynn's return impacted the store?"

I glanced at Flynn, who was watching from behind the camera with an encouraging smile. "Flynn's return has been a game-changer. He brought fresh ideas and a new energy that we desperately needed. He's helped us modernize without losing the charm that makes Rewind Rentals special. And more than that, he reminded me why this place is worth fighting for."

Rory's next question was more personal. "What

has been the most challenging part of this journey for you?"

I took a moment to gather my thoughts. "The uncertainty has been the hardest part. Not knowing if we'd make it, if all the hard work would pay off. But every time I see a customer's face light up when they find a movie they loved as a kid, it reminds me we're doing something important."

Rory smiled warmly. "What do you hope for the future of Rewind Rentals?"

"I hope it continues to be a place where people can come to reconnect with the past and create new memories," I said. "I want it to be a community hub, a place that brings people together. And with all the changes we're making, I believe that can happen."

By the end of the day, we had a lot of material to work with. The back room looked incredible, and the store was coming together.

Rory approached me with a smile. "You were amazing, Amelia. Your passion for this place is truly inspiring."

"Thank you," I said, genuinely touched. "I'm glad we're doing this. It's going to help so much."

"That's the plan," Rory said with a wink. "We'll edit this footage and get it back to you in a couple of weeks. Flynn said he mentioned my movie to you and that we might be able to use the footage for our film?"

"Yes! Oh yes, please use whatever you like."

"You are a passionate woman who is all about saving the last video rental store on the west coast," Rory said with such enthusiasm. "You know these films in and out. More than that, you're passionate about film. I've been watching you today."

My cheeks grew warm. "I'm flattered you see me that way."

After Rory and her crew left, Flynn and I stood in the newly transformed back room, looking around with pride.

"This is incredible, Flynn," I said, my voice filled with awe. "Thank you for all your help."

"None of this would have been possible if it wasn't for you. This is all you, Ams. And it's not over yet." Flynn grinned. "We still have a lot of work to do. But we're getting there."

I nodded, my eyes meeting his. "Yeah, we sure are."

CHAPTER 6
FLYNN

THE TRANSFORMATION of Rewind Rentals was well underway, and our first movie night was finally here. We had spread the word through social media and flyers around town, hoping for a good turnout. I arrived at the store early to help Amelia set up.

Amelia and I hadn't talked about the kiss we shared the other day. The right time would come around, and I wasn't going to push it.

"Morning, Flynn," Amelia greeted me with a smile as she arranged stacks of candy on the counter.

"Morning, Ams. How are we feeling about tonight?" I asked, grabbing a stack of vintage movie posters that still needed frames before being hung.

"Nervous, but I think mostly I'm excited," she admitted. "I really hope this works."

"It will work," I said confidently. "We've put in a lot of hard work. People are going to love it."

As the day went on, we finished setting up the store, transforming it into a cozy, nostalgic haven. The bright yellow walls of the back room now showcased vintage VHS, DVD, and record players. There were old movie posters on the walls. We had expanded our inventory as well. It was all a work in progress, but there had been huge strides.

Upstairs, we set up the old projector and arranged two dozen couches and a half circle of bean bags in the front to create a cozy theater viewing area. There were stacks of blankets, lots of extra pillows, and I even installed drink holders on the sides of each couch. The room could comfortably hold one hundred audience members, and the fire chief said we could have one hundred twenty people in that space.

Before the customers headed upstairs, they could buy any number of different candies, sodas, and, of course, fresh hot buttery popcorn. We programmed an intermission halfway through the films so that customers could stretch, come downstairs, and replenish their snacks.

Every aspect of expanding the business with the single theater lounge and the system rentals was a strategic move to increase sales. Hypothetically, with five showings a week, Rewind Rentals' profits would increase at such a substantial rate, it would allow Amelia to stay open and for her parents to retire. If there was more than one showing a day, it could be more. She was struggling to believe it still, but tonight I hoped to give her a glimpse of the future I planned.

By the time evening rolled around, a crowd had gathered. Locals and tourists alike filled the store, their faces lighting up with excitement as they took in the new retro ambiance.

"Welcome to the first movie night at Rewind Rentals!" Amelia announced, her voice carrying a mix of nervousness and enthusiasm. "Tonight, we're showing *The Goonies*, a classic adventure film that we hope you'll all enjoy. If you haven't had a chance to purchase some of our fresh popcorn or grab an icy cold drink, you still have time before the movie starts. After you've got your tickets, head upstairs to find a comfy spot."

As the movie started, I watched the crowd settle in, their eyes glued to the screen. There was a palpable sense of community in the air, a shared appreciation for the nostalgia and magic of old movies.

About halfway through the movie, right before we called intermission, something strange happened.

During the scene where the kids find the treasure map, suddenly the room went bright white before going back to the film. No one was bothered, thank the stars above. We'd have to look at the film and projector. I thought I'd fixed the issue from the last time. But I guess not. I wondered if maybe it was missing a cell? I'd have to call someone to be sure.

Amelia and I went downstairs to run the concessions. It was the oddest thing. Behind the counter, hanging on the wall, was an old map that looked an awful lot like the one in the movie upstairs. I blinked, not quite believing what I was seeing.

"Amelia, when did you buy that?" I whispered, nudging her.

She turned, and her eyes widened. "I assumed that was you."

"It was not. I have no idea where it came from," I said, taking it off the wall. "I don't remember it being here earlier."

"That's because it wasn't," Amelia said. "Jake?" she called out.

Jake popped his head out from behind a shelf. He was working this evening. "What's up?"

"When did you hang this map?" I asked.

"I didn't," he said. "These changes are all you."

We exchanged puzzled looks, but just then a group of folks trotted down the stairs for more concessions, gossiping about how much they loved the new space. Customers quickly surrounded us, inundating us with questions.

By the time the intermission was over, I'd forgotten about the map. The rest of the movie played, and when the film ended, Amelia and I stood up to address the crowd.

"Thank you all for coming tonight!" Amelia said, beaming. The crowd erupted with applause. "We hope you enjoyed the movie. We're planning to host themed movie nights and film trivia nights, and private events, so please spread the word. The calendar is up downstairs, and you can grab a flyer of events on your way out. We want Rewind Rentals to be a place where the community can come together and share their love for movies."

As people filed out, a few of them approached. "So, we were just having a debate, and we were hoping you could clear something up for us. You know the map hanging behind the register? That wasn't there earlier, was it?"

Amelia and I locked eyes.

"Well, you see that old projector up there?" I said, really leaning into the question. "I'm not saying it was the projector, but I'm also not not saying it was the projector."

They all chuckled at my joke. But the reality was,

we had no idea. We weren't the only ones to notice its arrival. We were excited about the gift all the same.

Once everyone left, the store was quiet, the excitement of the night still lingering in the air. Jake went home after complaining that he had to be up early for work. This left Amelia and me alone to clean up the remnants of popcorn and empty cups.

"That was an unequivocal success," I said, smiling at her. "People really seemed to enjoy themselves."

"They did," she agreed, her eyes shining with happiness. "And that map... I don't know how it got here, but it definitely added to the mystique of this place."

"Right? It was the cherry on top of a nearly perfect evening," I said.

We stood there for a moment, the energy between us crackling with unspoken words.

"What would have made it better?" Amelia asked, her voice growing husky.

Before I could think twice, I reached out and pulled her close, our lips meeting in a fiery kiss. All the tension and longing from the past six years exploded between us in that moment.

The time we'd lost melted away. A rush of memories and firsts. Amelia was my entire world and every one of my favorite memories.

With her hands tangled in my hair, she pulled me closer, silently begging for more. My hand gently wrapped around her waist, exploring the softness beneath her shirt and reveling in the intimate warmth between our bodies. Outside the store, the bustling sounds of the town faded into a distant murmur, creating a tranquil bubble for just the two of us.

The past collided with the present as if nothing could come between us again. I unhooked her bra and slipped her shirt off, exposing her supple breasts. Amelia had my top off in an equal frenzy.

"Flynn," she said, her voice breathless as she urgently tugged on my belt loop, leading me to a soft beanbag. With a sudden force, she tugged me on top of her, our bodies pressed together.

"Amelia, I..." I trailed off, unable to finish the thought, too enamored by the scent of her and the way her nails dug into my back, pulling me closer.

"Shhh," she whispered. "Make love to me?"

"Your wish is my command," I murmured, my kisses tracing a delicate line from her neck down to the gentle curve of her breast. I took a nipple into my mouth, savoring its sweetness, while my free hand explored all of her soft curves.

Amelia's moan of pleasure echoed through the room, a testament to the sheer bliss she was experiencing. "More," she demanded.

I took my time, sliding her pants off with care, relishing the sight that unfolded before my eyes. She was round in all the right places, with the most luscious, bitable thighs.

She squirmed under my gaze. "Flynn?"

"I'm drinking you in, baby," I said before finding her lips again. With each passing second, our kiss became more passionate, igniting a primal urge within me that I struggled to contain.

Instead, I explored her body with my lips, planting kisses and teasing bites along the way until I discovered the intense warmth and moisture at her core. I gently spread her legs further apart, then I wrapped them over my shoulders and pulled her wet pussy closer. Her slick heat tantalized my taste buds, and I relished savoring every last drop.

"Oh god," Amelia panted.

I lapped at her pussy, slowly making my way to her clit. I flicked it with my tongue, writing a love poem, willing it to find her heart.

I sucked gently, feeling her body tense beneath me. Her breath came in shallow gasps, and her hands gripped my hair, urging me on. Her moans grew louder, echoing off the walls as she reached the peak of pleasure.

I let the pleasure climb before laying her back down, stripping the last of my clothes. My aching cock found her center, poised to join us together.

Before I entered her, I met Amelia's eyes. She nodded, her gaze filled with trust and longing, and in one smooth action, I was inside her. Her heat enveloped me, and it almost sent me over the edge.

"Please," Amelia begged, her voice a sultry whisper.

I thrust again, and again. Faster and faster, our bodies moving in perfect harmony. She clung to me, her nails making art on my back, and I felt the sweet, intoxicating pull of pleasure building within me.

As I shifted, I lifted one of her legs for better access to her clit, entering her again with renewed urgency. That was all it took; Amelia cried out in pleasure, her release washing over her in waves. I reveled in her ecstasy, feeling her body quiver around me. For a brief moment, I wondered if she'd stir the attention of the neighbors. It was a fleeting thought, gone quicker than it came. I pumped inside her again and found my own release, the world fading away until there was only us.

When we finally broke apart, we were breathless, our eyes locked on one another. Her skin glowed, and her smile was radiant, as if she had been waiting for this moment as long as I had.

"Flynn," she whispered, her voice trembling with either emotion or the aftershocks of orgasm. Which, I couldn't tell.

In the dim light of the store, I confessed, "I've missed you so much, Amelia." I brushed a strand of hair from her face, my heart swelling with emotion. "This feels right," I mumbled. "Being here with you, working in this place... it all feels like it was meant to be."

She shifted slightly, her expression growing serious. Her smile faltered for just a moment as if she was wrestling with an unspoken thought. "Why did you leave me then?"

I blinked, surprised by her question. "I'm here right now," I said, not sure where this was coming from. I thought we'd moved past it. Left the past in the past.

Her eyes shifted, downcast. "Why did you leave six years ago?"

I hesitated, the weight of her question settling heavily in the space between us. "I..." I began, my voice faltering. I took a deep breath, realizing that now, more than ever, she deserved the truth.

CHAPTER 7
AMELIA

OUR FIRST MOVIE night was a wild success. Customers poured out in support of the lovingly named The Rewind Theatre. We had to turn people away when we met capacity.

Jake explained that those who couldn't catch the film rented movies. He'd even rented out half of our stock of VHS players and had reservations come in for future dates. In every possible way, this marked the greatest accomplishment the store had ever experienced.

It was an undeniable success.

Yet, as I lay here in the dim light, tangled in Flynn's arms, the question I'd buried for so long rose to the surface, insistent and relentless.

"Why did you leave six years ago?" I asked, my voice barely above a whisper. The words hung heavy in the air between us, casting a shadow over the warmth we'd just shared.

"I…" Flynn's eyes searched mine, and I could see the conflict warring inside him. "Amelia, it wasn't about you. It was never about you."

"How could it not be?" I wondered. "Then what was it?" I pressed, my heart aching with the memories of his sudden departure.

He sighed, running a hand through his tousled hair. "I got an offer I couldn't refuse—a job that promised everything I thought I wanted. I was young, Amelia. Ambitious and scared of being tied down before I had the chance to find out who I was."

My chest cracked open at his words. I pushed back, needing more space between us. "So, you just left?" I asked, the bitterness creeping into my voice despite my efforts to suppress it.

"I know it sounds selfish," Flynn admitted. "I needed to prove to myself that I could make it on my own. I got so caught up that I completely lost sight of what mattered."

"And what about us?" I asked, feeling the old wound reopening. "Did I mean anything to you?"

"How can you ask that? Of course you did," Flynn said, his eyes earnest. "You meant everything, but back then, I wasn't ready for everything. I thought I needed to be someone else. I thought I had to find my own success, and instead, I found I was wrong. I'd given up the most important thing in my life to chase a dream that left me unfulfilled."

"You didn't even call." I reached for a blanket, wrapping it around myself.

"Because I knew if you asked me to stay, I would have stayed. There was no way I could have looked into your October eyes and said no. I would have given up everything for you. I would have bent the world in two just to see you smile. I stayed away because I couldn't be who you wanted me to be."

"I only ever wanted you," I said, tears falling down my cheeks. "You didn't have to be something different for me."

"I know," Flynn said, his voice a whisper.

"And what's changed? How do I know you won't just pick up and leave again when something better comes along?"

Flynn reached for my hand, but I pulled away, needing space between us to breathe and think. "I've changed, Amelia. I've seen what life is like without you, without Coral Cove, without family. It's not where I want to be. I'm here now because this is where I belong."

I couldn't meet his eyes.

"I spent the last six years trying to be the kind of man you could come home to. You are everything.

You always have been. Since that first time we met as kids."

"You were Jake's friend," I said, a bit harsher than I intended.

"Because I was too afraid to ask to be yours."

Silence settled between us, thick with unspoken doubts and lingering hurt. I wanted to believe him—I really did. But part of me was still that young girl who watched him walk away without a backward glance.

The weight of our past pressed down on me, threatening to drown out the happiness we'd found again. I took a deep breath, trying to calm the storm brewing inside me. "I want to believe you, Flynn, but I don't know how."

He nodded, understanding in his eyes. "I know, and I don't blame you. But I'm going to prove it to you, every day. I'm not going anywhere, Amelia. I'm in this for the long haul."

I nodded, my heart torn between hope and fear. "I guess we'll see."

Flynn gave me a small reassuring smile, but the tension between us lingered, a reminder of the unresolved issues we still had to face.

The success of The Rewind Theater brought in a wave of new customers, and with it, new challenges.

The store was busier than ever, and we juggled the increased demand with the logistical issues of running a growing business. Flynn and I worked tirelessly, side by side, for four days, but the strain of our unresolved conversations simmered beneath the surface.

Things weren't right between us yet. I don't know if they ever would be. The sudden rush of customers provided a welcome distraction, allowing me a few precious moments of reprieve.

The town buzzed with excitement over the magic at Rewind Rentals. Word spread quickly about the mysterious map, and soon enough, people were flocking to the store, hoping to witness some magic for themselves.

The next night, when we showed the film *Rear Window*, a pair of binoculars appeared on a shelf in the theater with over seventy witnesses. Everyone wanted to know the secret to the magic. We didn't have any more answers now than the first time it had happened. It was great for business.

Flynn was busy fixing the old sound system. We weren't quite ready for that upgrade just yet, when a man in a sleek suit walked into the store. He introduced himself as David Reed, a representative from a "larger entertainment company"—as if he couldn't just tell us who he was really with. He was interested in purchasing Rewind Rentals and The Rewind Theater in key ready.

"You are all the buzz," David said, flashing a polished smile. "We believe this place has incredible potential. I came here today to make you an offer, Ms. Bennet."

I was taken aback. "Buy the store? But why?" Not that I hadn't thought about it. Before deciding to try and save it myself, I carefully considered and explored every available option.

David leaned forward, his expression serious. "We think Rewind Rentals could be the centerpiece of a new chain of retro movie experiences. With your unique touch and our resources, it could be something spectacular."

My mind raced. On one hand, I'd be lying if I didn't say the offer was tempting. It promised financial security and the chance to expand on a scale I hadn't dared to dream of. But on the other hand, the store was my family's legacy. Could I really sell it?

Flynn joined us, his expression guarded. "What kind of offer are we talking about?"

Flynn's eyes widened as I showed him the folder with a neatly typed proposal. The amount they were willing to pay was staggering. I glanced at him, seeing the same conflict mirrored in his eyes.

"I can see that you'll need some time to think on

it," David said, smoothing his suit. "Take all the time you need."

I couldn't find the words to reply.

"Thank you," Flynn said, his tone firm.

"I'll be in touch," David said before leaving the store.

As Flynn and I stood there, the weight of the choice bore down on me, filling the silence. It was my family legacy, and ultimately, my decision.

"What do you think?" I finally asked, breaking the tension.

Flynn rubbed the back of his neck, deep in thought. "I think his timing is weird. Like, where did he come from? Why would he want to buy something in this little town? But on the other hand, it's a lot of money, Amelia. More than you'd ever likely see otherwise. But is it worth giving up what you've built here?"

"I don't know," I admitted, my heart heavy with indecision. "This place means so much to me, to my family. I don't want to lose that."

"You should probably sleep on it. Weigh your options. We've worked hard to make this place what it is. You don't have to decide now if you want to keep fighting for it."

As I nodded, a strong sense of resolve settled

deep within me. "This place has always been more than just a business to me. It's my home."

Flynn smiled, reaching out to take my hand. "I'll support whatever decision you make. If you want to sell, I know a lawyer in town that could offer some advice. If you want to fight to keep it, I'll fight with you."

I let him hold my hand. The warmth of him was reassuring. It seemed I had two choices to make now.

THE DAY after meeting David Reed, the air felt thicker, filled with the weight of his proposal and the uncertainty it brought with it. Rewind Rentals had always been a haven, a constant in my previously chaotic life. Now, it felt like it was on the precipice of change, teetering between the familiar past and an uncertain future.

Amelia's parents had called her earlier that morning, announcing their official retirement. I knew this was something she had been anticipating for a while, but the timing couldn't have been worse. It was as if everything was happening at once, converging into a singular point of stress and decision.

"Amelia, your parents called again," I said, putting down the phone after they'd asked to speak with her. "How are you feeling about everything?"

She sighed, running a hand through her hair. "It's a lot to take in. I mean, I always knew they'd retire someday, but now it's real. They want to travel, spend time with friends. It's like they're finally letting go, and I have to be ready to carry this legacy on my own."

"You're not alone, Amelia. I'm here," I reassured her.

"I know. It's just a lot," she said, her voice laced with a mix of excitement and apprehension. "I just need to make sure we don't lose everything they've worked so hard for."

"We won't," I said firmly, trying to instill confidence in her and myself. "Whatever happens, whatever you decide, it will be okay," I said, as if saying it out loud would make it true.

Amelia nodded, taking the phone. "Hey, Mom."

With the store bustling and new customers flocking in to see the "magical" Rewind Rentals, I found myself increasingly fascinated by the mysterious events that were unfolding. The old map, the binoculars, and now we had a baseball bat from *Pride of the Yankees* and a yearbook from *The Graduate* with actual pictures from the high school in the film...they couldn't all be coincidences. There had to be something more, something tied to the very essence of this place.

Driven by curiosity and the need to understand, I dug deeper into the store's origins. Maybe there was a logical explanation as to why Rewind Rentals always seemed to be at the epicenter. I wanted to know why Amelia's grandparents had stopped showing films if they knew about the magic and what it could mean for us now.

I made my way to Spellbound Stories, the local bookstore known for its eclectic collection of rare books on local lore. The inside of the cozy little shop was designed to look like you've just walked into a fantasy novel. There were towering shelves and the comforting smell of new and aged paper. As I entered, I was greeted by a dark-haired man with an easy smile.

"Welcome, I'm Park. Let me know if there's anything specific you're looking for," he said, his voice warm and inviting.

"I'm Flynn," I replied, shaking his hand. "I'm actually looking for information about the history of Rewind Rentals. It's had some…interesting things happen recently, and I'm trying to figure out why."

Park raised an eyebrow, intrigued. "Rewind Rentals, huh? That place has quite a reputation. I think I might have something that could help."

He led me through the maze of bookshelves to a section dedicated to local history and legends. He pulled out a non-fiction book with a worn cover titled, *Mystical Happenings in Coral Cove*, and flipped through the pages until he found what he was looking for.

"Here you go," Park said, passing the book to me. "In a chapter about unusual spots in Coral Cove, Rewind is specifically mentioned. It turns out that even before it was a rental store, the place was known for its frequent occurrence of unexplained phenomena."

I scanned the page, taking in the stories of mysterious apparitions and objects appearing out of thin air. It was fascinating and unnerving at the same time. "This is incredible," I said, looking up at Park. "Do you know why these things happened there?"

Park nodded. "The book hints that the magic could be influenced by the original owner's deep connection to Coral Cove. The rumors were that they dabbled in the supernatural." Park shrugged. "But if you want to know more, you should talk to Lillian at the flower shop. She's been around a lot longer than most people realize, and she might have some insights that you won't find in any book."

"Can I buy this?" I asked, holding up the book.

"Sure thing," he said.

I thanked Park for his help and promised to return with an update if I learned anything. I left the store and couldn't shake the feeling that I was on the brink of discovering something monumental.

The Sunflower was a small, charming flower shop filled with vibrant blooms and the soothing scent of lavender in the air. Lillian, the owner, was tending to a display of sunflowers when I walked in. She was an elegant woman with a timeless aura about her. Her eyes twinkled with the wisdom of someone who had seen much in her lifetime.

"Flynn Callahan," she greeted me with a knowing smile. "I was wondering when you'd come by."

Her familiarity caught me completely off guard. "I'm sorry, but do we know each other?"

"Word gets around in a town like this," she said with a gentle laugh. "And I make it my business to know what's happening, especially when it involves magic."

I nodded, feeling slightly out of my depth. "I'm trying to understand the magic at Rewind Rentals. It's become a bit of a mystery, and I was hoping you could shed some light on it."

Lillian gestured for me to follow her to a small sitting area at the back of the shop. "I'm surprised that Amelia isn't here with you."

"She's feeling overwhelmed by all the attention the shop is getting," I said nervously. "I just want to help her understand her heritage a bit more. So she can make a sound decision with all the facts laid before her."

"Amelia's grandparents were quite special, you know. They were close friends of mine," Lillian said.

I tried not to show my skepticism. There was no way Lillian was a day over thirty.

She continued. "They had a deep connection with the magic that flows through Coral Cove. The projector you have was enchanted by them, a gift to keep the town's magic alive."

"But if that's true, why did they stop using it?" I asked, eager for answers.

"They didn't stop out of fear," Lillian explained. "They stopped because they were worried about the attention it was drawing. Not everyone sees magic as a gift. Some see it as something to be exploited."

I frowned, the weight of her words sinking in. "So, the objects appearing in the store... they're manifestations of the films?"

Lillian nodded. "Yes, and more. They're a reflection of the town's history, its stories coming to life. The magic preserves the heritage of Coral Cove, to remind people of the wonders that lie beneath the surface."

I sat back, absorbing the enormity of what she was saying. "And what should we do with this information?"

"Embrace it," Lillian said with a soft smile. "Use it to bring people together, to celebrate the uniqueness of Coral Cove. It's a legacy worth protecting."

Her words resonated with me, and I knew I had to share this revelation with Amelia. But first, I needed to tell my cousin, Rory. She was making a film about the store. I needed to give Amelia a real choice and a store worth fighting for.

I thanked Lillian for her time and insights, promising to keep her updated on our plans. This was no longer just about saving a store, it was about honoring a legacy, preserving the magic that made Coral Cove special.

Back at Rewind Rentals, I called Rory, eager to fill her in on everything I'd learned.

"Hey, Flynn," Rory answered, her voice bright with anticipation. "How's everything going?"

"You're not going to believe this," I said, launching into the story of my meeting with Lillian and the book from Park.

"Wow," she said, her voice tinged with awe. "That's incredible. We have to include this in the film."

"Exactly," I agreed. "I'll send you copies of everything I've found. This could really add depth to your project."

"Thanks, Flynn. I'm excited to see where this goes," Rory said.

"Can you help me with one other thing?" I asked.

"Anything."

After hanging up, I felt a renewed sense of determination. We were on the brink of something amazing, a beacon of magic and community. I'd only have to wait a little longer till I could tell Amelia.

CHAPTER 9
AMELIA

IN WHAT FELT LIKE AN INSTANT, another week slipped away. Flynn and I were still tiptoeing around the beanbag sex.

I tried to focus on the task at hand, but my mind kept drifting back to the kiss we had shared. It was as if the memory of it had seared itself into my skin, every brush of his lips replaying in my mind. I could still feel the way his hands had gripped my waist, the way his breath had mingled with mine, the taste of him lingering on my lips.

The tension between us was palpable, even when we weren't touching. Flynn seemed to sense it too, his gaze following me whenever I moved, his body gravitating toward mine like a magnet. He was always just a little too close, his voice dropping to that low, intimate tone that made my insides flutter. I knew we needed to talk, to address what had happened, but the thought of it terrified me. What if he regretted it? What if he didn't feel the same way?

The uncertainty gnawed at me, making me short-tempered and distracted. But I couldn't bring myself to confront him, to risk shattering the fragile connection we had built. So, I avoided him, avoided being alone with him, even though every fiber of my being ached to be near him again. I knew I couldn't give him the attention he craved.

Besides, he made me wait six years. He could cool it for a couple of weeks.

Life at Rewind Theater and Rentals had found a new rhythm. The store was bustling, the movie nights were selling out, and we were constantly on our toes to keep up with the demand. The chaotic pace had become strangely comforting, a welcome distraction from the heavy decisions looming over me.

Last week, I overheard Flynn speaking quietly on a phone call. No matter what I did, that feeling stayed with me the entire week. I'd convinced myself he was accepting another job, and the anxiety gnawed at me. He was going to leave, again.

His voice was barely a whisper, but the few words I managed to catch sent a wave of dread crashing over me. "Yeah, I know it's a big opportunity… I'll consider it for sure… I'm just not sure if I'm ready to make a move. There's a lot at stake for me right now… Okay, I look forward to hearing from you again…"

I froze, my hand hovering over the doorknob. The conversation echoed with a seriousness that immediately sent my mind spiraling to the worst possible scenario.

Was Flynn actually considering leaving again?

Had he found another job that promised him everything he said he didn't want anymore?

Was I ever going to be enough?

I waited until the conversation ended before walking into the office, trying to act as casual as I could despite the knot tightening in my stomach.

"Who was that?" I asked, keeping my tone light.

Flynn looked up, his face unreadable. "Just… someone about an opportunity," he said, his eyes not quite meeting mine.

"What kind of opportunity?" I asked. My chest tightened as the weight of the unspoken goodbye settled in.

"Umm," he cleared his throat. "For me."

"Are you thinking about taking it?" I pressed, unable to keep the concern out of my voice.

He hesitated, and I could see him weighing his

words. "I'm still thinking things over. Honestly, it doesn't matter."

Part of me wanted to push for more information, to demand to know what was going on in his head. Despite my inner conflict, I restrained myself. If he wanted to leave, he knew where the door was.

I forced a smile and nodded. "Okay, well, let me know if you need to talk about it."

"Of course," he said, offering a smile that didn't quite reach his eyes.

After overhearing Flynn's phone call, a sharp pang of jealousy and fear gripped my heart. The idea of him leaving again, of walking out of my life just when I was starting to let him back in, was unbearable. The thought consumed me, making me even more aware of the tension between us.

That evening, when we finally had a moment alone, the air was thick with unspoken words. Flynn stood close, too close, his hand brushing against mine as we talked. The contact sent a jolt through me, and I could feel the heat radiating off his body, drawing me in.

"Amelia," Flynn murmured, his voice low, almost a whisper. He stepped closer, his chest brushing against mine, his breath warm on my skin. "We need to talk."

My heart raced, and I knew we were standing on

the edge of something irreversible. But before I could respond, his hand found my waist, pulling me closer until our bodies were pressed together. I could feel the hard planes of his chest against me, the tension in his muscles as he held himself back.

"Flynn," I breathed, my voice trembling with the weight of everything I wanted to say.

But before I could say another word, he kissed me again, hard and desperate, as if he were afraid this might be our last chance. The kiss was a storm, wild and untamed, and I surrendered to it, letting the waves of desire crash over me. We were both on fire, consumed by the heat that had been building between us for weeks.

I pulled away first, the sudden distance between us feeling like a cold shock. I cleared my throat, running a hand down my shirt as if smoothing out the fabric could also smooth out the feelings churning inside me. I took a step backward, creating a necessary physical barrier. Without meeting his eyes, I spun around and busied myself with the nearest task, anything to distract from the moment that had just passed between us.

THE REST of the day passed in a blur of customer interactions and managing logistics, but Flynn's evasiveness lingered in the back of my mind. I couldn't shake the feeling that something was going on, something that he wasn't telling me. Conflicting emotions bubbled and resurfaced. I didn't enjoy any part of it.

As the week drew to a close, I found myself more and more excited about the upcoming grand reopening. The renovations were almost complete, and the store had undergone a stunning transformation. The theater was a hit, the profits were better than I could have ever imagined, and everything seemed to fall into place.

Despite the success, the question of whether to sell the store loomed. David Reed's offer was still on the table, and while I had decided not to worry about it until after the reopening, it was hard to ignore the financial security it promised.

Even with the tension, the reality was Flynn had been a rock through all of it. From helping me make minor changes and tweaks to optimize the store's operations, he had a knack for spotting what worked and what didn't, and his suggestions were invaluable.

As we ushered the last customer out and locked up for the night, Flynn turned to me with a mischievous grin. "I have a surprise for you."

"A surprise?" I asked, raising an eyebrow. "What kind of surprise?"

"Something special. I wanted to wait until after everyone's gone home and we're all locked up. I want to show you a film. It's something I think you'll really appreciate."

A flutter of excitement moved through me, and I followed him upstairs. "This isn't going to be a repeat of last time, is it?" I teased, trying to keep things light.

Flynn chuckled, a warm, genuine sound. "Would that be so bad?"

Heat pooled in my center at the memory, reminding me of all the feelings I still had for Flynn. Feelings I needed to sort out. "Okay, show me this surprise of yours."

The lights dimmed, and the only sound was the hum of the old projector.

"I promise this is something you'll want to see."

The film began, and the opening scenes immediately captivated me. It was Rory's documentary, featuring Rewind Rentals, its history, and the magic that had become part of its identity. The footage was beautifully shot, interwoven with stories about the town and its unique charm.

As I watched, a whirlwind of emotions stirred deep within me, my heart expanding. There were interviews with locals, tales of the magical events that had taken place, and glimpses into a past I hadn't known about. It was a love letter to the store, to my family, and to Coral Cove itself.

Flynn sat beside me, his presence reassuring. As the film continued, I realized what he had done. He had preserved part of my history forever, ensuring that the legacy of Rewind Rentals would be known to the world no matter what decision I made.

Tears filled my eyes as the credits rolled. I turned to Flynn, overwhelmed by the gratitude I felt. "This is incredible. Flynn, I don't even know what to say."

He took my hand, his eyes soft and earnest. "No matter what you decide, Amelia, whether you sell the store or keep it, what you've made here will always be preserved. Several film circuits picked the documentary up, and people will know about Rewind Rentals and its magic."

I was at a loss for words, happiness and disbelief mingling in my chest. But the joy was tempered by the lingering doubt about the phone call I'd overheard more than a week ago. I had to know the truth.

I took a deep breath. "Flynn," I started.

He met my eyes.

"I overheard you talking on the phone about a job. Are you leaving?" My voice trembled as I asked, feeling the weight of it in every word.

He looked at me, his expression one of surprise, before a flash of understanding crossed it. "No, Amelia, I'm not going anywhere. I was talking to Rory. I wanted this to be a surprise, and I didn't want to spoil it. The film was the enormous opportunity we were talking about. She asked if you were still considering selling the store. I told her I didn't think you were ready to decide. That's all."

As the puzzle pieces fell into place, relief washed over me, and I felt foolish for doubting him. "So, you're not leaving?"

He shook his head. "I'm not leaving, Amelia. I'm here, and I'm staying."

"I'm sorry. I just... I've been so scared that you'd leave again."

He pulled me into his arms, holding me close. "You have nothing to be sorry for, Amelia. I understand where your fear is coming from. It's okay, I'm not leaving. I'm here for the long haul. I love you, and I want to be with you, Amelia Bennet."

Tears slipped down my cheeks. "I love you too, Flynn. I want to give us another chance. A real one."

He smiled, brushing the tears from my face, and kissed me with a tenderness that made my heart flutter.

The plush seat surrounded us in a cocoon of intimacy. The air seemed to crackle with anticipation as

Flynn leaned in, his lips meeting mine in a lingering kiss. His touch was soft at first, exploring and teasing, until a spark of hunger ignited between us.

Eagerly, I threaded my hands through his hair, drawing him closer. The world outside ceased to exist. There was only Flynn. His presence was a heady mix of desire.

Our kiss deepened. Flynn's hands explored every inch of my body, discovering all the secret spots that would make me quiver with delight. He broke away, his warm breath caressing my skin as he whispered. "I've been thinking about this for weeks."

My pulse quickened at the promise in his voice. "Then stop thinking," I whispered.

His chuckle was low and wicked. Flynn kissed me again, more insistent this time. The air was thick with tension, a tangible force pulling us closer together.

Flynn's hands moved to my waist, lifting me effortlessly onto his lap. As I straddled him, my knees on either side of his hips, I could feel the undeniable presence of his erection pressing against me. It made my breath catch in my chest.

He pulled back slightly, eyes dark with need as he gazed into mine. His voice grew deeper as he murmured, "You're beautiful."

A flush of heat spread through me at his words. I reached for the hem of my shirt, tugging it over my head and tossing it aside. Flynn's eyes drank me in, his hands skimming over my bare skin with a touch that made me shiver.

His lips followed, trailing kisses along my neck and collarbone, each one a promise of the pleasure to come. I arched into him, my body aching for more of his touch.

With a playful grin, Flynn leaned back, his hands moving to my hips as he guided my movements. I gasped as he rocked me against him, feeling the evidence of his arousal pressing against my center.

"Flynn," I breathed, my voice dripping with desperate need and longing.

He responded with a soft groan, his hands tightening their grip on my hips as he pulled me closer. "I want to taste you," he said, his voice thick with desire.

I licked my lips, nodding as my body trembled with excitement. Flynn's gaze held mine as he gently shifted me off of his lap, helping me to stand. He knelt before me, his hands sliding down my sides, fingers curling around the waistband of my jeans.

I watched, captivated, as he slowly undid the button and slid the zipper down, his eyes never leaving mine. There was something deliciously wicked about the way he looked at me. It was a promise.

With a deft motion, Flynn eased my jeans down, leaving me exposed to his gaze. His hands lingered on my hips as he pressed a soft kiss to my stomach, warmth pooling in my belly.

I let out a soft moan, my fingers tangling in his hair as I guided him lower. Flynn obliged, his kisses trailing down my thighs, each touch setting my skin on fire.

Flynn paused, looking up at me with a devilish grin that made my heart skip a beat. Then, with deliberate slowness, he leaned in, his mouth a source of exquisite pleasure as he tasted me, his tongue tracing patterns on my clit that made my toes curl and my mind lose all focus.

My world narrowed to this moment, the sensation of Flynn's touch driving me to the edge of madness. My fingers tightened in his hair, urging him on as my body moved with a will of its own, lost in the ecstasy he gave me.

The first wave of pleasure crashed over me, and I cried out, body shuddering as Flynn continued his relentless assault, drawing out every last ounce of sensation until I was left breathless and trembling.

When I finally opened my eyes, Flynn was watching me, a satisfied smile playing on his lips. His voice, heavy with desire, whispered, "You taste even better than I remembered."

I laughed softly, pulling him up to me for a searing kiss, tasting myself on his tongue. My fingers worked at his belt, eager to free him from the confines of his clothes. Flynn helped, shrugging out of his shirt and jeans, and soon we were skin against skin, the heat of our bodies mingling in a dance of passion.

Flynn sank back into the seat, and I straddled him once more, my heart pounding with anticipation. I took him in, inch by inch, savoring the feel of him filling me completely.

Once he filled my core, we moved slowly, a languid rhythm that built with each heartbeat. My breath came in soft pants as I rode his exquisite cock, my body moving in time with his, our connection a symphony of shared desire.

Flynn's hands gripped my hips, guiding my movements with skill. The tension inside me built, a tightening coil of sensation that threatened to unravel at any moment.

"Flynn," I breathed, my voice a plea for release.

He responded with a soft groan—his eyes darkening with desire. With a sudden burst of energy, he flipped me onto my back, my body cradled by the plush seat as he thrust into me with a newfound urgency.

I cried out, my senses overwhelmed by the intensity of his movement. Flynn's hands were everywhere, tracing patterns on my skin, his mouth claiming mine in a kiss that spoke of possession and love.

The world around us faded to nothing, leaving only the two of us entwined in this intimate dance. His thick, hard shaft thrusting inside of me, the feel of his body moving in time with my own, drove me to the brink, and I surrendered to the pleasure that washed over me in waves.

Like a sudden storm, the climax engulfed me with intensity. I couldn't control the shudders that ran through my body as he held me, and all I could do was call out his name. Flynn followed soon after, his own release, a powerful surge, leaving him breathless.

We lay together, wrapped in the aftermath of our shared passion, the theater a silent witness to the bond we'd forged. I rested my head against Flynn's chest, listening to the steady beat of his heart as I savored the warmth of his embrace.

With all inhibitions abandoned, we made love

again, our hearts open and our emotions unleashed. It was better than before, a connection that felt right and true. In this moment, I knew without a doubt that this was where I belonged—in the arms of the man I loved, in the sanctuary of our shared world.

THE EXCITEMENT in Coral Cove was palpable as word spread that the documentary featuring Rewind Rentals had been accepted into several film festivals. The phone hadn't stopped ringing for days, with journalists, bloggers, and film enthusiasts eager to know more about the magical rental store that had captured the hearts of so many.

It was surreal to think that our little slice of nostalgia was making such waves. I couldn't help but smile every time I saw the look of pride on Amelia's face as she read through the emails and social media comments, praising her dedication and vision.

"Flynn, can you believe this?" Amelia said one afternoon, her eyes wide with disbelief as she scanned through the latest message on her phone. I kissed her neck. "I've been invited to present at the Coastal Film Festival next month!"

I grinned, my chest swelling with pride. "You deserve this, Amelia. You and Rewind Rentals both. This is your legacy, and it's finally getting the recognition it deserves."

She looked up at me, her expression softening. "I couldn't have done any of this without you, you know. Your support and belief in this place have meant everything to me."

I reached across the counter and squeezed her hand, feeling the warmth of her touch. "We make a pretty great team, don't we?"

Her smile was answer enough, and it filled me with a sense of contentment that I hadn't felt in years.

As the buzz around the documentary continued to grow, we threw ourselves into planning the grand reopening event for the store. It was the perfect opportunity to unveil the film to the community and celebrate the transformation of Rewind Rentals into a beloved local attraction and tourist destination.

The preparations were intense. We wanted everything to be perfect—the decorations, the refreshments, the screenings—and we worked tirelessly to ensure that the event would be a memorable one.

Amelia and I spent hours in the theater room, tweaking the seating arrangement and testing the sound system to make sure it was just right. We organized a lineup of classic films to be shown throughout the reopening day for free, interspersed with clips from the documentary.

"I think we're ready," Amelia said, stepping back to admire our handiwork. "The place looks incredible."

I nodded, taking in the newly polished floors, the vintage posters lining the walls, and the cozy seating area that had become the heart of Rewind Rentals. "It really does. You've created something amazing here."

The night of the grand reopening arrived, and the store was buzzing with anticipation. The line stretched down the block, a mix of folks eager to experience the magic of The Rewind Theater.

As the doors opened and the crowd poured in, I watched with a sense of pride as Amelia greeted guests, her energy infectious. The documentary played on a loop in the rental shop downstairs and upstairs between showings. It drew in a lot of "oohs" and "ahhs" from the audience as they marveled at the story of our store and its mystical legacy.

The event was a resounding success. People laughed, reminisced, and shared stories of their own experiences with movies and magic. By the end of the night, Rewind Rentals had cemented itself as a cherished part of Coral Cove, a place where memories were made and dreams came to life.

As the last of the guests trickled out, Amelia and I sat together on one of the theater couches, exhaustion mingling with satisfaction.

"We did it," I said, wrapping an arm around her shoulders. "Rewind Rentals is officially the hottest spot in Coral Cove."

Amelia leaned into me, her head resting on my chest. "I can hardly believe it. It feels like a dream."

"It's real," I assured her. "And it's all because of you."

She lifted her head, her eyes meeting mine with a mixture of gratitude and love. "Flynn, I don't think I've ever been happier."

"Does this mean you're not going to sell?" I asked.

"I already called to tell him thanks, but no thanks."

Relief washed over me. "I'm glad to hear it," I said, my heart pounding as I prepared to take the next step. "Because there's something I want to ask you."

Amelia sat up, curiosity sparkling in her eyes. "What is it?"

Taking a deep breath, I reached into my pocket and pulled out a small box, feeling a wave of nerves crash over me. "I know we've been through a lot, and we've worked so hard to get here, but I can't imagine spending another day without you by my side. Amelia Bennet, will you be my partner—not just in business, but in life?" I opened the box to reveal a morganite ring. "Will you marry me?"

I watched as her eyes widened in surprise, and my heart skipped a beat, fearing I had pushed her too soon. But in an instant, her expression transformed into a beaming smile, and she enthusiastically wrapped her arms around me, almost causing us to tumble from the couch.

"Yes!" she exclaimed, laughter bubbling up from her chest. "Yes, Flynn, a thousand times, yes!"

Relief and joy flooded through me as I kissed her, feeling the last of my doubts melt away. We were in this together, now and forever.

EPILOGUE

AMELIA

THE SUN SET over Coral Cove, casting a warm, golden hue that danced across the waters and painted the sky in shades of pink and orange. Standing at the entrance of Rewind Rentals, I took a deep breath, savoring the sweet smell of popcorn and the sound of laughter that drifted from inside the store. The grand reopening had been everything I could have hoped for, and more.

In the weeks that followed, the buzz from the documentary continued to grow. It had not only been accepted into multiple film festivals, but it also won awards, garnering attention far beyond what we had imagined. Each award brought a new wave of visitors, eager to experience the magic of The Rewind Theater for themselves. The store had become a cultural landmark, offering not just movie rentals, but a nostalgic and enchanting experience that resonated with people from all walks of life.

Flynn and I were amazed by the response, and as our days grew busier, our relationship blossomed alongside the success of our store—a seamless intertwining of our lives. The magic of Coral Cove had found its home in Rewind Rentals, and we embraced it wholeheartedly, hosting special events that celebrated the town's unique history and enchantment.

We expanded our business model, collaborating with other local shops and artists to create a vibrant community hub. These partnerships breathed new life into the store, attracting an even broader audience and making Rewind Rentals a centerpiece of the community. We even planned to turn the third and fourth floors into additional theaters in time.

I walked to the counter, where my parents stood, their faces beaming with pride as they watched the bustling store. It was a busy Saturday afternoon, and every corner of the store was filled with life—families picking out movies, couples holding hands as they browsed, and groups of friends laughing as they reminisced about old film favorites.

"You've done us proud, Amelia," my mother said, clapping me on the back. "Your grandparents would be overjoyed to witness the amazing things you have achieved."

Tears shimmered in my eyes, and I hugged them both tightly. "Thank you. I couldn't have done it without you," I said, feeling the familiar warmth of love and gratitude wash over me.

As the evening drew on and the crowd thinned, I found myself at the counter, watching the store buzz. I felt a deep sense of fulfillment and purpose, knowing that Rewind Rentals was more than just a business; it was a testament to what could be achieved when people came together with a shared dream.

Flynn joined me, slipping his hand into mine, his presence grounding and reassuring. "What are you thinking about?" he asked.

"Just how far we've come," I replied, squeezing his hand. "And how grateful I am for all of it."

He smiled, the kind of smile that reached his eyes and made my heart skip a beat. "I'm grateful too. We make a pretty good team, don't we?"

"The best," I agreed, feeling the truth of it resonate in my bones.

Together, we stood there, savoring the moment as the store hummed around us, creating a comforting symphony. It served as a powerful reminder of how community, love, and the invisible threads of magic intertwined to create something truly remarkable.

As the night settled over Coral Cove, I knew that whatever the future held, we would face it side by side. The magic of this town had woven its spell around us, and I was more than happy to be caught in its enchanting embrace.

Rewind Rentals would always be a place of wonder and nostalgia, a beacon of magic in Coral Cove. And as Flynn wrapped his arm around me, pulling me close, I felt a profound sense of peace and joy.

"This is where we belong," I said softly, leaning into him.

Flynn nodded, his gaze warm and full of love. "This is our home, Amelia. It's our story."

———

SIGN up for Jax Wilder's newsletter and receive a collection of unpublished Coral Cove short stories. Meet familiar characters and dive deeper into the love and romance that Coral Cove is known for. Don't miss out on this exclusive content!

Jax Wilder

If you enjoyed Love Rewound, you'll want to check out Amelia and Flynn's story in the Tarot Fantasies series

Six of Cups

Some love stories need to be rewound to be truly understood.

Amelia:

I'm haunted by memories of my first love, Flynn. Can revisiting the past help me finally move on, or will it pull me back into the love I've never fully let go of?

FLYNN:

Amelia always saw the best in me, even when I couldn't. Now, I'm back in her life, but only as a memory. Can I help her heal, or will our past keep haunting us both?

IN THE MYSTICAL heart of the Arcane Room, where memories come alive and the past intertwines with the present, Amelia is on a quest for closure. Haunted by the lingering emotions of her first love, she returns to the enigmatic room to confront the memories that have held her captive for years. But as the past unfurls before her eyes, she discovers that some memories are more powerful—and more painful—than she ever imagined.

Guided by the Six of Cups tarot card, a symbol of nostalgia and childhood innocence, Amelia is drawn into a world where the lines between reality and fantasy blur. Each memory brings her closer to the truth about her relationship with Flynn, forcing her to face the joys and sorrows of their love story.

As the memories unfold, Amelia must decide if she's ready to finally let go of the past or if she'll be forever bound by the love she lost. In this emotionally charged journey, "Six of Cups" weaves a tale of love, loss, and the enduring power of memories.

Perfect for fans of romantic fantasy, magical realism, and emotional journeys of self-discovery, "Six of Cups" will take you on a heart-wrenching ride through the most cherished and painful moments of a love that was never meant to be forgotten.

THE PERFECT LOVER SPELL

A SHORT TIME TRAVEL, ACCIDENTAL
MAGIC ROMANCE WITH HEA

For my witchy kin.

I see you.

CHAPTER 1
JESSA

ZEUS, in his cruelty, tore humans apart, leaving us fractured and incomplete, destined to roam the earth in search of the missing pieces of our souls.

More specifically, our soulmates.

Most of us stumble through life, swiping left or right, convinced that a filtered selfie of a random stranger might somehow unlock the door to true love. Honestly, it's laughable. I've swiped right more times than I can count, but not one of those digital matches has ever led me to anything resembling love.

Take Mason, for instance. He was a charming ex-Mormon who had a serious grudge against caffeine and a terrifying knack for emotional manipulation. He chipped away at me, slowly eroding my confidence like he had done to countless women before me. But the final nail in the coffin? His blatant homophobia. That was the moment I realized I had absolutely no room in my life for bigots.

Then there was Lawrence. He was suave, sophisticated, and completely married—though he conveniently left out that minor detail. He invited me on what I thought was a romantic moonlit stroll after a party, where we shared secrets and flirtatious banter. That is, until we bumped into his wife, who was casually leaving the same party. Talk about an awkward encounter. Nothing says "run for the hills" like being the unintentional side piece.

Mutton Chops—yes, that's how I remember him —looked like the perfect match on paper. Punctual, good-looking, and brimming with confidence, he seemed like someone I could actually have fun with. But the moment he arrived at my place, he chose to park himself on the tiniest chair in my apartment instead of sitting next to me on the couch. That was red flag number one. Five minutes in, he was snoring like a chainsaw. Nothing says romance like falling asleep mid-date.

And let's not forget about the cute guy who claimed he was twenty-five, in town for the summer, and looking for some casual romance. He was sweet, almost too sweet—innocent, even. I should've known something was off. We went out for drinks, but when we got to the bar, he was denied entry. Turns out my "summer fling" was a nineteen-year-old carny, fresh off the circus circuit.

Seriously, what is wrong with me?

To say that my dating life has been a disaster is putting it lightly—like calling a shipwreck a minor inconvenience. But unlike the spinster I'm determined not to become, I keep throwing myself into the fray, hoping that the next swipe or awkward first date might lead to something real. Yet, here I am again, on the cusp of another evening, not planning to meet Mr. Right but instead heading toward something more reliable: a good book.

Right now, the only thing I can think about is heading to the bookstore, finding tonight's perfect book boyfriend, and curling up in bed with a glass of wine. It's not exactly the kind of passion I'd envisioned for my life, but it's dependable—and there's something comforting in that.

Stepping into Spellbound Stories feels like slipping into a warm bath after a long, cold day. This little corner of the world is my sanctuary. The fantasy décor, with its floating bookshelves and enchanted forest murals, stirs something magical inside me every time. And then there's that unmistakable new book smell that greets you at the door, lingering in every nook and cranny. It's pure bliss.

And, of course, there's Park. The adorable, off-limits clerk who's been the subject of one too many of my fantasies. Unfortunately, those fantasies were dashed when I learned that we're both playing for the same team—team "seeking men." But if nothing else, that revelation has given us a solid foundation for friendship. Plus, he always knows exactly which book will get me through the night, which is a skill I value almost as much as his good looks.

"Welcome!" Lea's voice chimed from behind the counter, carrying that sing-song cheerfulness that made her the perfect fit for a bookstore like this. "How are you doing today, Jessa?"

"Doing as well as can be expected," I replied with a smile. "Just here to find my date for the night."

"Park's putting out a couple of new titles right now," Lea said, nodding toward the back of the store.

"Perfect, thanks!" I followed her gesture, weaving through the aisles until I spotted Park, carefully arranging books on a shelf. "Hey, cutie," I called out.

He glanced over his shoulder, a playful smirk already forming on his lips. "If it isn't my favorite spinster," he teased.

I nudged his shoulder with mine, rolling my eyes. "Spinster or not, I'm on the hunt for love tonight. Think you can hook a girl up?"

He leaned back against the shelf, crossing his arms with a grin. "What's the request?"

"I'm looking for the perfect lover," I said, my voice taking on a dramatic tone. "Tall, confident, maybe a little on the kinky side. Any chance he's hiding out in an obscure corner, just waiting for me to discover him?"

Park raised an eyebrow, his expression turning thoughtful. "Hmm... well," he began, setting the books down on a nearby table. "Considering your... let's say, eclectic reading tastes..."

I shot him a mock-indignant look. "What exactly is that supposed to mean?"

He laughed, the sound warm and familiar. "Let me clarify—considering your willingness to dive into whatever weird and wonderful book I hand you, I think I have just the thing."

I tried to stifle my grin but failed miserably. "When you put it that way, you know I'm game. Bring it on."

Park didn't say another word. Instead, he led me to a section of the store that seemed almost hidden from the rest—an alcove tucked away. He ran his fingers along the spines, finally pausing at a thick, leather-bound book. He pulled it off the shelf and handed it to me with a flourish.

I took the book. "What do we have here? The Beginner's Guide to Romance Magic," I said hesitantly. "I was thinking something I could read one-handed, if you catch my drift."

Park chuckled. "Oh, I hear you loud and clear, Jessa. Turn to page seventy-eight. I think you might find something interesting there."

I flipped through the book and stopped on The Perfect Lover Spell. "Well, I mean, I did say I was looking for the perfect lover. I just didn't think, you know, magic was the answer."

"Hey, if it doesn't hurt anyone, what's the harm in trying it?" Park suggested.

"Okay, let's say I bite. I buy the book and add," I glanced at the page, "cloves to a potion. What happens? Will the man of my dreams come knocking on my door? Like magic?"

Park shrugged. "I don't know. But what I will say is that I did one of the spells, and then I met Ben. I'm not saying I met him because of the spell, but I'm not saying I didn't either."

"You liar. This book just came out, and you met Ben last Thanksgiving." I crossed my arms.

"Okay, well, that's true. But please?" he pouted.

"I'm not your guinea pig, Park."

"Yes, you are. And I need to know if it works. For research," he said, his eyes growing larger and more puppy-like.

"Fine," I conceded.

"You'll do the spell?" Park asked, far more excited than he should be.

"Yes, but you're giving me your employee discount on this one," I said. "Especially if I have to go to the store to buy ingredients for this experiment."

"Done."

CHAPTER 2
BRYCE

THE SUN HUNG low in the sky, casting a golden glow over the rolling hills that stretched beyond the village of Glenmore. I stood at the edge of my family's farm, leaning against the old wooden fence, watching the cows lazily grazing in the meadow. The air was fresh and crisp, a perfect reflection of the quaint life I led in this corner of Scotland.

"Oi, Bryce!" called a voice from behind me. It was Hamish, my neighbor, ambling down the path with a wide grin on his face. "Daydreaming again, are we?"

I chuckled, turning to face the older man. "Aye, just wondering what it would be like to see the world beyond these hills."

Hamish shook his head, a knowing twinkle in his eye. "Ah, the wanderlust of youth. But ye'll find there's plenty of adventure to be had right here in Glenmore if ye look hard enough."

I smiled, though my thoughts lingered elsewhere. While I loved my village, the longing for something more tugged at my heart. At thirty, I felt the weight of the years that had passed without the adventures I'd dreamed of in my youth. I imagined bustling cities, vibrant cultures, and the thrill of the unknown —all things I could only dream of while tending to the farm.

As we chatted, the faint sound of bagpipes drifted through the air from the village square, where the annual Glenmore Highland Games were underway. The event was a local highlight, a blend of tradition and friendly competition that brought everyone together.

"Are ye comin' to the games later, Bryce?" Hamish asked, his eyes alight with anticipation. "Ye might even find a bonnie lass to keep ye company."

I laughed, though I felt a familiar pang of yearning. "Perhaps, Hamish. But the lass who'll steal my heart might need to have a bit of magic about her," I said with a wink.

With a final wave, Hamish continued on his way, leaving me to my thoughts. As I made my way back to the farmhouse, I couldn't shake the feeling that my life was meant for more than this pastoral existence.

Inside the cozy kitchen, the aroma of freshly baked scones filled the air, and my mother, Moira, bustled about, her hands dusted with flour. "There you are, Bryce. I thought I'd heard you outside."

I kissed her cheek with a grin. "I thought I'd come and steal one of your scones, Mum."

Moira laughed softly, her eyes filled with affection. "You remind me so much of your father at your age. Always dreaming. But remember, sometimes the greatest adventures come when you least expect them."

As I helped set the table for tea, my mind wandered to the stories my father used to tell of our ancestors: fierce Highland warriors who embraced the unknown with courage. It was a legacy I felt in my bones, a reminder that the world was vast and full of possibilities.

Later, as twilight descended upon Glenmore, I walked the familiar path to the village square. The sound of laughter and music grew louder with each step, drawing me into the heart of the celebration. The Highland Games were in full swing, with kilt-clad competitors showcasing their strength and skill.

I joined a group of friends near the caber toss, exchanging jokes and playful banter. Despite the lively atmosphere, my mind wandered elsewhere. I was lost in thought when a sudden gust of wind swept through the square, causing the banners to flutter wildly. I shivered as a strange sensation coursed through me, as if the universe were shifting around me.

The feeling was fleeting, but it left me with an inexplicable sense of anticipation. I shook my head, dismissing it as the excitement of the games. Yet, deep down, I couldn't shake the feeling that something extraordinary was on the horizon.

As the night wore on, I found myself alone on a hill overlooking the village, the stars twinkling like a thousand distant dreams. I sighed, the cool breeze ruffling my hair.

"Maybe tomorrow," I whispered to the night sky. "Maybe tomorrow will be the day everything changes."

CHAPTER 3
JESSA

The list of ingredients are as follows:

A cauldron of water – Boil then turn to down to a simmer.

Cinnamon

Ginger Root

Star Anise

Lavender

Cloves

Fresh Rose Peddles

1 Pink Candle

DROPPING ginger root into the simmering pot, I scanned the list of ingredients again. I double-checked my grocery haul splayed out on the coun-tertop—everything seemed to be here. I stole another bite of my orange chicken and fried rice before going back to the spell book.

With any love spell, your intentions must be clear, infused with positive energy, and come from an honest heart. What you're asking from the universe must be in harmony with the world you live in. Remember, anything you put into the universe will come back three-fold—whether positive or negative.

Be sure to carefully consider what you ask for. There's nothing worse than asking for someone you think you want in your life, only to find out they're quite horrible for you—and worse, difficult to get rid of. Instead, focus on the feelings and qualities you desire in a lover.

Do you want a one-night stand or marriage? Do you need someone who's a caretaker or someone who can take control? What kind of sex life do you desire? What values should your future mate have? Considerations like money, family, kids, and religion are all crucial for a successful love spell.

The Perfect Lover Spell is best performed on a Friday, as Friday is the day of Aphrodite. When you have a clear idea of what you want in a lover, you're ready to perform the spell.

"Light a pink candle," I read aloud, spinning

around to grab the candle. The only pink one the grocery store had was a seven-day candle with a picture of Dolly Parton on the outside. "Alright, Dolly, let's do this thing." I struck a match. "Let there be light."

Add the cinnamon, cloves, lavender, ginger root, and star anise, to the cauldron.

I grabbed the last two ingredients on the list, then dropped in the ginger root and the little star anise into the simmering pot. "Okay, Perfect Lover Spell, let's make some magic."

Before you start the incantation, it's best to be naked. Nudity helps break down our walls and allows us to be more open and vulnerable. No barriers between you and the life you desire.

Per the instructions, I stripped off my clothes. If this is some stupid joke, Park will never hear the end of it.

Naked, standing over a pot of bubbling water with the lit Dolly candle at the ready, I couldn't help but smile.

After you say the first part of the incantation, add one

rose petal for every attribute of your perfect lover. Then,
say the final incantation.

I assumed my silver pot would do instead of a cauldron. But if this goes awry—again—I'm blaming Park. Plain and simple.

I took a deep breath.

"You must believe for it to work," I said aloud. Wasn't that what Park told me before I left?

I closed my eyes and thought about all the horrible dates and boyfriends I've had. All the shitty lovers who made me doubt my own attractiveness. The boys who toyed with my heart and made me feel less than. I didn't want to bring that kind of nasty energy into this experience. If I'm going to do a love spell, I'm going to give it everything.

I took another deep breath and tried to channel the future I wanted. The book said manifestation is about speaking as if you already have everything you desire.

You're bringing your future to the present. Try saying,
"I have the perfect lover," instead of, "I want the perfect
lover."

I don't know if I fully understand the larger

universal implications, but I can play ball. Okay, I think I'm ready for this.

I took a long pull from my glass of wine. Yeah, I wasn't about to perform magic for the first time sober. I read the incantation to myself one more time.

It's now or never, Jessa.

"Aphrodite, Goddess of love and beauty, bring to me a lover worthy of me, and I worthy of them," I began, taking a breath and grabbing my rose petals. I dropped one into the pot with each desire. "My lover is a kind man. He is a caregiver who understands what it means to care for your partner. My lover makes me laugh. I never worry about how they feel or what we mean to each other; there is complete honesty and trust between us. We complete each other—mind, body, and soul. Intellectually, sexually, and spiritually. There is an understanding between us that transcends this human existence. We fulfill each other sexually. He was made for me, and I for him. Our desire for one another never wavers. He is my perfect lover, partner, and soulmate," I said, feeling my words resonate through every fiber of my being.

"Oh, and he has a birthmark on his ass," I added, just to ensure I'd know if the spell worked. Letting my last petal fall into the water, I felt something inside me begin to grow.

I glanced at the book again for the closing words. "Goddess Aphrodite, I submit myself to you. Bring my perfect lover to me. So mote it be, three by three by three."

THE WOOD SHOP was my sanctuary, filled with the scent of freshly cut lumber. I spent countless hours here, surrounded by the comforting aroma of sawdust and the rhythmic sounds of tools shaping wood. On any given day, you could find me crafting furniture, restoring antiques, or simply tinkering with ideas that danced around in my mind. The family business wasn't bustling by any means, but it was familiar, and it was mine. Today, however, was different.

I was sanding down a rough edge on an old chair when a sudden gust of wind whipped through the open window. The weather in Scotland was as fickle as a cat, but this breeze felt peculiar. It carried an energy, a strange tingling that seemed to hum through the air and settle in me, penetrating my skin, worming its way down into my bones.

Brushing it off as nothing more than an odd draft, I refocused on my work. But the feeling didn't leave. It intensified, becoming almost electric, like the air before a storm. I set the sandpaper down—something prickled at the back of my neck.

Before I could ponder further, the world around me twisted and blurred. My workshop dissolved into a whirlwind of colors and light. My heart pounded, threatening to break free from my chest. Panic rose as I grasped at the bench, trying to anchor myself in reality.

"What the bloody—" I began, but the words were snatched away as the vortex swallowed me whole.

The sensation was dizzying, like being caught in a maelstrom, tumbling through space and time. My stomach lurched, and my mind raced with a thousand questions. What was happening? Was this some sort of dream? Had I inhaled too many varnish fumes?

Then, just as suddenly as it began, the storm ceased. I landed with a thud on a soft carpet, blinking against the sudden brightness.

Disoriented, I took in my surroundings. I was no longer in my workshop, that was for sure. Instead, I found myself in a cozy living room filled with the scent of lavender and vanilla. Books lined the walls, and a simmering pot bubbled nearby, emitting fragrant steam.

I blinked again, struggling to make sense of the impossible. It was like stepping into a scene from one of the old stories my father used to tell about High-landers lost to time and another world.

"W-where am I?" I muttered to myself, still trying to catch my breath.

From the corner of my eye, there was movement. A woman, wide-eyed and clearly as startled as I was, stood just a few feet away. Her hair cascaded in wild curls, and her skin was flushed from what I assumed was a combination of shock and embarrassment.

And then it hit me: this goddess was stark naked.

My brain short-circuited for a moment, and all I could do was stare, my mouth opening and closing like a daft fish. The woman let out a startled yelp, snatching a nearby blanket and wrapping it around herself with a speed that would have impressed an Olympic athlete.

"Who are you?" she demanded, eyes narrowing suspiciously. "And what are you doing in my apartment?"

I tried to find my voice, but it seemed to have taken a temporary leave of absence. "I—uh—well, I was just in my workshop, and then there was this—

this whirlwind, and now I'm here." My words tumbled out in a thick Scottish brogue, no doubt sounding as bewildered as I felt.

Her expression shifted from suspicion to confusion, her grip on the blanket loosening slightly. "A whirlwind? What, like you caught a tornado here, Dorothy?"

I shook my head. "I don't know who Dorothy is. It was like a magical teleportation spell or something." I put my hands up. "I've never been the subject of magic or tornado-induced transportation before. It's all new to me."

Her eyes narrowed.

I shrugged helplessly. "One moment I was in Scotland, and the next, I'm in your living room."

"Scotland?" she echoed, eyebrows shooting up. "You're saying you're from Scotland?"

I nodded, trying to make sense of the situation while attempting to ignore the surge of awareness that came with her standing so close. "Aye. Name's Bryce MacGregor," I said, my voice a bit huskier than I intended. "And you are?"

"Jessa," she replied, her gaze softening slightly. "Jessa Owens."

We stood there, both of us grappling with the absurdity of the situation. It felt like a scene straight out of a romance novel, where destiny—or perhaps a touch of magic—intervened in the most unexpected ways. The air between us seemed to hum with unspoken possibilities, leaving me wondering if fate was playing a cruel joke or if there was something more at play.

"Okay, let's just take a breath," Jessa said, her voice betraying her effort to regain composure. "There's got to be some logical explanation for this."

I chuckled. "Logical explanation? Lass, I've just been whisked across the globe and landed in a room with a naked woman. Logic seems to have taken a holiday."

To my surprise, she laughed—a bright, genuine sound that cut through the tension, making the situation feel a little less surreal. "Fair point. This is... unusual, to say the least."

I couldn't help but grin. Jessa was undeniably charming, her wild curls framing a face that managed to look both fierce and soft at the same time. Even in this bizarre scenario, I found myself drawn to her—a pull that was more than just the situation. It was in the way she carried herself, a blend of confidence and vulnerability that stirred something deep within me. I realized, with a jolt, that I didn't want to look away.

"Where is here?" I asked, scanning the room for any context clues that might ground me in reality.

"You're in Coral Cove. The Pacific Northwest of the United States," she replied.

"Really?" I asked, eyebrows raising in surprise.

Jessa nodded, a hint of amusement in her eyes.

"Weird," I murmured, still processing the strangeness of it all, yet unable to shake the feeling that there was something extraordinary about this moment—and about her.

"So, Bryce," she said, her voice softening as her eyes met mine, a curious blend of amusement and something else flickering in their depths. "Do you have any idea how we're going to get you back to Scotland?" The way she said my name, like a secret only the two of us shared, sent a shiver down my spine.

I shrugged, glancing around the room as if the answer might be hiding in a corner. "I've no clue. But maybe there's a reason I ended up here."

Jessa eyed me thoughtfully, the corners of her lips twitching in a half-smile. "A reason, huh? Like destiny or magic?"

I tilted my head, weighing the possibility. "Perhaps. Or maybe the universe just has a peculiar sense of humor."

We both laughed, a shared moment of camaraderie amidst the chaos. Neither of us had the answers, but there was something oddly comforting about facing the unknown together.

"Well, until we figure it out," Jessa said, her voice dropping to a low, almost conspiratorial tone as she gestured toward the couch, "make yourself at home. I'm going to find some clothes." She turned to leave, but not before our eyes locked for a heartbeat longer than necessary, the air between us charged with a tension neither of us dared to acknowledge. Yet.

"Don't do it for me," I teased, winking as I settled into the plush cushions, marveling at the strange twist of fate that had brought me here. An adventure indeed, I thought, as I watched Jessa move around the room with an air of determination.

In that moment, as I sat in her living room, the reality of my situation began to sink in. But instead of fear or confusion, what I felt was a pulse of pure, unfiltered excitement. My eyes followed Jessa as she moved around the room, my mind spinning with possibilities. Maybe, just maybe, this was the adventure I'd been waiting for all along—and perhaps, if the universe had its way, it wasn't just an adventure of place, but of the heart as well.

THE SILENCE in the room was almost comical. If someone had told me this morning that I'd be standing in my living room, wrapped in a blanket, talking to a Scotsman who looked like he'd stepped out of a Highlander romance, I would've laughed in their face. Yet, here we were, both of us equally perplexed and trying to make sense of it all.

"What's the date?" Bryce asked, his brow furrowing slightly as he scanned the room like a time traveler trying to place his coordinates.

I shook my head, trying to keep the absurdity from overwhelming me. "You look pretty present-day to me," I replied, my voice barely masking the rising hysteria.

"Is it twenty-fourteen?" he asked again, his tone

insistent, eyes locking onto mine with a seriousness that sent a shiver down my spine.

I blinked, my brain doing somersaults. "Are you serious?"

"I mean, I think life is more enjoyable with a laugh, but on this point, I'm wholly serious," he replied, his thick Scottish brogue making even the most ridiculous statements sound like sweet promises.

I watched him settle onto my couch as if he belonged there, a bemused grin tugging at his lips. He looked far too comfortable for someone who'd just been plucked from his cozy workshop in Scotland and dropped into my living room like a very sexy, very confusing gift from the universe. The whole situation felt like a fever dream, and I half-expected to wake up any moment.

But Bryce... well, he didn't seem like he was in any rush to leave. In fact, he looked almost amused by the whole ordeal, like this was just another quirky adventure life had thrown his way. Maybe it was the rugged charm, or the way his eyes sparkled with mischief despite the craziness, but I found myself relaxing, if only a little.

"I suppose putting you on a plane is out of the question. You're about ten years behind," I said, attempting to inject some humor into the madness.

"Ten years?" Bryce echoed, his brows knitting together in surprise. "Was it a good ten years?"

I cringed, not sure how to sugarcoat the past decade.

He waved a hand dismissively, his tone light despite the bizarre situation. "Don't tell me. I'd rather find out for myself."

I turned away, beginning to pace the room, clutching the blanket around me like it was a lifeline. Magic wasn't real. Or, at least, that's what I kept telling myself, even as the evidence sat there, looking every bit the part of a displaced Scotsman.

"Okay, Jessa," I muttered to myself, trying to regain control of my racing thoughts. "Let's break this down. Somehow, you performed a spell and conjured up a man. Not just any man, but a man from Scotland, and apparently, from ten years in the past. What are the odds?" I paused, wondering if my friend Park had spiked my drink with something hallucinogenic. This couldn't be real.

"Ye look like you're trying to solve a grand mystery, lass," Bryce observed, his voice teasing yet warm, like a gentle nudge out of my spiraling thoughts.

I stopped pacing and faced him, trying not to be distracted by how ridiculously handsome he was. "I just don't understand how any of this is possible. I mean, I did a spell as a joke," I admitted, throwing my hands up in exasperation. "Magic isn't real. People don't just appear out of thin air."

"If magic isn't real, why were you practicing it?" Bryce asked, his tone curious yet pointed, like he was genuinely trying to understand the logic—or lack thereof.

That pulled me up short. "I... well, maybe a tiny part of me wanted to believe in something more," I confessed, suddenly feeling very exposed under his gaze.

"So maybe people do appear out of thin air after all?" Bryce smirked, leaning back on the couch as if he'd just won an argument. "I'm living proof of it, am I not?"

I wanted to argue, to cling to some semblance of reality, but the evidence was sitting right there, all six feet of him, rugged and undeniably real. "This can't be happening," I muttered, more to myself than to him.

Bryce leaned forward, resting his elbows on his knees, his eyes gleaming with a mix of amusement and seriousness. "Ye're not the only one feeling out of sorts. I was just a simple man, working on a chair, and now I'm here, talking to you. And if magic's the culprit, then we'll just have to figure out how to make it work in reverse, aye?"

I sighed, the weight of the situation finally sinking in. "Yeah, about that… Even if we figure out how to reverse the spell, you're kind of stuck around here for the moment."

His brow furrowed deeply, a hint of vulnerability seeping through his confident demeanor. "What do you mean?"

I hesitated, trying to find the right words. "Well, you said you're from Scotland, right? From ten years ago?"

He nodded, the confusion evident on his face.

"Even if we could get you a plane ticket, you don't have any ID, and it's not just that," I continued, watching as the realization began to dawn on him. "You're technically not even in the right year. If you go back, your friends and family will think you've been missing for the last decade. You can't just pop back into their lives like nothing happened."

The realization hit him, and his expression shifted from bemusement to concern. "Ten years? That's… quite a long time to be gone. My family would think I disappeared, or worse."

"Exactly," I said, the gravity of the situation settling heavily between us. "We need to figure out how this happened and, more importantly, how to reverse it. Until then, you're stuck here."

Bryce leaned back, rubbing his chin thoughtfully,

a slow grin spreading across his face. "Stuck in the future with a beautiful woman. There are worse fates, I suppose," he quipped, though the smile didn't quite reach his eyes.

I couldn't help but chuckle, despite the storm of emotions swirling around us. "Don't get any ideas, MacGregor. This isn't some romance novel where we fall in love at first sight."

He raised an eyebrow, his playful demeanor returning. "Who said anything about love? I'm just trying to make the best of a strange situation."

I crossed my arms, the blanket slipping slightly, reminding me of my less-than-ideal wardrobe situation. "Good. As long as we're clear on that. No magic spell is going to make me fall for a man I accidentally conjured."

Bryce nodded, but I could see the hint of challenge in his eyes. "Understood, lass. But I'm still curious about this magic of yours. How exactly did you manage to bring me here?"

I sighed, realizing it was time to come clean. My cheeks warmed under his gaze. "I was just messing around with a book that a friend recommended. It was called *The Beginner's Guide to Romance Magic*. There was this spell—The Perfect Lover Spell—and, well, I guess it worked a little too well."

His eyes lit up with interest, a mischievous glint

appearing. "And what exactly were ye hopin' to conjure with this spell?"

I felt the blush deepen. "Not a real person, that's for sure. Just, you know, the idea of the perfect partner. Someone who's kind, funny, and maybe a little bit magical."

Bryce chuckled, the sound warm and rich, sending a shiver down my spine. "And here I am. Though I'm not sure how magical I am, beyond the whole time-travelin' Scotsman thing."

Heat bloomed in my center. "Yeah, well, you've got a lot to live up to, MacGregor," I teased, feeling the tension between us ease slightly.

We shared a moment of silence, both of us lost in thought about the bizarre twist our lives had taken. Despite my initial disbelief, I couldn't deny the connection forming between us. It was as if the universe had thrown us together for a reason, even if I wasn't ready to admit it.

"So, what's our plan, then?" Bryce asked, breaking the silence with that same playful tone. "How do we unravel this mystery?"

I considered the question, feeling the weight of our predicament settle in. "First, we need to do some research. I'll check the book and see if there are any clues about reversing the spell. Maybe we can find answers online, too."

Bryce nodded, determination in his eyes. "And until then, I suppose we're partners in this strange adventure?" He reached out his hand.

"Yeah, partners," I agreed, slipping my hand into his. My heart fluttered at the contact.

"The perfect lover, aye?" he said, gently rubbing the back of my hand, his voice dropping to a low, teasing rumble.

I nodded, unable to tear my gaze away from his. His touch sent a jolt of electricity through me, making my heart skip a beat. There was a softness in his eyes, a mischievous glint that made me both nervous and excited. I couldn't deny it any longer—Bryce was gorgeous. His dark red hair was tousled in a way that suggested he was born to star in a Highland fantasy, and his piercing blue eyes seemed to see right through me, right into my soul.

Bryce didn't let go of my hand. Instead, he gently pulled me down onto the couch beside him. The world seemed to tilt on its axis as I sank into the cushions, feeling the heat radiating from his body.

"I've got to say, you did quite a job with that spell, lass," he teased, his voice a delicious rumble that made my skin tingle. "If you were aiming for the perfect lover, I'm afraid I might disappoint. But I'll do my best to rise to the occasion."

"Is that right?" I challenged, feeling bolder than I

had in years. "Well, I'm a pretty demanding woman, you know. You might have your work cut out for you."

His grin widened, full of confidence and that irresistible charm. "Aye, but I'm a quick study."

Without another word, he leaned in and kissed me, his lips soft and tentative against mine. The world fell away, leaving just the two of us in that moment, suspended in time. It was like fireworks behind my eyes—dazzling, electric, and utterly breathtaking.

I melted into him, my mind a whirl of emotions as the kiss deepened. My thoughts flickered back to the spell, how I conjured him out of thin air with nothing but words and wishes. Yet in that moment, he felt as real and solid as anything I'd ever known.

Bryce's hands moved to my waist, pulling me closer until I was practically in his lap. The blanket slipped, exposing more of my skin to the cool air. I gasped against his mouth, and he chuckled, a low, sexy sound that made my pulse race.

"Ye're more beautiful than I could have imagined," he murmured, his fingers tracing delicate lines along my bare shoulders, leaving a trail of fire in their wake.

I shivered, both from his touch and his words. "You imagined me?"

He pulled back slightly, his eyes twinkling with mischief. "Of course. A woman who could conjure me from ten years in the past and halfway around the world had to be something extraordinary."

I laughed, feeling the tension melt away, replaced by a delicious heat that spread through my entire body. "Well, I did say I wanted someone a little magical."

"And here I am," he replied, shifting beneath me so that I straddled him, the blanket slipping further down my body.

His hands moved with a gentle but insistent purpose, sliding the blanket away to reveal my breasts. His gaze traveled over me, reverent and appreciative, and I felt a flush of heat that had nothing to do with embarrassment.

"You're incredible, Jessa," he said, his voice hushed with awe. "I don't think I've ever seen anyone so stunning."

A smile tugged at my lips, but words seemed to fail me. Instead, I reached up, threading my fingers through his hair, loving the feel of his dark red locks against my skin.

With each kiss that Bryce trailed along my collarbone, my skin erupted in a symphony of goosebumps, amplifying the sensation of his touch. His hands followed the path his mouth set, exploring with a touch that was both teasing and tender.

"I suppose I'm just about the luckiest man alive to have been conjured by someone as remarkable as you," he murmured against my skin, his lips curving into a playful smile.

"Don't get too cocky, MacGregor," I warned, though my voice was breathless, and my heart was pounding in my chest.

"Ah, but ye like me cocky," he playfully teased, leaving a trail of gentle kisses along my shoulder, his hands caressing every inch of exposed skin. Every place he touched me left fire in its wake.

I sucked in a breath as his touch moved lower, tracing lines down my body and removing the blanket entirely. It was all I could do to hold onto him, to keep from losing myself completely in the sensations he stirred.

"Words," I whispered, my voice a mere breath of sound. "I need words."

Bryce chuckled, lifting me effortlessly in his arms. "Words are overrated, love. Actions speak louder, don't ye think?"

He carried me toward the bedroom, every step sending anticipation humming through me. I couldn't help but giggle, feeling like a teenager sneaking away for a forbidden tryst.

"This way?" he asked, nudging the door open with his foot, his grin wide and irresistible.

I nodded, unable to find my voice, pointing him toward the bed that awaited us.

He laid me down gently, straddling over me with a grace that belied his strength. "Ye know, your room is as enchanting as you are," he said, casting a glance around the eclectic décor that filled the space. "I half expected unicorns and fairy dust."

I laughed, feeling warmth blossom in my chest. "Sorry to disappoint. Just me and a lot of books."

"Well, that's a sight I'll never tire of," he replied, his fingers tracing a line along my jaw before capturing my lips in another searing kiss.

It was everything I'd imagined and more—the perfect blend of passion and playfulness that left me breathless. I tugged at his shirt, eager to feel more of him, to discover every inch of the man I'd somehow conjured.

"Too many clothes," I murmured against his lips, my hands deftly working to free him from the fabric that separated us.

He obliged with a smirk, tossing his shirt aside to reveal a physique that was lean and muscular. I drank him in, my eyes wide with appreciation as I traced the lines of his muscles with eager fingers.

"Ye approve, then?" he asked, his voice a low rumble that sent heat pooling in my belly.

"Very much," I breathed, feeling the connection between us deepen with every touch, every kiss.

His hands explored my body with a reverence that sucked all the air out of my lungs. All words died on my lips. Soon we were tangled together, a symphony of limbs and laughter and teasing caresses.

I found myself above him once more, straddling his hips as he gazed up at me with an intensity that made my heart skip a beat. He was beautiful, all tousled hair and smoldering eyes. The mere thought of him being here, with me, in this moment sent a thrill coursing through my veins.

As his hard cock entered me, a moan escaped my lips. The world fell away, leaving only us, wrapped in a magical cocoon of warmth and desire. We stayed like that for a long moment, my body adjusting to the girth of him. I moved above him, each slow thrust igniting a firestorm of pleasure that built with intensity.

Bryce's hands found my hips again, guiding me with a firm touch, his thumbs tracing patterns across my skin that sent delicious shivers racing through me.

His touch drifted lower, finding my clit, the sensitive bundle of nerves that sent shockwaves of plea-sure coursing through my veins. My breath hitched, my insides coiling in on themselves. With one touch, I was lost to the sensation, to the overwhelming bliss that surged through me in waves.

When release finally claimed me, it was with a force that shattered every thought, every worry, leaving only the blinding euphoria of the moment.

I cried out, my body trembling with the after-shocks of the most explosive orgasm I'd ever expe-rienced.

As I collapsed against him, breathless and spent, Bryce wrapped his arms around me, holding me close. The world slowly came back into focus, and I found myself nestled against him, feeling a sense of peace and contentment that was wholly unexpected.

"Ye're quite the enchantress, Jessa," he said, pressing a soft kiss to my temple. "I've a feeling this adventure is just beginning."

I smiled, unable to deny the truth of his words. Maybe magic was real after all. And maybe, just maybe, I'd found my perfect lover in the most unex-pected of ways.

CHAPTER 6
BRYCE

THE MORNING LIGHT filtered softly through the curtains, casting a warm, golden glow over the room. I lay still, listening to the rhythmic sound of Jessa's breathing beside me, her chest rising and falling in a slow, peaceful rhythm. My mind, however, was anything but peaceful—a whirlwind of thoughts raced through it, trying to make sense of the past few hours.

This morning, I'd been nothing more than a man sanding down a chair in Scotland. Now, I was lying in bed with a woman who had somehow conjured me out of my life and into the future. It was surreal, impossible even, but there was something about it that felt... right. And that scared the hell out of me. The longer I lay there, the more doubts crept in.

Sure, Jessa was enchanting—wild hair, expressive

eyes, a laugh that could light up the darkest room. She was the kind of woman who turned heads, made you forget your own name. But the idea that I could fall in love with her? That seemed far-fetched. I couldn't stay with someone who'd summoned me with magic. I had a life back in Scotland—one I needed to return to, for better or worse.

Careful not to wake her, I slipped out of bed and quietly pulled on my clothes before wandering into the living room. The remnants of our night together were scattered around, but my thoughts were elsewhere. I had to figure out how to reverse this spell, how to get back to my time.

Despite the undeniable chemistry between us, this was temporary. A fluke of magic that needed fixing. I wasn't meant to be here, in this time, with this woman. As I paced the room, though, part of me couldn't help but be drawn to her—like maybe there was a reason for all of this, something more at play than just magic.

A soft rustle of sheets signaled that Jessa was waking up. I turned to see her standing in the doorway, wrapped in a blanket, her eyes sleepy but curious as she looked at me.

"Good morning," she said, her voice heavy with sleep. "You're up early."

"Aye," I replied, trying to keep my tone light. "Too many thoughts running through my head."

She joined me on the couch, tucking her legs beneath her and pulling the blanket tighter around her shoulders. "I get it. It's a lot to take in."

We sat in comfortable silence for a moment, the events of the night still hanging between us like a charged wire. I knew we had to talk, figure out what had happened and, more importantly, how to fix it.

"So," I began, turning to face her. "This spell of yours—the one that brought me here—any idea how to reverse it?"

She sighed, running a hand through her tousled hair. "I was hoping you had some brilliant insight. I've never done anything like this before."

"Well, we've got to start somewhere," I said, trying to be practical even as my mind raced with a thousand questions. "Maybe that book you mentioned? It might have some answers."

Jessa nodded, her eyes meeting mine with a spark of determination. "I'll grab it. There might be something we missed."

She retrieved the book from the table, flipping through its pages with a focused intensity that made her even more attractive. There was something about the way she tackled problems head-on that I found irresistible—her strength, her resolve, the way she didn't back down.

We spent the morning poring over the book, jotting down notes, tossing around ideas on how to reverse the spell. It was like working on a complex puzzle, each piece needing to fit perfectly for us to see the full picture. And as strange as it was, I found myself enjoying it—the challenge, the way our minds seemed to sync in this strange dance of problem-solving.

"Here," Jessa said, pointing to a passage in the book. "This part talks about reversing spells. Maybe we can use some of these principles to send you back."

I leaned in closer, reading over her shoulder. Her scent—fresh and floral with a hint of spice—filled my senses. "Aye, it's worth a shot. If we can gather the right ingredients, maybe we can make this work."

As we discussed our plan, the connection between us seemed to grow stronger, as if the universe was weaving our fates together for a reason. Despite my initial resistance, I couldn't deny the attraction, the bond that was forming. It felt as real as anything I'd ever known.

After what felt like hours of intense focus, my stomach rumbled loudly enough to make us both pause. I looked at Jessa, and she smiled, a playful glint in her eyes.

"Sounds like someone's ready for a break," she teased.

I chuckled, rubbing the back of my neck. "Aye, it seems spellcasting is hungry work."

Jessa stretched, closing the book with a soft thud. "Why don't we take a break? I could use a bite to eat too."

I glanced at her, feeling a tug of familiarity despite the strangeness of our situation. "I'd be happy to make us something, though I cannae promise much beyond a simple meal."

"Be my guest," she said with a wave toward the kitchen. "Just don't be surprised if you find more condiments than actual food in there."

Curious, I opened the fridge, only to find it nearly barren—some takeout containers, a half-empty carton of milk, and a lone stick of butter. I raised an eyebrow, turning back to her with a wry grin.

"Looks like I'd need a bit of magic to make a meal out of this," I quipped.

Jessa laughed, the sound bright and infectious. "Guilty as charged. How about we head out for lunch instead? There's this little place—Golden Chopsticks. Nothing fancy, but they make the best orange chicken."

The idea of stepping out into this unfamiliar world felt daunting, but something about her smile put me at ease. "That sounds perfect," I agreed. "Though if we're going out, I might need to clean up a bit."

Jessa's eyes sparkled with a teasing glint. "I was just thinking the same thing. I need a shower, and you, my dear Scotsman, are more than welcome to join."

A thrill shot through me at her invitation, and I found myself grinning. "When in Rome, aye?"

She led me to the bathroom, revealing a space that was nothing short of a modern marvel. The shower was immense, the kind you'd find in a luxury spa, with no doors or curtains—just sleek tiles and an open design with three showerheads arranged to hit you from every angle.

"This is... impressive," I admitted, taking it all in. "Dare I say, intimidating."

Jessa chuckled, stepping into the shower with a grace that was downright mesmerizing. "It's why I chose this place. The shower made it worth it."

I followed her, the warmth of the water cascading over us as the showerheads sprang to life, enveloping us in a steamy, sensual embrace. The sensation was divine, washing away the remnants of doubt and worry that had been gnawing at me since I'd arrived here.

Jessa turned to face me, her gaze locking onto mine as the water traced rivulets down her skin. I was captivated, unable to tear my eyes away from the woman who had somehow brought me into her world. Her hair clung to her shoulders, droplets glistening on her skin like diamonds.

"You're beautiful," I murmured, stepping closer until our bodies were almost touching.

She smiled, reaching for the soap and lathering it in her hands before gently applying it to my chest. Her touch was tender yet electrifying, exploring every contour and muscle with a care that made my pulse quicken and my knees weak.

"You have a birthmark on your bottom," she said.

"Me whole life," I say as she traced fingers on it.

As she worked my body, I took the soap from her, returning the favor by running my hands over her back, her shoulders, and down the curve of her spine. The intimacy of it all was intoxicating, the heat of the shower matching the warmth that blossomed between us.

"Feels nice," she sighed, leaning into me.

I began washing her hair, my fingers massaging her scalp as the fragrant suds enveloped us. It was a simple gesture, but it felt incredibly intimate—like we were sharing something far deeper than just a shower.

As the soap and water rinsed away, Jessa wrapped her arms around me, pressing her body against mine. I held her close, inhaling her scent—fresh, floral, and utterly irresistible.

"Ye smell amazing," I whispered, my lips grazing her ear.

She shivered, and I felt her pulse quicken against my chest. "You're not so bad yourself," she replied, her voice playful but laced with desire.

I couldn't resist any longer. My hands traveled lower, finding her center and coaxing soft moans from her lips. She leaned into me as I explored her with deliberate, gentle strokes, each one drawing her closer to the edge. Her gasps and trembles spurred me on, the fire between us burning hotter with every touch.

Jessa arched against me, her breaths coming in ragged gasps as I continued to pleasure her, my fingers dancing over her sensitive skin. The world narrowed to this moment, this connection, as the water cascaded around us.

Her release was exquisite, a symphony of cries and whispered curses as she reached her peak. I held her through it all, savoring the way she clung to me, the way her body responded to my every touch.

When the aftershocks of her climax finally subsided, Jessa looked up at me with eyes that sparkled with satisfaction and something deeper, something that made my heart skip a beat. "That was... wow," she breathed, still catching her breath.

I grinned, a swell of pride warming me from the inside out. "Glad to be of service, lass."

She kissed me then, a deep, lingering kiss that spoke volumes—more than words ever could. It was a kiss that promised so much more than just physical connection; it was a merging of our worlds, our lives, in a way that felt undeniably right, despite the madness that had brought us together.

As the heat of the moment cooled, Jessa lowered herself to her knees, her intentions clear in the sultry gaze she gave me. My heart raced as I watched her, anticipation building in every fiber of my being.

"Now it's my turn," she purred, her voice dripping with seduction.

Her hands moved with a confident grace, exploring every inch of me as she took me into her mouth, her touch igniting a blaze along my skin. The world around us faded away, leaving only the two of us, the water, and the pure ecstasy that unfurled in a tidal wave between us.

I was lost to it, to her, as her mouth moved over me with a skill that left me gasping, my control slipping with every moment. The tightening in my core grew, an intense, burning pleasure that built with every stroke, every flick of her tongue up and down my thrumming erection.

And when the release finally came, it was like nothing I'd ever experienced—a torrent of pure bliss that left me shaking, my mind adrift on a sea of satisfaction. I couldn't hold back the moan that escaped my lips as I let go, my hands tangling in her wet hair, anchoring me to the moment.

We stayed like that for a while, her holding me through the aftershocks, our breaths mingling in the steam-filled air. When the last of my strength left me, I pulled her up to her feet and into my arms, holding her close as the water continued to rain down on us, a soothing lullaby.

It felt like a dream—this beautiful, impossible escape from reality that I wished could last forever. But as we stood there, wrapped in each other's arms, I realized that maybe, just maybe, this was real. That this connection between us was something more than just the result of a spell gone wrong.

As the water finally began to cool, I pressed a kiss to the top of her head. "We should probably get out before we turn into prunes," I teased, my voice light, but my heart heavy with the weight of what lay ahead.

Jessa chuckled softly, the sound vibrating through me in the most delicious way. "Yeah, probably a good idea," she agreed, though neither of us made a move to separate just yet.

Eventually, with a reluctant sigh, we turned off the water and stepped out of the shower, drying off with the towels she handed me. The easy banter from before returned, filling the space between us as we dressed.

But there was something different now—an unspoken understanding that this was more than just a fling, more than just a result of magical interference. There was a connection between us that defied logic, defied time itself, and as we got ready to step out into the world, I knew that no matter what happened next, I wasn't ready to let her go.

"Ready for that orange chicken?" she asked, a playful smile tugging at the corners of her lips as she slipped on her shoes.

I nodded, returning her smile with one of my own. "Aye."

CHAPTER 7

JESSA

THE DAY WAS SUNNY, and the warmth on my skin felt like a gentle reminder that my world had shifted in ways I never could have imagined. As Bryce and I strolled side by side toward Golden Chopsticks, the events of the last twenty-four hours played like a reel in my mind—a surreal mix of magic, disbelief, and an undeniable attraction that had me questioning everything.

Bryce glanced around with wide eyes, his gaze darting from the cars to the people bustling along the sidewalks. He looked like a tourist in a strange new world, and I found it utterly endearing.

"So this is the future," he mused, shaking his head slightly, a mix of awe and confusion in his expression. "Hardly seems real."

"Trust me," I said with a chuckle, nudging him

playfully with my elbow. "It feels the same to me. But I have to admit, having a time-traveling Scotsman by my side does add a certain charm to it."

He laughed, a rich, genuine sound that sent a pleasant warmth through my chest. Despite everything, his presence was comforting, like I'd known him forever—even if forever had only been a day.

When we arrived at Golden Chopsticks, the mouthwatering scent of soy sauce and sesame oil clung to the air. The small restaurant was bustling with lunchtime patrons, but we managed to snag a cozy booth by the window.

"This place is delightful," Bryce said, his eyes taking in the lively atmosphere. "Reminds me of the pub back home—always full of life and chatter."

I settled into the booth, grabbing a menu and sliding one across the table to him. "You should try the orange chicken," I suggested, winking at him. "It's like a party in your mouth. Trust me."

He scanned the menu with interest, looking adorably out of place yet somehow perfectly at home in my world. I found myself studying him—how his strong hands held the menu, the way his eyes lit up when he found something intriguing. He was fascinating, and I wanted to know everything about him.

"So," I said, eager to learn more about the man

who had quite literally tumbled into my life. "Tell me about Scotland. What's it like?"

Bryce's face lit up, his eyes shining with warmth. "Ah, Scotland. It's beautiful—rolling hills, sweeping moors, the kind of landscape that makes you feel small in the best way possible. You can lose yourself in the mist and feel like you're the only person on earth." He took a sip of water, his gaze far away as he reminisced. "When I left, it was the time of the Highland Games. The air was filled with the sound of bagpipes and the laughter of people gathering for the festivities."

I could almost picture it in my mind, imagining the vibrant colors and lively atmosphere he described. "It sounds magical," I said softly, my voice tinged with longing.

He nodded, his expression thoughtful. "Aye, it is. I run my family's furniture shop there, restoring antiques. There's something about bringing an old piece of wood back to life that just feels... right."

"That sounds fulfilling," I said, genuinely intrigued. "I imagine you must be pretty good with your hands."

Bryce smirked, his eyes sparkling with mischief. "Oh, lass, you've no idea."

I blushed, thinking about the shower—I had some idea. Thankfully, the waiter arrived to take our order, saving me from further embarrassment. As we waited for our food, the conversation flowed naturally, a comfortable rhythm settling between us.

I told him about my job as a high school English teacher, how I loved introducing my students to the world of literature and the power of words.

"You're shaping the future," he said, admiration clear in his tone. "That's no small feat."

I shrugged, feeling a bit shy under his praise. "I try my best. Though, shouldn't you be in a classroom right now, shaping those young minds?"

I laughed, shaking my head. "Today's Saturday, Bryce. You really have lost track of time, haven't you?"

He chuckled, running a hand through his hair, a sheepish grin on his face. "Aye, I suppose I have. This whole time-travel business has me feeling a bit out of sorts."

When our food arrived, Bryce's eyes widened in delight as he tasted the orange chicken. "This is incredible! They don't make anything quite like this back home."

We ate in comfortable silence for a moment, the satisfaction of a good meal adding to the pleasantness of the day. But curiosity got the better of him, and soon he was looking at me with those inquisitive eyes of his.

"So, what's happened in the last ten years? Anything I should be aware of?"

I paused, searching for the right words to distill the last decade into something manageable. "Well, let's see… technology's pretty much taken over every aspect of life. Robots are everywhere, and if you're not careful, they'll be taking your job next. Social media isn't just on your phone anymore—it's in your glasses, your watches, even your TV. Politics? Well, that's been one hell of a rollercoaster. Honestly, I'm not sure you're ready for that ride. And, oh yeah, we survived a global pandemic—not that we've fully figured out what that means yet."

Bryce's eyes widened, clearly startled by the mention of a pandemic. "A pandemic?"

I nodded, giving him a reassuring smile. "Yeah, it was intense. Lockdowns, masks, the whole nine yards. If you're thinking about where to put your money these days," I added, letting a smirk slip through, "ByteDance a solid bet."

Bryce chuckled, the sound tinged with a mix of disbelief and amusement. "That's a lot to process. Maybe being stuck here a while longer isn't such a bad thing. Gives me time to get up to speed."

As we finished our meal, a sense of contentment settled over me. Bryce's company was easy, enjoyable, and it was hard to believe we'd only just met.

THE PERFECT LOVER SPELL

But the reality of our situation loomed over us, and I knew we needed answers.

"Ready to hit the bookstore?" I asked, hoping we might find some clues about how to reverse the spell. After all, that's where I'd bought the book in the first place.

Bryce nodded, his expression turning serious. "Aye, let's see if we can make sense of this mess."

We left the restaurant and made our way to Spellbound Stories, the bell above the door chiming as we entered. I spotted Park organizing a display near the back.

"Jessa!" he exclaimed, his eyes lighting up when he saw me. But when his gaze shifted to Bryce, his jaw dropped. "Wait a minute… Is this…?"

"Park, meet Bryce MacGregor, straight from 2014," I said, introducing them with a flourish.

Park's eyes widened as he approached, studying Bryce with a mix of awe and disbelief. "I can't believe it. You're really from the past?"

Bryce nodded, extending a hand with that charming smile of his. "That I am. Pleasure to meet ye."

Park shook his hand, still looking incredulous. "I don't know whether to be amazed or terrified."

"We're hoping you can help us figure out how to reverse the spell," I said, cutting to the chase.

Park hesitated, scratching his head. "Well, I got the book from The Arcane Room. Ms. Vesper recommended it. She's kind of an expert in these things."

"Ms. Vesper?" Bryce echoed, glancing at me with curiosity.

"She's kind of a local legend," I explained. "If anyone knows about reversing spells, it'll be her."

Park nodded, a sheepish smile on his face. "I might have mentioned you to her, Jessa. I'm a bit of a romantic meddler, and I thought you deserved more. I had no idea this would happen."

His admission warmed my heart, and I pulled him into a hug. "Thank you, Park. It means a lot."

Bryce chuckled, watching the exchange with amusement. "Looks like I've got ye to thank for bringing a bit of magic into my life."

We left Spellbound Stories with a renewed sense of hope. With Park's information, we had a lead—a chance to unravel the mystery of the spell and perhaps find a way to send Bryce home.

But as we made our way to The Arcane Room, a pang of uncertainty settled in my chest. We were getting closer to finding a solution, but that also meant we were getting closer to saying goodbye. I pushed the thought down, determined to focus on the task at hand.

The Arcane Room was nestled on a quiet street,

its exterior as mysterious and enchanting as its name suggested. As we approached, I felt a tingle of anticipation, a mix of excitement and nerves swirling in my stomach.

We entered, and the air was thick with the scent of incense, the walls lined with crystals, tarot cards, and various mystical trinkets. The atmosphere was hushed, as if the very walls held ancient secrets.

"Ah, Jessa and Bryce," a voice called from behind a curtain. Ms. Vesper appeared, her eyes twinkling with an otherworldly wisdom. "I've been expecting you. I could feel the energy shift yesterday."

Bryce and I exchanged a glance, both of us caught off guard by her foresight. "You knew we were coming?" I asked, incredulous.

Ms. Vesper nodded, a knowing smile playing on her lips. "Indeed. Magic has a way of guiding those who need it to where they must be."

A shiver ran down my spine, the weight of our quest settling in. We were bound by the spell that had brought us here and by the connection that had formed between us—a connection that, despite everything, felt as real and unbreakable as the very magic that had started it all.

CHAPTER 8
BRYCE

THE ARCANE ROOM was unlike any place I'd ever seen. The walls were lined with crystals and trinkets that glimmered under dim lights, casting an otherworldly glow over everything. The air was thick with the intoxicating scent of incense, carrying an almost euphoric energy that made the shop hum with possibilities. It was the kind of place where anything could happen, and I wasn't sure if that excited or terrified me.

Ms. Vesper watched us with a knowing smile, her eyes twinkling with the kind of wisdom that only comes from years of experience in matters far beyond the ordinary.

I exchanged a glance with Jessa, feeling a mix of curiosity and uncertainty. Ms. Vesper motioned for us to sit at a small table draped with a deep purple cloth. As we settled in, her gaze seemed to pierce right through us, as if she could see every thought, every fear, every unspoken word.

"It's not every day that a spell like yours takes effect," she began, her voice soft but filled with an authority that demanded attention. "But when it does, it speaks of desires that run deep and true."

I shifted in my seat, trying to wrap my mind around what she was saying. "What do you mean by that?" I asked, genuinely intrigued but also slightly unnerved.

Ms. Vesper leaned back, folding her hands in her lap, her eyes never leaving ours. "The spell Jessa used only works when the caster is honest about what they truly need in life. It requires more than just words—it demands a piece of your soul."

A piece of your soul. The phrase echoed in my mind, and I found myself glancing at Jessa. She was looking down, her expression contemplative, as if she was trying to piece together the same puzzle. There was a blush creeping up her cheeks, and something about her vulnerability in that moment touched something deep within me. I felt a warmth spreading through my chest, a connection that I hadn't expected but couldn't deny.

"You poured a part of yourself into the spell," Ms. Vesper continued, her eyes locked on Jessa. "And what you asked for was not merely a passing fancy. It was a desire for love and for a connection that transcends time and space."

Jessa's blush deepened, and I couldn't help but feel a surge of protectiveness, an instinct to reach out and comfort her. But I was also caught off guard by the intensity of my own emotions. Was it possible that this crazy, magical mishap had unearthed something I didn't even know I was searching for?

I cleared my throat, trying to regain some semblance of composure. "And what about the other person?" I asked, my voice a bit steadier. "What part do they play in this magic?"

Ms. Vesper turned her gaze to me, her eyes twinkling with a knowing look that made me feel exposed in the best way possible. "The spell would only draw someone who shared those same desires. A person who, whether consciously or not, longs for the same things—a partner who fulfills their soul's need."

Her words hung in the air like a challenge, daring me to confront the truth I'd been avoiding. Deep down, beneath the stoic façade I'd perfected over the years, I'd always yearned for something more than the ordinary. I'd dreamed of a love that defied logic and expectation, a connection that went beyond the mundane.

Jessa and I exchanged a glance, a silent understanding passing between us. The gravity of the situation settled over me like a weight, the realization that we were bound by something far more profound than mere circumstance.

Ms. Vesper's voice broke the silence, pulling us back to the present. "You must reverse the spell within twenty-four hours, or it will become permanent."

I tensed at the urgency in her words. A quick glance at my watch told me we had only a few hours left. My heart sank at the thought of leaving, but I knew it was the only way to set things right.

"How do we reverse it?" Jessa asked, her voice tinged with resolve, her fingers tightening around the edge of the table.

Ms. Vesper nodded, rising gracefully to gather a few items from around the shop. She returned with a blue candle and a small bag of herbs, handing them to Jessa with the kind of reverence you'd give a sacred relic.

"You'll need to create a simmer pot with these herbs," she explained, her tone steady and assured. "Light the candle, and repeat this incantation together. The spell will begin to unravel, but be warned, the bond you've formed will not simply disappear. It will remain a part of you both."

I took a deep breath, the weight of her words settling in like a bittersweet truth. The bond between us—real and undeniable—would linger, even as we parted ways. The thought was both comforting and heartbreaking.

Ms. Vesper's eyes softened as she looked at us. "Remember, love is the most powerful magic of all. Even if the spell is reversed, its effects may last longer than you realize."

I slipped my hand into Jessa's, feeling her fingers entwine with mine in a gesture that spoke louder than words. It was a silent promise, a commitment to face whatever lay ahead together. She squeezed my hand, and in that moment, I knew we were on the same page, even if we didn't know what the next chapter held.

"Thank you, Ms. Vesper," I said with genuine gratitude.

She smiled, a wise, knowing smile that seemed to carry the weight of lifetimes. "It's been a pleasure, dears. Trust in yourselves and in each other. Magic has a way of leading us to where we truly belong."

As we stood to leave, I felt a pang of sadness at the thought of saying goodbye to this newfound connection. But I also felt a sense of peace, knowing that whatever happened next, we were on the right path.

Jessa and I left The Arcane Room, the door closing softly behind us. The afternoon sun was warm on our faces as we made our way back to her apartment, the world around us seemingly unchanged. Yet inside, everything had shifted.

With the clock ticking down, we had only a few hours left to savor this unexpected adventure and the bond that had formed between us. Despite the inevitable farewell, I couldn't help but feel a sense of hope. Jessa had touched my life in ways I never could have anticipated, and the thought of letting go now seemed impossible.

We walked hand in hand, the warmth of her touch a constant reminder of what we were fighting for. I couldn't help but wonder what the future had in store for us—for both of us. The magic we'd stumbled into might have been an accident, but the connection we'd found felt like destiny.

"Jessa," I murmured, my voice low and filled with a hunger I could no longer deny. "No matter what happens, I don't regret a single moment of this."

She looked up at me, her eyes wide and filled with the same desire that was coursing through my veins. "Neither do I, Bryce."

With that, I captured her lips in a kiss that was both a promise and a plea—a promise that we would face whatever came next, and a plea that this moment, this connection, would last beyond the spell, beyond time itself. I knew that no matter what magic had brought us together, it was nothing compared to the magic we'd found in each other.

Not now. Not ever.

CHAPTER 9
JESSA

THE WALK back to my apartment felt both endless and all too brief. Each step brought us closer to goodbye—a word that tasted bitter on my tongue. I squeezed Bryce's hand tighter, not ready to let go of the warmth and comfort it provided. My heart ached with the knowledge that soon, he would be gone, back to his own time and place. It was a cruel twist of fate, and I wasn't ready to face it.

We entered my apartment, the space feeling somehow different now—imbued with memories and emotions I hadn't anticipated. The clock ticked softly in the background, a reminder of the precious time slipping away, each second a reminder that we were on borrowed time.

Bryce closed the door behind us and turned to face me, his expression a mix of determination and sadness. "We don't have much time," he said, his voice gentle yet firm, a painful reminder of the task at hand.

I nodded, though my heart protested. "I know, but—I wish it didn't have to be this way."

His eyes softened, and he stepped closer, brushing a strand of hair from my face. His touch sent shivers down my spine. "Jessa, I want you to know that the past day with you has been more than I could have ever imagined for myself. You've given me something I never thought I'd find—a glimpse of love that feels real."

The sincerity in his words moved through me like a wave, and tears pricked at my eyes. "I don't want you to leave," I admitted, my voice trembling with the weight of the truth. "I didn't expect any of this, but now that you're here, everything else feels wrong."

He cupped my face in his hands, his touch tender and reassuring. "And yet, I must go back. I have responsibilities, a life waiting for me in Scotland. But know this, lass—I've got feelings for you too, feelings I can't ignore."

Bryce's confession filled me with a bittersweet joy. We were two people caught in a whirlwind of magic and fate, destined to part but undeniably connected. I leaned into him, savoring the warmth of his embrace, wanting to hold on to this moment for as long as possible.

We stood like that for a moment, wrapped in silence, each of us silently acknowledging what we had found together. Then, as if sensing the urgency, Bryce leaned in and kissed me—a soft, lingering kiss that conveyed more than words ever could.

As our lips met, the world fell away, leaving only us in a bubble of time suspended between what was and what might be. It was a kiss filled with longing, with the knowledge that this might be our last chance to truly be together.

His hands found my waist, pulling me closer until I was pressed against him, feeling the steady beat of his heart against mine. "Let's not waste what little time we have left," he whispered, his voice low and filled with a promise that sent heat pooling in my belly.

Without another word, he scooped me into his arms, and I laughed softly, the sound wrapping around us like a shared secret. He carried me to the bedroom, where the soft glow of the room set the stage for what was to come.

In the dim light, a sense of intimacy wrapped around us as we took our time undressing each other, savoring every moment, every touch. Bryce's eyes locked onto mine as he reached for the hem of my top, slipping it gently off my shoulders. His fingers brushed against my skin, leaving a trail of tingling warmth in their wake.

He leaned in, his lips following the path of his touch, trailing kisses along the curve of my neck and down to my shoulders. I shivered under his caress, the heat between us building with each passing second, an irresistible pull that defied reason and time.

Bryce's hands moved with deliberate care, tracing the outline of my collarbone before drifting lower, his fingers grazing my breasts. He paused, his gaze darkening with desire as he took one breast into his mouth, his tongue flicking over the sensitive peak with expert precision.

A soft moan escaped my lips as he lavished attention on me, his hands kneading and exploring with a reverence that made my heart race. He moved to the other breast, repeating the motion, and I arched into him, craving more of his touch, more of him.

His kisses trailed lower, down my stomach, each one a promise of what was to come. My body responded eagerly, every nerve alive with anticipation as he knelt before me, spreading my legs with a gentle insistence that left me breathless.

Bryce's eyes met mine, a playful glint dancing in their depths as he lowered his head, his tongue finding my most intimate place. He tasted me with a rhythmic skill that sent waves of pleasure coursing through my body, his touch teasing and precise, driving me wild.

He playfully nipped at my thigh, sending a delicious shiver up my spine before returning to his task, his focus unwavering. The sensation built, a symphony of ecstasy that crescendoed with each flick of his tongue and every whispered sigh, every gasp of my name.

As his expert mouth worked its magic, I felt the tension coil tighter, my breath quickening, heart racing. With a final, exquisite caress, he pushed me over the edge, and I shattered around him, a cry of pure bliss escaping my lips, my body trembling in release.

Before the aftershocks of my orgasm had fully subsided, Bryce rose to his feet, the heat in his gaze matching the fire that burned within me. He entered me slowly, his movements deliberate, a testament to the connection we shared.

We moved together, bodies entwined in a dance, a rhythm that spoke of a love that transcended the boundaries of time. Each thrust felt like a declaration, each caress a reminder of our bond, of what we had discovered in each other.

Bryce explored my body as if committing it to

memory. Our breaths mingled in the air, our moans filling the room, a symphony of pleasure that seemed to stretch into eternity. Time stopped, and for a moment, we were suspended together in this perfect, impossible love.

In the aftermath, as our breathing slowed and reality seeped back in, I clung to him, unwilling to let go. The world outside seemed distant, the ticking clock a cruel reminder of what was to come.

Bryce pressed a kiss to my forehead, his touch a soothing balm to the storm inside of me. "It's time," he whispered, his voice filled with a sadness that mirrored my own. I blinked back tears, the thought of losing him tearing at my heart. He wiped away the single tear that fell, his thumb gentle on my cheek. "It's going to be okay, my love."

Reluctantly, we rose from the bed and returned to the living room, where the blue candle and simmer pot awaited. The herbs Ms. Vesper had given us were arranged with care, the incantation ready to be spoken.

We stood together, hand in hand. As we lit the candle, its flame flickered, casting a warm glow that illuminated the room and our faces, a soft reminder of the love we had found.

Bryce squeezed my hand, and I met his gaze, seeing the same mixture of hope and sadness reflected in his eyes. "Let's do this," I said, my voice steady despite the turmoil that churned within me.

Together, we recited the incantation, our voices weaving a tapestry of magic that resonated with the power of our connection. The words flowed like a melody, carrying with them the weight of what was and what could have been.

As the final syllable left our lips, I felt a shift in the air—a gentle tug, as if the universe itself was acknowledging our decision. The room seemed to shimmer, the magic coalescing around us in a vibrant display of light.

I turned to Bryce, tears brimming in my eyes, blurring my vision. "I don't want you to go," I breathed, the words a plea and a farewell wrapped into one, my heart breaking at the thought of losing him.

He smiled, but it didn't reach his eyes. "I'll always remember you, Jessa. You've changed my life in ways I will never have words to explain."

With that, he kissed me—a tender, lingering kiss that held the promise of eternity. And then, as if swept away by the very magic that had brought him to me, Bryce began to fade, his form dissolving into the shimmering light.

In an instant, he was gone, leaving only the echo of his presence and the ache of absence in his wake.

I stood there, the room silent and still, my heart heavy with loss. I curled up on the couch and broke down, sobbing uncontrollably. I couldn't breathe—everything hurt. The spell had been reversed, but the bond lingered, a memory of what I could never have.

The promise of hope had soured in my stomach, threatening to make me sick. It felt like hours had passed as I sat there, caught between the echoes of the past and the emptiness of the present. The silence threatened to overwhelm me, crushing me beneath its weight, when a soft knock sounded at the door.

Hope flared within me, tentative and bright. I rushed to the door, flinging it open.

Bryce stood there, warmth in his eyes, though marked with the subtle changes of time—wrinkles at the corners of his eyes, a maturity that spoke of the years that had passed since we last stood together.

"What? How?" I stammered, disbelief warring with the joy that surged through me. "You just left…"

He smiled, that same irresistible smile that had captured my heart from the very beginning. "I wait-ed," he said simply, stepping forward to close the distance between us. "I waited ten years for you, Jessa. It was the longest ten years of my life, but I knew I had to come back. I couldn't let you think I'd forgotten."

"But how did you find me?" I asked, reaching out

to touch his face, needing to confirm that he was real, that this wasn't some cruel trick of the mind.

He chuckled softly, his hand covering mine as he leaned into my touch. "I couldn't remember the name of the town, but I remembered The Arcane Room and Ms. Vesper. So, I called her."

"When?" I whispered, still trying to process the fact that he was standing in front of me.

"Years ago," he replied, his voice filled with the kind of patience and love that only comes from waiting for something you believe in with your whole heart.

I blinked, a wave of understanding washing over me. "That's why she knew your name? You contacted her? Is that why I got the book when I did?"

Bryce nodded, his eyes twinkling with a mixture of amusement and sincerity. "Aye, I think perhaps a part of me was always meant to find you."

His words washed over me, filling the void that had opened in my heart when he'd left. I reached out, tracing the lines of his face, seeing the man he had become—the man who had chosen me, despite the odds, despite the passage of time.

"You came back?" I breathed, emotion choking my voice, the tears that had dried now returning in full force.

He nodded, his gaze steady and filled with love.

"I got my visa, just like we talked about. Invested in ByteDance, made a life for myself. But it was all for this moment. It was all for you."

Tears spilled down my cheeks, but this time they were tears of joy, of relief. Bryce had returned, against all odds, proving that magic wasn't the only force at play—love was its own kind of magic, a magic that transcended time and space.

He pulled me into his arms, holding me close as if afraid I might vanish if he let go. "I couldn't imagine spending another moment without you," he murmured, pressing a kiss to my hair.

I looked up at him, seeing both the changes and the constants—the wrinkles, the maturity, but also the same twinkle in his eyes, the same warmth in his smile.

"You're still my perfect lover," I whispered, feeling the truth of those words resonate in my soul, grounding me in the reality that this was happening, that he was here, and he wasn't going anywhere.

We stood there, wrapped in each other's arms, the door to the apartment still open, the world outside forgotten. It was a moment of magic and love that felt destined from the start, as if every step we'd taken had led us to this point.

And as we kissed, sealing the promise of a future together, I knew that this was only the beginning.

Not just of our love story, but of a lifetime of moments where time no longer mattered, where the past and future blurred, leaving only the present—the here and now—where Bryce and I belonged.

Together.

EPILOGUE

Jessa

One Year Later

THE SUN HUNG low in the sky, casting a golden hue across the rolling hills and the quaint village of Glenmore. The warmth of the Scottish summer enveloped me as I stood on the porch of our cottage, my gaze fixed on Bryce as he worked in the garden. His sleeves were rolled up, revealing strong fore-arms, and his hair was deliciously tousled by the gentle breeze.

He glanced up, catching my eye, and flashed that grin that never failed to make my heart flutter—yes, even after all this time. Life in Glenmore was different from Coral Cove, but it was exactly where I wanted to be. The magic of our love had turned this picturesque village into our personal fairy tale.

"Fancy giving me a hand, lass?" Bryce called out, his voice laced with teasing warmth.

I chuckled, making my way down the steps to join him. "Only if you promise not to laugh at my gardening skills. We both know I'm more of a city girl than a green thumb."

He took my hand, pulling me closer until our bodies were flush against each other. His lips brushed my forehead in a soft kiss that sent shivers down my spine. "With you by my side, everything's perfect," he murmured, his eyes locking onto mine with a promise that made my knees weak.

We'd been living in Scotland for nearly nine months now, a decision that felt as natural as breathing. After Bryce returned to my life, we spent weeks catching up on the years we'd lost, savoring every moment as we built a life together that was as vibrant and full of love as the wildflowers in our garden.

Bryce had introduced me to his family, who welcomed me with open arms and an enthusiasm that was both heartwarming and slightly overwhelming. They'd woven me into the fabric of their close-knit community, and before I knew it, Glenmore felt like home. I'd even found a job at the local school, teaching English to eager young minds who quickly stole a piece of my heart—though not as thoroughly as Bryce had.

Our days were filled with the simple pleasures of life—morning strolls through the village, evenings by the fire, and nights spent tangled in each other's arms. Every day was a new adventure, and every moment was infused with the magic that had brought us together. It was as if the very air we breathed was enchanted, every touch between us sparking a flame that never seemed to dim.

I glanced over at Bryce, who was now tending to a patch of vibrant wildflowers, his touch gentle and sure. Watching him work, I marveled at how seamlessly he'd transitioned into this new chapter of his life, balancing his love for furniture restoration with his commitment to our shared dreams. The man could make a garden grow just by smiling at it.

"So, what do you think?" he asked, gesturing toward the garden with a flourish. "Will these flowers be ready for the harvest festival? Or should we consider them a decorative attempt at best?"

I smiled, admiring the burst of colors that seemed

to dance in the sunlight. "They're beautiful, Bryce. Just like everything you do. And if they don't win any prizes, I'm sure we can bribe the judges with your charm."

He laughed, the sound rich and full of life, and before I could react, he'd pulled me into his arms, spinning me around until I was breathless with laughter. When he finally set me down, he captured my lips in a kiss.

"You're the one who's made everything beautiful, Jessa. I wouldn't have it any other way," he whispered against my lips, his hands still holding me close.

As we stood there, in the warmth of the afternoon, I couldn't help but think about how far we'd come—from a spell gone awry to a love that had surpassed the boundaries of time. It was a story that defied logic, a testament to the power of fate and the magic that resided in every heartbeat. And it was a story that I never wanted to end.

Later that evening, as we sat on the porch, the sky painted with hues of pink and orange, I rested my head on Bryce's shoulder, feeling the steady rise and fall of his chest. It was the most comforting sound in the world, a melody that grounded me in the present moment.

"Do you ever wonder what would've happened if the spell hadn't worked?" I asked, my voice a soft whisper against the tranquil night.

Bryce was silent for a moment, his hand gently stroking my hair in a soothing rhythm. "Sometimes," he admitted, his voice thoughtful and laced with a hint of that Scottish lilt I loved. "But then I realize it doesn't matter. We found each other, Jessa. And that's all that counts."

I felt his words deep in my soul. We were living proof that magic wasn't confined to fairy tales—it was real and tangible, a force that had shaped our lives in the most wondrous ways. A force that had given us the greatest gift of all—each other.

As the stars began to twinkle above, Bryce turned to me, his eyes reflecting the brilliance of the night sky. There was a playful glint in his gaze, the kind that always made me brace myself for whatever mischief he had in mind. "You know, there's something I've been meaning to ask you," he said, his tone light yet serious.

I raised an eyebrow, intrigued by the shift in his demeanor. "Oh? And what might that be? Are you finally going to admit that I'm the better gardener?"

He chuckled, shaking his head. "Not quite, lass. But close." He took my hand, his gaze steady and unwavering, the humor fading into something deeper. "Marry me, Jessa. Make this life we've built official."

My heart skipped a beat, joy bubbling up inside me so fiercely I thought I might float away. The answer was as clear as the constellations that stretched above us.

"Yes," I whispered, tears of happiness glistening in my eyes. "A thousand times, yes."

He pulled me into his arms, lifting me off the ground in a move that made me squeal with laughter, his lips finding mine in a kiss that promised forever. As he set me down, our foreheads resting together, I knew that this was the moment we had been building toward—where magic and love met, creating a bond that would never break.

And as we sat there, wrapped in the embrace of the Scottish night, I knew that our story was just beginning—a tale of love, destiny, and the magic that would continue to guide us through every chapter of our lives. Because with Bryce by my side, I knew that our happily ever after was guaranteed, and every day was a new adventure waiting to unfold.

———

Sign up for my newsletter and get a free book today!
https://mailchi.mp/158597581671/jax-wilder

If you enjoyed this book be sure to check out my
Tarot Fantasies series:

THE DEVIL'S TEMPTATION

Dottie:

I never believed in fairy tales, but the moment I stepped into The Arcane Room, I felt a magic I'd always denied myself. Ms. Vesper's velvety voice was a spell of its own. She offered me a chance at the forbidden—all I had to do was draw a tarot card. I drew the Devil card. His name was Lucian, His touch was electric, awakening parts of me I'd kept hidden for so long. I wanted to forget every rule I'd ever made for myself and live in this moment forever.

. . .

DOROTHEA HAS ALWAYS PLAYED it safe, her life confined to the walls of her bakery in the quaint town of Coral Cove. But when she steps into The Arcane Room, an unassuming new age shop, she's thrust into a world where her deepest fantasies come to life. Guided by the enigmatic and dangerously seductive Lucian, Dottie enters a magical experience where her untouched innocence and hidden passions are brought to the surface.

At twenty-nine, Dottie has never experienced the complexities of intimacy. Her untouched innocence is a stark contrast to Lucian's experienced hands. As he guides her through a series of sensually charged encounters, Dottie learns to confront her fears and embrace the desires she's long kept buried. Lucian's dark allure pushes her boundaries, helping her to uncover her inner strength and face the temptations she has always denied herself.

Within the enchanted simulation, Dottie's journey is one of self-discovery and empowerment. In the heart of The Arcane Room, she learns that true strength comes from within, and living fearlessly is the key to unlocking her greatest desires. Through each tantalizing experience, she discovers the courage to embrace her passions and the power to transform her life.

Will Dottie emerge from the magical realm with

the confidence to live her life fully, or will her fears continue to hold her back? Enter a world of seduction, secrets, and self-discovery in "The Devil's Temptation," a spellbinding tale that will leave you breathless and yearning for more.

RED, WHITE, AND RAVISHED

A SHORT FTM/M SECOND-CHANCE TRANS ROMANCE

This is a romance for all trans men and women.

You deserve love, you deserve passion, and you deserve to be cherished—body and soul.

And yes, you deserve a good pounding too.

This one's for you.

CHAPTER 1
MICHELLE

"HURRY UP, we're going to be late," Mom yelled up the stairs.

"How am I going to be late to a fireworks show? It's not even dark out yet," I replied as I walked down the stairs, pulling my hair back into a ponytail.

"I wish you'd wear your hair down; it's so pretty," she said. "We need to get there early, or we'll never find a parking spot."

We hurried out of the house, and I glanced at the setting sun over Coral Cove. The sky was already streaked with hues of orange and pink, promising a spectacular evening. As we climbed into the car, I could hardly contain my excitement. The annual fireworks show was the highlight of the summer, and this year was special because Thomas and I had planned to meet up before the show at a secret spot we had found months ago.

We approached the cliffs of Coral Cove and traffic thickened, and the scent of saltwater and grilled food filled the air. The town's streets buzzed with families, couples, and kids running around with colorful cotton candy. Coral Cove's charm always seemed to amplify during these events, the magic of the seaside town blending with the festive atmosphere.

Mom maneuvered the car through the crowded streets, and we found a parking spot a short walk from the park at the top of the cliffs. It would have a perfect view of the fireworks. As we made our way to the event, I spotted Thomas waiting near the entrance, his face lighting up as soon as he saw me.

"Michelle! Over here!" he shouted, waving enthusiastically.

I waved back, a broad smile spreading across my face. Thomas and I had been best friends since the 4th grade in Ms. Winthrop's class. He had been bullied for wearing a pink shirt by one of the mean boys, Clayton. A rage had fueled inside me, and I punched Clayton in the eye.

Ever since then, my anger had become legendary, and no one messed with Thomas or me. Instead of feeling emasculated that a 'girl' had beaten someone up for him, Thomas was elated that someone had stood up for him. We'd been inseparable ever since.

But now that we were in high school, things had started to change. Our handshakes lingered, our friendly hugs felt deeper somehow. I found myself enjoying my alone time with Thomas more and more, but I wasn't sure what it meant.

"So, how was the movie last night?" Thomas asked, bringing me back to the present as we walked down the street, out of earshot of my mother.

"Oh, uh, it was okay," I said. "Dad was going overboard again to make up for 'lost time' or whatever. He let me get whatever I wanted from the concessions and seemed disappointed that I only wanted popcorn and a Coke."

"That sounds alright," Thomas said.

"Yeah, he means well. Divorce is hard. Even harder when he lives so far away, and I only get to see him every few months," I said.

"Yeah," Thomas agreed. "Are we going to the spot?"

"Oh, right. I have to tell my mom," I said jogging back to my mom, who was meeting up with her sister and my cousins under the large oak tree we claimed every year. My aunt Kathy always got there before noon and camped out until the rest of the family showed up. "Mom, this year, Thomas and I found an alcove up at the end of the road. We want to watch the show from there."

Mom looked me up and down. "Okay," she said, glancing over at Thomas. She glanced at my clothes, then up to my face. "Why don't you wear prettier clothes? I don't understand those baggy pants and rocker T-shirts you always wear."

"Thanks, Mom," I said sarcastically before I walked away.

Thomas and I headed to a grassy area with a clear view of the sky. We walked down a narrow deer trail that led into thick shrubbery and shoved our way through to the ledge we had discovered before I went to visit my dad.

We laid out our blanket and sat down, the anticipation building as we chatted about the rest of our summer plans and caught up on Thomas's life.

"It's been pretty good," Thomas said, taking a sip from his Coke. "Just busy with my cadet stuff."

Thomas had been working as a cadet for the local fire department for the past year. As a minor, he couldn't do much, but he got to wear a uniform, carry a radio, and ride along in the fire trucks and ambulances. He even got to flip the switch to turn on the sirens. On scene, he had to maintain his distance while the paid firefighters worked, but he got to observe and take notes. Some crews even let him call up on the radio to dispatch updates.

I never understood why he enjoyed it so much. It sounded kind of boring, aside from riding in the fire truck, I guess. He had asked if I wanted to become a cadet with him, but with my semi-regular visits to my father out of state, I couldn't commit to it. Honestly, I wasn't as jazzed about it as he was.

"Oh, I forgot to tell you about this one dead guy," Thomas said, his eyes sparkling with excitement. Only Thomas could speak of such morbid things with a glimmer in his eyes. I chuckled to myself at his ridiculousness, though he probably thought it was at his story. "He was so large that we had to stay on scene to help the medical examiner get him on a stretcher. I actually got to help move him because they needed extra muscle."

Thomas flexed his arm muscles, but I tuned out the rest of the story.

As the sun continued to dip below the horizon, the crowd around us began to buzz with excitement. I felt a thrill of anticipation—tonight was going to be unforgettable.

Bam!

The first firework shot off. A bright green streak of fire zigzagged through the air, rotating three times in the sky before heading directly toward us. Thomas and I huddled together as we waited for the firework to hit, but just before it could, it exploded. The bright white embers sprinkled down on us.

"What the hell?" Thomas said.

"I thought these embers would be hot," I said, reaching out and letting one land on me. It tingled and tickled as it touched my arm.

The fireworks were like burning stars in the sky, destruction and creation all wrapped into one. As the embers floated down like tiny, twinkling lights, they enveloped us in their majesty. I couldn't help but feel the weight of the moment as Thomas's laughter broke through the soft crackling. I looked over at him, his face lit by the cascading embers above, and something stirred deep inside me—something more than the usual warmth I felt when we were together.

The next burst of color exploded near us, casting a dreamy purple hue above, but my attention was fixed entirely on him. My heart raced as I realized what it was: I was in love with Thomas. The kind of love that had been creeping up for years but was only just now bursting into full bloom, like the fireworks themselves.

He turned toward me, eyes bright with excitement, and it was as if he could sense it too. His hand brushed mine, sending sparks of its own. My breath caught in my throat as he leaned in, his gaze lingering on my lips, his intent clear.

But just before his lips could meet mine, a wave of panic rushed through me, stopping me cold. The secret, the one I could never share—not even with him—loomed large in my mind. I froze, pulling away, my heart pounding with more than just excitement now.

"I… I can't," I stammered, backing up, the magic of the moment crumbling around me. Without another word, I turned and ran, disappearing through the shrubbery and into the sea of people. My heart ached as I left behind the embers of something I couldn't let burn.

CHAPTER 2
THOMAS

"I'M SORRY!" I yelled, but I wasn't sure if Michelle could hear me.

I lost my footing trying to get off the ledge, chasing after her, and by the time I made it through the thick brush back to the smooth grass of the park, I had lost her in the crowd. My heart sank—I felt terrible for trying to kiss her. We had been best friends for years, and now I had messed everything up.

I maneuvered my way through the throngs of people back to the large oak tree. Her mother was there, along with her aunt and all her cousins, but Michelle was nowhere to be found. I thought about asking them if they had seen her, but I didn't want to worry them and cause a panic.

"Come on, the show's about to start," a kid next to me yelled.

"Start?" I muttered to myself, glancing over the cliff toward the water. The show hadn't even begun. So what was that firework that almost hit us?

The loud boom of the fireworks drowned out any noise from the crowd as smoke filled the park, making any search for Michelle impossible. I looked back at the fireworks display—the typical circular blasts of red, white, and blue filled the sky. But without my best friend, they felt dull and bleak.

I didn't wait for the show to end. I walked home, defeated and upset.

Weeks passed, and school started, but I hadn't heard from Michelle all summer. Mom and Dad asked why she hadn't been around, and I couldn't bring myself to tell them what had happened. Instead, I invented excuses.

"Oh, she has a family event when I'm free, and when she's free, I'm working at the fire department."

"She's out of state, visiting her dad again."

"Yeah, we just haven't found a good time to get together."

Eventually, they stopped asking. But I never stopped worrying.

The school year began like any other day, except Michelle wasn't there. I kept hoping she'd show up, maybe just running late. But each time the classroom door opened, it was never her. I must have glanced at her empty seat a hundred times, my stomach twisted in knots.

By lunchtime, I was starting to panic. She never skipped school. Something must have happened. My mind raced with possibilities. Maybe she was hurt? Maybe something terrible had happened after she ran off that night? My chest tightened with guilt—it had to be because I tried to kiss her.

But as the hours dragged on, I started to calm down. If something awful had happened, surely someone would have said something by now, right? It would be all over the news; her family would have called... something. But there was nothing. No announcements, no whispers of concern. Everyone else seemed to be going about their day like normal.

Still, the worry gnawed at me. I had to know. So after school, I decided to go straight to her house. Her mom always liked me, maybe she'd let me know what was going on. Maybe Michelle just needed time to cool off.

I drove over as fast as I could, my heart pounding the entire way. When I reached her house, her mom answered the door, a kind but tired smile on her face. "Thomas! It's good to see you, honey."

I shifted awkwardly on the porch. "Hi, Ms.

Winters. Is Michelle home? I haven't seen her in a while, and I wanted to check on her."

Her expression softened with empathy. "Thomas, sweetheart… Michelle isn't here."

"What do you mean?" My voice wavered.

She sighed, glancing down for a moment before meeting my eyes. "Michelle decided to move in with her father. She… she wants to live with him now. I'm sorry she didn't tell you."

My heart dropped. "But… why?" The word came out as a barely audible whisper. I knew why. It was all my fault.

"I'm not sure. She didn't give much of an explanation, honey. Just that she needed a change. I know you two were close, and this must be hard to hear."

The ground felt like it had shifted beneath me. Michelle was gone. Just like that, without saying goodbye. Without even a word to me.

I forced a nod, my throat too tight to speak. "Thanks, Ms. Winters."

As I walked away from her house, my mind raced. The pain of losing her as my best friend was overwhelming, and deep down, I couldn't shake the feeling that it was all because of what happened on the Fourth of July.

No, I was certain. It was all my fault.

CHAPTER 3
BLAKE

"BLAKE, before you go, I sent you that email about your upcoming travel dates," Roger said as I was about to walk out the door for the day.

"Is it crucial that I look at it right now?" I asked, my annoyance evident. Roger had a knack for catching me just as my shift was ending.

"I'm sorry, but I just got final approval from Cynthia upstairs a few minutes ago. I need your confirmation so Carlos can start booking your hotel rooms," he explained.

I groaned, turning back to my desk. Logging in, I quickly located the email. I skimmed through the cities and dates. "Roger," I called from my desk.

"Yeah?" he responded.

"This has me traveling over the Fourth of July," I

shouted, loud enough for him to hear me from his office.

"I'm sorry, it's just how the schedule worked out. Cynthia said you can come back for the Fourth, but you'd have to be right back up there by the fifth. Let Carlos know what you prefer," he said, his tone softening as he approached my desk.

I scanned the list again, hoping the town I'd be working in during the holiday would be somewhere exciting, like New Orleans. "Coral Cove?" I nearly choked on the words. "Coral Cove? Seriously?"

"Uhh, yeah, I guess," Roger said, peering over my shoulder at the schedule. "Do you know it?"

"Yeah, I'm from Coral Cove. My mother still lives there," I said.

"Oh, perfect! Then you can stay with her, and we don't have to pay for a hotel that week," Roger said with a grin.

"Oh hell no. I'll be getting a hotel," I shot back.

I spent another few minutes scanning the towns and dates before sending off my approval to Carlos with a note. 'Be sure to book Coral Cove first—it's a tourist town, and rooms will likely fill up fast. And don't listen to Roger; I'll need a room in Coral Cove.' And send.

I shut my laptop with a sigh and slung my bag over

my shoulder. My mind was racing. Coral Cove. I hadn't been back in years. Too many memories were tied to that place—both good and bad. Seeing my mother again was one thing, but being back in that town, with all its ghosts? That was something else entirely.

"Everything good?" Roger asked, still standing awkwardly behind me.

"Yeah, fine," I muttered, heading for the door again.

"Great. We really appreciate your flexibility on this, Blake. I know it's not easy traveling over the holiday."

I nodded, not in the mood for more of his corporate praise. The door closed behind me with a soft click, and I took a few deep breaths before continuing. Coral Cove. Of all the places I could be sent, it had to be there.

I walked to my car, the summer heat hitting me full force, but I barely felt it. My mind was already miles away, back in that seaside town with its familiar winding roads, the boardwalk, the sound of the ocean crashing against the rocky shore. And then there was Michelle.

I hadn't thought about her in years, but now her name echoed in my mind, her face etched into every memory. That's who I was in Coral Cove all those years ago, the person people still remember. The thing about dead names that no one ever tells you is that they carry weight, like a chain you've long since broken but can still feel around your neck. You can change everything about yourself, become who you truly are, but when you go back, it's like the world is still waiting for you to be the version of you that doesn't exist anymore.

I threw my suitcase on the bed with a sigh, already feeling the weight of the trip ahead. As I packed both my business clothes and casual wear, I couldn't help but chuckle, thinking of my mother. She always wanted me in skirts and floral dresses, but here I was, packing the same baggy jeans and loose-fitting tees. A small reminder that I was always Blake, even inside that little girl in Coral Cove.

As I zipped up the bag, I caught my reflection in the mirror. The face staring back was mine—stubbled, sharper, more defined. It felt right. But the thought of seeing old friends for the first time since transitioning? That was something else. Would they even recognize me? Should I acknowledge that they knew me back then?

Technically, they didn't know the real me until I transitioned anyway. Perhaps a better approach would be to act like we're meeting for the first time. I'm sure a lot of them have changed too. I haven't seen anyone from high school in my adult life—especially not Thomas.

I froze at the thought of him. The last time I saw Thomas was at the fireworks show, the night everything shifted for me. I remembered how he leaned in for a kiss, how I panicked and bolted. That memory has always haunted me, but it was hard to imagine what Thomas was like now, after all these years. Probably working as a firefighter. That made the most sense.

I shook my head and finished packing, adding my toiletries to the bag. No point in worrying about it now. The flight was early, and by this time tomorrow, I'd be back in Coral Cove.

The drive to the airport was quiet, but my mind was anything but. Memories flooded back—my mom's prying but kind questions, high school football games, hanging out with Thomas and hearing his morbid stories, endless beach days. Coral Cove wasn't just a place; it was where I figured out who I really was.

When the plane started its descent, my pulse quickened. A rental car counter and an hour's drive were all that stood between me and my past. Funny how the last time I was in town was also the Fourth of July.

CHAPTER 4
THOMAS

"ARE you going to be at the fireworks show this week?" Mom asked as I was heading out.

"Obviously. The Fourth of July is the fire department's busiest day," I said with a hint of sarcasm. "I'm so excited to be hunting for fingertips and dealing with third-degree burns all weekend."

"I guess that makes sense," Mom said. "Well, I hope it's not too crazy busy." She reached up, pulling my head close so she could sneak a kiss on my cheek.

"Thanks, Mom. I love you," I said, heading out the door.

Mom and I have dinner together every Sunday. It's been our tradition for years now, ever since I graduated college, went to medic school, and started working full-time for the Coral Cove Fire Department. As I got busier, I saw my family less and less, but she insisted on these dinners, and honestly, I'm grateful. Without them, I probably wouldn't see anyone outside of work.

As I pulled out of Mom's driveway, I couldn't help but think about the week ahead. I hated the Fourth of July. It was always the busiest time of the year for the fire department. People treat fireworks like toys, and every year, without fail, someone loses a finger—or worse. I could already see the lineup of calls: fires from bottle rockets, kids lighting M-80s like they were sparklers, and the inevitable backyard shows that end in a trip to the ER.

But there was another reason I despised the Fourth of July—it was the anniversary of losing my best friend.

The sun was setting, casting a soft orange glow over the streets as I drove home. This job defined my life now. High school felt like a lifetime ago. Now, it was all late-night shifts and emergency calls that came in at all hours. The adrenaline rush of the job was addicting, but the rest of my life? That felt like it was always on hold.

As I turned onto my street, my house came into view—a modest two-bedroom tucked at the edge of town. Nothing fancy, but it was home. The lights were already on, and I knew Duke, my Great Dane, would be waiting at the door like he always did. Sure enough, the moment I unlocked it, I was greeted by the sound of paws thudding across the floor and Duke's oversized head nudging into my side, practically knocking me off balance.

"Hey, big guy," I said, scratching behind his ears as he wagged his tail, thudding into the wall like a drum. Duke had been my constant companion since I adopted him as a puppy a couple of years back. He was a good dog—too big for most people's liking, but he fit well in my quiet life.

I tossed my keys onto the counter and grabbed a sparkling water from the fridge, walking over to the sliding glass door that opened onto the backyard. Duke followed, plopping down beside me as I stood outside, watching the last bits of sunlight fade away. The cool evening breeze felt good after the heat of the day.

Dating? Yeah, I'd been doing that off and on, but nothing ever seemed to stick. I'd been on the apps, met people at bars, but it always fizzled out before anything serious could happen. Maybe it was me. Maybe it was the job. Either way, I was single, and honestly, most nights, I didn't mind coming home to an empty house. But sometimes, I wondered what it would be like to have someone there. Someone to talk to after a long day, or share breakfast with before heading out to the station.

I finished my water and headed inside; Duke followed me to the bathroom. The house was quiet as I got ready for bed. Tomorrow would be the start of the madness, and I needed to be ready for whatever came my way.

As I lay in bed, I could hear Duke stretching out on his bed beside me. I stared at the ceiling for a while, letting my thoughts wander. It was funny how life had turned out—how different things were from what I imagined back in high school. I hadn't seen most of my old friends in years. And Michelle... I never seemed to think much about her until it was the Fourth of July. The memory of her hit me like a jolt sometimes, but I always pushed it down. It was easier that way.

I closed my eyes, feeling the exhaustion settle in. Tomorrow would be chaos, but for now, I let sleep take over, drifting off to the sound of Duke's steady breathing beside me.

CHAPTER 5
BLAKE

"WHO'S THAT HANDSOME MAN?" my mom yelled from the house as I got out of my rental car.

"Hello, Mom," I said, doing a model walk up the driveway toward her.

"He is style, he is grace, turning heads in every place," Mom catcalled. I smiled and pulled her into a tight embrace.

"How are you, sweetie?" she asked, her voice warm with affection.

"I'm really good, thank you," I said, surprised by how true it felt. "I thought it would be harder to come back here, but now that I'm here, it feels good."

"Great! So you'll cancel your hotel room and just stay here?" she asked, almost pleading.

"Well, the company is paying for it..." I started, "so I'll just keep it and hang out here anyway."

Mom beamed with happiness and quickly scut-
tled upstairs to make up my old room. As I watched
her disappear up the stairs, I glanced around the
house. Everything looked the same, but something
about coming back made my chest tighten just a bit.
It was the first time I'd stepped foot in this house
since high school. The walls, the furniture, even the
creaky floorboards—all held memories. It felt like I
was standing in a different life.

I followed her upstairs, the familiar creaks
beneath my feet reminding me of long, sleepless
nights spent thinking about things that didn't make
sense back then. But as I reached the doorway of my
old room, the unease began to shift. It wasn't a
haunting feeling or one of discomfort. It was almost
as if I was finally making peace with this part of me.
This room, these four walls, had witnessed a lot of
confusion, frustration, and sadness. But now, stepping in as Blake, I wasn't the same person who had
left.

The full-length mirror on the far wall caught my
reflection. I took a moment and really looked. My
broad shoulders, square jaw, and the definition in my
arms—I couldn't help but feel a sense of accomplishment, like I had reclaimed something in this space. It
was as if this old room needed to see me now, the
person I'd worked so hard to become.

"Room's all set," Mom said, bustling around and straightening things unnecessarily.

"Thanks, Mom," I said softly, leaning against the doorway.

She looked up at me, her eyes bright. "You've come a long way, you know that?"

"Yeah," I nodded, taking in the room one last time. "I know."

It wasn't just pride; it was peace. As I stood there, I knew this wasn't the room of who I used to be. It was mine, all over again.

"So, what is it that you do now?" Mom asked as she set a tray of crackers and cheese down on the coffee table.

"I'm a field service technician for a software company. We do all sorts of point-of-sale systems, and they've just rolled out a huge update. So, I get sent out to all of our vendors to make sure their systems upgraded correctly and to train the owners on the new system," I explained. I had a list of clients that I would be visiting while in Coral Cove and handed it over to my mom.

"Oh yeah, most of these are the small businesses in the downtown area," Mom said.

"Yep! We have a few larger clients, but we specialize in small businesses. I'm very fortunate that I get to travel around as a part of this and really connect with the business owners," I said, beaming with pride at my job.

"Well, I'm proud of you, sweetie," Mom said. "I wouldn't have the first clue how to do what you do."

I just laughed. My mom could handle technology if she would just sit down and commit herself, but she constantly dismissed her abilities with 'oh, I'm too old' or 'I just don't understand those new-fangled things.' I know several people, especially women her age, who embrace today's technology and do just fine. She's incorrigible.

I smiled at her and shook my head. "Mom, you could figure it out if you really wanted to. I think you just like making me do all your tech stuff."

She laughed, the familiar sound filling the room with warmth. "Maybe I do. But that's what kids are for, right?"

I took a deep breath, letting the comfort of being home settle into my bones. It wasn't just the room, or the town, or even Mom. It was the sense that I had returned to a place I had left behind, but as a completely different person. And yet, I was still connected to it, like a thread pulling me back.

"I think it's time for me to settle in. I have an early day tomorrow," I said.

"Good night, sweetie," Mom said, pulling me in

for a kiss on the forehead. "I love you, and I'm so glad to have you back."

THE NEXT MORNING, I stood in front of the bathroom mirror, the steam from the shower still lingering in the air. The man staring back at me was strong, confident, and undeniably handsome. My polo fit snugly over my broad shoulders, the sharp lines of my jaw were clean after a fresh shave, and my hair was perfectly styled. It all came together in a way that made me feel like I had finally arrived.

I'd worked hard to get here, both physically and mentally. There was a time when looking in this mirror was a painful reminder of everything I wasn't. But now, it was different. I saw someone who had overcome, who had taken control of his life and his body, and who was now standing tall because of it. There was a quiet pride in knowing I had earned every bit of what I saw.

With one final check, I straightened my collar and smiled. Today was going to be a good day.

My first stop was Spellbound Stories, the local bookstore. The owner, Lea, would be my contact. I put the address into my phone and drove downtown.

A cute young Asian guy was behind the counter

as I walked in. "Welcome! Let me know if you need help finding anything."

"Thanks. I'm actually with TransactPro Technologies, and I have a meeting with Lea Lovegood. Is she in?" I asked.

"Yes, she's in the back. Follow me," he said with a smile, his eyes lingering on me. He was handsome, and I couldn't help but notice the way he looked me up and down. It gave me a boost of confidence as I followed him to the back of the store, weaving between the bookshelves.

He knocked gently on a door marked "Office" and pushed it open. "Lea, your meeting is here," he called out.

Lea, a self-assured, curvy goddess with flowing red hair, looked up from her desk with a warm smile. "Blake, right? Come on in."

"Thank you, and yes," I said, stepping inside. As the door closed behind me, I stole a quick glance at the guy who led me back, catching him watching me once more before he turned away.

Lea stood and extended her hand. "Nice to meet you. That was Park, by the way. I don't know if he introduced himself or not."

"He didn't," I smiled.

"So, you're here to help us get the new system up and running?"

I shook her hand firmly, grinning. "Yep, I'll make sure all of the new software uploaded correctly. Then I'll walk you through all the fun updates. Shouldn't take too long, and once it's set up, I'll train your staff."

"Perfect. That won't take long either, as it's just Park and me," Lea said. She led me to the checkout counter, and I couldn't help but think about how surreal it felt to be back in Coral Cove. I went over the software update, and everything appeared to have imported successfully.

Every few minutes, I couldn't help but scan the bookstore for the handsome Park. Apparently, I wasn't being as covert as I thought.

"Park is very handsome, but he's got a man," Lea whispered.

I was so stunned that I didn't know what to say. My jaw dropped, and I quickly returned to the computer.

"Oh, don't be embarrassed. He catches the eye of a lot of boys. Don't worry, I have a tingle in my stomach about you," Lea said, her voice taking on an ominous tone.

"A tingle?" I raised a brow.

"Yeah, I have a sixth sense about these things. You have an aura around you. Someone is coming you're your life," she said, leaning in close. "Enjoy it. I sure did."

I was once again stunned silent. She gave me a wink and walked over to assist a customer who had just come in. Park made his way back to the checkout counter, and I told him I was ready to show him the new software. He was trained up in less than fifteen minutes.

Handsome and smart.

"Very good. Now I've just got to make sure Lea understands all of this, and I can be out of your hair," I said.

The door creaked open with a soft chime, and three young kids burst in, leaving trails of green sparks in their wake. The sparks fizzled in the air, disappearing just as quickly as they appeared, almost like the remnants of an old sparkler. The kids were a whirlwind of energy, chasing each other in wild circles, their movements impossibly smooth, as if they weren't quite touching the ground. Their outfits struck me as odd—suspenders with knee-high socks, a vintage dress with a lace collar, and a jaunty cap tilted over dark curls—clothing that seemed like it belonged in a sepia-toned photograph rather than in the present day.

"Hey, slow down!" Lea called out, her voice

wavering between amusement and mild exasperation. "No running in the store."

I couldn't take my eyes off them. There was something about the way they moved—too fast, too fluid, as if they were skating on air rather than solid ground. One of them, the boy with the cap, knocked over a stack of books near the front counter. The books tumbled to the floor with a series of dull thuds, yet the kids didn't pause or even glance back at the mess they had made.

"Sorry about that, Blake," Lea sighed as she bent down to pick up the scattered books.

"No problem," I replied, though my focus remained on the children as they darted deeper into the store. I couldn't shake the feeling that something was... off. A chill ran down my spine, like a ghostly finger tracing my skin, but I couldn't put my finger on why. It wasn't fear, exactly, but a strange sense of nostalgia mixed with unease. The air around them seemed to shimmer, the faint smell of sulfur and burnt sugar lingering in the air, like fireworks on the Fourth of July.

Suddenly, a small green firework burst from the floor near the center of the store, spiraling upward with a soft whistle before exploding into a shower of emerald sparks. The light danced in the air, casting ghostly shadows on the walls before fading into nothing. I blinked, half expecting to see the kids standing there, but they were gone. The store was eerily silent, the only sound the soft crackle of the dying sparks.

Lea hadn't noticed the firework, still focused on gathering the books. I stepped closer to where the kids had vanished, peering down the aisles. There was no sign of them, no hint of their presence, yet the air still buzzed with an odd energy.

As I turned back toward the front, I saw one of the kids reappear briefly near the exit, his hand reaching out as if to steady himself, but in a bizarre series of events, his fingers brushed against the fire alarm on the wall, and in that instant, the alarm blared to life. A piercing bell filled the store

The door swung open on its own, and the kids darted outside, their forms flickering like old film reels before they vanished entirely. The last thing I saw was the boy with the cap, tipping it in my direction as if to say goodbye.

"They're gone," Lea said, standing beside me, her voice tinged with confusion.

"Yeah," I murmured, my mind racing. I didn't know how to explain it, but deep down, I knew those kids weren't just playing a game of tag. They were something more—a ghostly reminder of a time long past, of a Fourth of July that had faded into memory, leaving only echoes and sparks behind.

CHAPTER 6
THOMAS

THE FIRE TONES RANG OUT, but our desensitization to the bells was evident as none of us immediately jumped up. We waited for the dispatch before moving.

"Engine six, fire alarm activation, Spellbound Books—hand-pull activation. Engine six, fire alarm activation. Spellbound Books—hand-pull activation," the dispatcher broadcasted over the radio.

"Engine six en route," I responded. "A hand-pull activation? We better get a move on. A bookstore is a tinderbox."

The other firefighters and I hustled into the rig and pulled out of the station with lights and sirens blaring.

We arrived at Spellbound Books within minutes. It was a small bookstore nestled in downtown Coral

Cove, its sign crooked from years of being battered by the sea breeze. As we pulled up, I didn't see any smoke or flames, but the front door was wide open with a few people lingering outside.

I stepped out of the rig, already suspecting it was a false alarm. "Looks clear, but let's do a sweep anyway," I told the crew as we headed inside.

Lea, the store's owner, waved from behind the counter. "Sorry about that," she called out. "A group of kids were running around, and one of them must've pulled the alarm on their way out. Nothing's burning here, just some over-enthusiastic little troublemakers."

I nodded. "No worries. We'll reset the alarm and clear the building just to make sure it won't go off again."

We moved through the store and I spotted a man standing at the register. He was adjusting something on the countertop. He glanced up briefly, and our eyes met. There was something about him... Familiar. He had a strong jaw, broad shoulders, dark hair neatly styled, and an easy confidence about him that tugged at some distant memory.

Who was this guy?

I tried not to stare, but something about the way he moved, the way his brow furrowed when he was focused, stirred something in the back of my mind. A flicker of recognition, but I couldn't place it.

I watched him for a moment longer as my crew cleared the bookstore, something tugging at the back of my mind. The guy at the counter—there was something about him, something familiar I couldn't place. His eyes locked on mine, and suddenly, his entire expression shifted. He went still, staring at me like he'd seen a ghost.

"Thomas?" he said, his voice soft, almost hesitant.

The way he said my name—it sent a jolt through me. My heart dropped, and everything clicked into place in a way that knocked the wind out of me.

Michelle.

But not Michelle.

I felt the ground sway beneath me as my mind scrambled to catch up. I hadn't seen her in years. She'd vanished after that night at the fireworks show, after I'd tried to kiss her, after everything had gone wrong. And now here she was standing in front of me. Except it wasn't her. It was... him.

My throat tightened. "Michelle?" I whispered, the name slipping out before I could stop it.

He gave a small, almost nervous smile. "It's... Blake, actually. Now."

Blake. The name felt foreign on my tongue, but I couldn't deny the truth of it. He wasn't Michelle anymore. My head spun, the air around me thickened as a flood of emotions hit all at once—shock, confusion, sadness for the years we'd lost. And then there was something else, something deeper. A warmth I hadn't expected, like seeing a part of my past I thought was gone for good.

Blake stood there, so different, yet still familiar. The broad shoulders, the square jaw, the self-assuredness that hadn't been there before. But those eyes, those damn eyes, still carried the same kindness I remembered.

"Blake," I repeated, feeling a shake in my voice. "I... I didn't recognize you."

He nodded, the smile fading into something more vulnerable. "It's been a while."

I swallowed hard, trying to wrap my head around it. "Yeah, it has." I didn't know what else to say. Memories of us flashed in my mind. Laughing together, sitting under the oak tree at the park, sitting on the ledge that night with the fireworks... and the way everything had fallen apart.

"You look..." I hesitated, my words catching in my throat. "You look amazing."

Blake's smile returned, small but genuine. "Thanks. You do too."

I wanted to say more. Ask him how he'd been, what had happened after all those years. My stomach twisted painfully as I realized how much time had passed, how much I hadn't known about him. About who he really was. A sadness washed over me, mingling with an overwhelming sense of relief at seeing him alive, well, and happy.

"I didn't expect to see you here," I said, trying to steady my voice. "After... everything."

"Yeah, I've been away for a long while. Only came back for work," he explained, leaning casually against the counter. "I'm here for a bit though. We should catch up."

I nodded, feeling my heart pound in my chest. The flood of emotions inside me was almost too much to bear. And underneath it all, that familiar flicker of something deeper. I couldn't be sure. It felt complicated, messy, like everything between us always had been.

"Yeah," I said, my voice rough. "That sounds good."

Blake gave me an understanding nod, as if sensing the storm of feelings inside me. "How about after your shift? We can grab a drink or something, just... talk?"

"Yeah," I agreed quickly. "After my shift."

"Okay," he said, smiling again, that same warm smile I remembered all too well. "I'll be around. Just let me know."

I nodded, my knees shaky as I turned to leave. My mind was spinning, my heart in a tangle. Michelle was gone, but Blake... Blake was here, and I didn't know how to feel about any of it. Part of me was overjoyed to see my old friend again, and another part of me was grieving the years we'd lost, the girl I thought I knew, and the person standing behind me now.

He tapped on my shoulder and handed me a piece of paper. "Here's my phone number."

His hand brushing against mine sent a signal throughout my entire body. The sting met at the base of my neck, and I could feel my heart rate quicken. I smiled and looked down at the scrawled-out number underneath, his name once more. Blake.

But most of all, I felt that spark, the one that always burned quietly inside me, flaring up again—uncertain, raw, and undeniable. I simply nodded and headed back to my rig.

The fire truck's interior was filled with the low hum of the engine as we headed back to the station, but my mind was anything but calm. I stared at the piece of paper in my hand, the digits written in Blake's handwriting. His name felt achingly familiar as if it appeared in a dream. The sensation of his hand brushing against mine was still vivid, the warmth lingering like a gentle burn.

I replayed our brief encounter over and over, trying to piece together the emotions swirling inside me. It was a whirlwind of confusion and excitement, nostalgia mixed with a rush of something I couldn't quite name. Blake was back, and I couldn't mess this up again.

The fire alarms had been a false alarm, just a prank by some kids. The bookstore was fine, and nothing else had happened that day. But for me, the day felt charged with a new kind of energy, a rush of new possibilities.

When the shift finally ended, I found myself eager to head home, though my thoughts were far from calming. I'd been so consumed by my encounter; it made the hours drag by.

I drove home with a sense of anticipation, my thoughts drifting back to the brief but intense interaction with Blake. The way his eyes had locked onto mine, the hesitant yet hopeful tone in his voice. It made me wonder about the path we would take from here.

Pulling up to the house, I was greeted by the enthusiastic barks of Duke. I let him out into the yard, watching as he raced around happily. His boundless energy was a sharp contrast to the turmoil inside me. I took a deep breath and walked inside, determined to keep my mind occupied with something other than the paper crumpled in my pocket.

After grabbing a quick bite to eat, I decided to take a shower. The hot water was soothing, and as I stood there, the steam swirling around me, I found my mind returning to the bookstore. To Blake. The memory of his touch lingered, the fleeting brush of his fingers against mine sending a shiver through me even now. I could feel the subtle strength in his grip. I closed my eyes under the cascading water, letting it wash over me, but my thoughts remained with him.

I let my hand glide over my body, the water mingling with the heat of the memory. The way Blake looked at me, with that intense, almost burning gaze made my pulse quicken and my cock stiffen. I imagined him closer, his body pressed against mine, his hands tracing the lines of my muscles. His lips brushing against mine, the warmth of his breath against my skin. These fantasies pulsed through me, making me breathe heavier.

The steam enveloped me, adding to the sense of intimacy, as if it were a cocoon holding all my private thoughts.

He reached over and kissed my neck. I started to tug at myself as I grew harder. He gently massaged my chest, following the lines of my pecs. I stroked faster, my breath quickening. Our lips met, and I welcomed his tongue, sucking gently at it all while never letting up on my cock.

The more I thought of him, the quicker I stroked. He kissed at my chest, his mouth tracing a path down to my bellybutton. He kissed gently before continuing south. His eyes, hungry as he took me wholly into his mouth.

My cock slid in and out of his mouth rapidly, Blake's eyes locked onto mine, making my pulse quicken even more. I felt a tingle in my center as Blake focused on the tip, moving quicker.

"Blake," I moaned, releasing my hot load into his mouth.

As the water finally began to cool, I took a deep breath, trying to steady my racing heart. I turned off the shower and wrapped myself in a towel, but the thoughts of Blake remained vivid and compelling. There was a new energy in my veins, a spark of hope and desire that promised something exciting, even if it was tinged with uncertainty.

With a final glance at myself in the bathroom mirror, I knew I was ready for whatever came next. The encounter had reignited something within me, and the promise of seeing Blake again was something I looked forward to with both anticipation and a touch of trepidation... but first, I needed to make the call.

Finally, I took a deep breath, picked up my phone, and dialed the number on the paper. It rang a few times before Blake's voice answered, smooth and comforting.

"Hello?" he said, and I could almost hear the smile in his voice.

"Hey, Blake, it's Thomas."

"I know," he said. "I'm glad you called."

"Uhm… should we go for a drink?"

"Yes," he said. "I think I saw a pinball bar downtown earlier. Would you like to meet there? I think it was called Middletown?"

"Yes, that sounds great. Twenty minutes?" I asked.

"I'll see you there," he said, and we disconnected.

CHAPTER 7
BLAKE

I ENTERED MIDDLETOWN DREAMS, a small pub with a double-sided bar. The front part had a row of stools backing up to the storefront, while the back was open for walk-ups. The rest of the bar was flanked by pinball machines on both sides, stretching all the way to the back of the establishment.

The glow from the machines painted the room with a vibrant energy that was almost palpable. The place was cozy, a little dim, with most of the light coming from the machines and a few hanging bulbs. The clinks of the games and soft chatter filled the air, but there was no sign of Thomas yet.

I slipped into a seat near the window, my heart fluttering with a mix of nerves and excitement. Memories of our friendship rushed back, mingling with a new, unfamiliar warmth. My thoughts kept drifting back to that Fourth of July—why I had to run, and what could have been if I hadn't.

The bell above the door chimed, and I saw Thomas walk in, his eyes scanning the room. When he spotted me, a broad smile spread across his face. He made his way over, his movements full of that easy confidence I remembered so well.

"Hey, Blake," Thomas said, sliding into the chair next to me. Hearing him call me by that name made my heart flutter. "You found this place pretty quick."

"Yeah, I'm good with directions," I replied with a grin.

We fell into easy conversation, the kind that felt like no time had passed at all, yet somehow still new. We caught up on each other's lives. He told me about Duke, his Great Dane. I was excited at the thought of meeting him—he sounded gorgeous. I let him know about my life in the city with my dad and my one-bedroom apartment. We ordered a round of drinks, which quickly turned into a second.

The conversation finally came to a gentle pause. I took a deep breath. "Thomas, there's no sense in avoiding it anymore. I need to tell you about that Fourth of July."

He raised an eyebrow, a curious glint in his eyes. "Alright."

I hesitated—the words tumbled out in a rush. "I

left because I was scared. Scared of what you'd think of me if you knew... about who I actually was. About my transition. I didn't want to deal with any judgments or awkwardness. I thought it would be easier to just disappear."

Thomas's expression softened, his eyes full of understanding. "Blake, you don't need to apologize for that. I wouldn't have cared. What stung the most was just how much I missed you. Missing my best friend. The not knowing what happened to you, why you vanished."

His words struck a chord deep inside of me. "I'm so sorry, Thomas. I should have been braver. I should have trusted you."

Thomas shook his head, a small smile tugging at his lips. "No, you don't owe me an apology. I think neither of us needs to apologize. We just need to figure out where we go from here."

I nodded, feeling a mix of relief and uncertainty. "Yeah, I guess we do. I've missed this—missed talking to you."

Thomas's smile widened. "Well, let's make the most of tonight. Catch up, have some fun. We've got a lot of lost time to make up for."

We clinked our glasses together, the weight of the past slipping away as we started to reconnect. The bar's ambiance wrapped around us, the pinball machines providing a whimsical backdrop to our newfound understanding. As we talked and laughed, it felt like we were picking up right where we left off—only now, with a deeper, more honest connection.

"Do you want to go for a walk?" I suggested, feeling the warmth of the booze twirling inside me.

"Yes," Thomas said. He paid for the drinks, waving me away as I reached for my card.

As we stepped out of the bar, the briny sea breeze swallowed us, mingling with the remnants of our shared laughter.

We strolled down Water Street, our steps in sync. The streets of Coral Cove felt both new and nostalgic under the streetlights. Every accidental touch of hands, every bump into each other, was electric. Thomas seemed to be savoring every second, though I could sense a hint of hesitation.

I brushed my fingers lightly against his hand, feeling the warmth of his skin. "You know, I've missed this place," I said, smiling. "And I've missed you."

Thomas glanced at me, a smirk playing at the corner of his lips. "I've missed you too, Blake."

His eyes searched mine, and I could feel the weight of unspoken words hanging between us. The last time he tried to kiss me, I had fled, leaving him without any explanation. I could see the hesitation in his eyes now, and I understood why.

I took a step closer, my heart pounding. "Thomas, I'm sorry for running away. I was scared, and I didn't handle it well. But I'm here now, and I want to be here with you."

Thomas's gaze softened, but there was a flicker of fear in his eyes. He leaned in slightly, then pulled back, as if unsure. "Blake, I…"

I gently cupped his face in my hands, forcing him to look at me. "It's okay, Thomas. It's been a long time, and we both have some catching up to do. But right now, I want to be close to you."

Before he could pull away, I kissed him. The initial hesitance quickly melted away as our lips met, and I could feel the spark that had always been there between us. His body relaxed into mine, and I deepened the kiss, savoring the connection.

When we finally pulled apart, Thomas looked at me, his expression a mixture of relief and awe.

"Thomas, I'm sor—" he cut me off. He pulled my face back to his, and we kissed again. His tongue parted my lips, deepening the kiss further. This was more passion than I had ever known.

When we pulled apart once again, he whispered, "I wasn't sure if this would ever happen again."

I smiled, brushing a stray lock of hair from his forehead. "It's happening now."

There was a pause, a stillness between us as we caught our breath, something unspoken lingering between us. I hesitated, then asked quietly, "Did you... ever think about this? About us? Even after I left?"

He looked at me, his eyes searching mine, as if deciding how much to reveal. "Yeah," he admitted, his voice barely above a whisper. "I've thought of you nearly every day."

I bit my lip, feeling the weight of the moment. "I always wondered... what was it about me, you know? I mean, back then, when I was presenting as Michelle."

Thomas's gaze softened, and he reached out, tracing his thumb along my jawline. "It was never just about who you were on the outside, Blake. I've always been attracted to the person, not the gender. I guess you could say I'm pansexual, though I don't think I ever put a label on it."

His words wrapped around me, offering a comfort I hadn't realized I needed. "So, you're saying... it wouldn't have mattered?"

He shook his head, a gentle smile playing at his lips. "No, it wouldn't have. It still doesn't."

Relief washed over me, and I felt a smile tugging

at the corners of my mouth. "That's... good to know," I said, my voice thick with emotion on the verge of tears.

Thomas leaned in, pressing a soft kiss to my forehead. "It's more than good," he whispered. "Let's head back to my place."

I nodded and followed Thomas back to his truck.

CHAPTER 8
THOMAS

BLAKE and I walked hand in hand down Water Street toward my truck, the soft glow of the street-lights casting long shadows as we strolled through the quiet night. The air was warm, with a faint breeze carrying the scent of saltwater and distant pine. It felt like the town was holding its breath, caught in the stillness that often comes just before dawn.

We passed closed storefronts, their windows dark and empty—a stark contrast to the memories I had of this place bustling with life, especially on the eve of a holiday. It was strange being here, but with Blake at my side, the town didn't feel so empty.

Suddenly, a sharp crack echoed through the night, followed by a bright flash of green light streaking across the sky in front of us. I jumped, instinctively squeezing Blake's hand as the light whizzed around us, spiraling in intricate patterns that seemed almost too perfect to be random.

"What the hell?" I muttered, furrowing my brow in annoyance. "Kids must be setting off fireworks early."

I watched as the green light zipped past us, looping around once more before shooting up into the air. It paused for a heartbeat, suspended above us like a star that had lost its way. Then, with a soft pop, it exploded into brilliant bursts of purple, the sky suddenly alight with an otherworldly glow. The light shimmered as it spread out, leaving behind delicate white embers that drifted down like snowflakes, landing gently on our skin.

I reached out, catching one of the embers on my palm. It danced across my skin before dissolving into a faint sparkle, leaving a warm, tingling sensation behind. "Blake, look…" I began, my voice trailing off as I realized what was happening.

Blake turned to me, my frustration giving way to confusion. "Thomas… it's after midnight," he said softly. "It's the Fourth of July."

I blinked, the realization dawning slowly. "But that firework… it looked just like…"

"Like the one we saw when we were kids," Blake finished, my heart pounding in my chest. "Remember? We thought it was a firework, but it wasn't. It was… something else."

I stared at the sky where the firework had exploded, the last of the purple light fading into darkness. "It felt… ethereal," I whispered. "Like it wasn't really of this world."

We stood there in silence, the weight of the moment settling over me like a blanket. The town was still quiet and unbothered by the explosion. It no longer felt empty. Instead, it was full of memories, of possibilities, of something magical we had both forgotten until now.

But then, as the white embers continued to fall, I froze. A wave of anxiety washed over me, tightening my chest. He left me last time. What if…

Before I could spiral further, Blake, seeing the worry on my face, grabbed my arm and pulled me into an embrace. The warmth of his body pressed against mine, his steady heartbeat grounding me.

"Don't worry, I'm not going anywhere," he whispered into my ear, his breath warm and reassuring. I closed my eyes, letting the tension seep out of me as I leaned into him. I wanted to believe him—I needed to.

I pulled back just enough to meet his gaze, a small smile tugging at my lips. "Maybe it's a reminder," I said, my voice soft but certain. "That some things, no matter how much time passes, never leave us."

The last of the white embers danced around us, fading gently into the night. And for the first time in years, I felt like I was exactly where I was supposed to be.

"Come on," I said, squeezing his hand. "Let's get out of here."

Blake nodded, and we climbed into my truck, heading toward my place. The silence between us was comfortable, filled with an unspoken under-standing. When we reached my house, the warm glow of the porch light greeted us. I fished my keys out of my pocket, feeling a sense of relief as I unlocked the door.

The moment we stepped inside, a massive shape bounded toward us, tail wagging furiously. "Whoa, Duke, calm down," I said, laughing as the Great Dane practically knocked us over in his excitement.

Blake chuckled, kneeling to greet Duke, who immediately nuzzled into his hand, his tail still wagging like crazy. "Hey, big guy," Blake greeted, scratching behind Duke's ears. The sight of them together made me smile. Duke usually took a while to warm up to strangers, but he seemed to have taken to Blake instantly.

"You've made a friend for life," I said, watching as Duke settled happily at Blake's feet.

Blake grinned, looking up at me. "Good, I like him."

We made our way to the living room, where I flicked on a lamp, casting a soft, warm glow over the space. Duke trotted over to his bed in the corner, circling a few times before flopping down with a satisfied huff. Blake and I sat down on the couch, the cushions sinking under our weight.

For a moment, we just sat there, side by side, the silence between us thick with anticipation. I glanced over at him, my heart pounding in my chest. The night felt charged with something electric, something I couldn't quite name.

Without thinking, I reached out, brushing an eyelash from his cheek. "Blake," I said, my voice catching in my throat.

He turned to me, his eyes dark and intense. Before I could second-guess myself, I leaned in. Our lips met softly at first, testing the waters. But then something snapped, and the kiss deepened, all the pent-up emotions from the past rushing to the surface.

Blake's hand slid up the back of my neck, pulling me closer as his lips moved against mine, insistent and demanding. I responded in kind, the world around us fading into nothingness as we lost ourselves in the moment. The couch cushions shifted beneath us as we pressed closer together, our bodies molding into each other's.

For a brief, shining moment, everything felt right. It wasn't just the physical connection—though that was intense, almost overwhelming. It was the emotional closeness, the sense that this, finally, was my person and we had been reunited.

I tugged at Blake's shirt, pulling it over his head. I took in the sight of his bare chest, a work of art— sculpted pecs, strong shoulders leading down to toned arms. He was a sight to behold, and I wanted to kiss every part of him. I twisted him around and gently pushed him down onto the couch. I climbed on top of him and started kissing his neck, his arms, his chest, sides, and stomach.

I worked my way back up his sides, breathing in at his hairy armpit. The scent of him intoxicated me, and I bit gently at his neck. He squealed and pulled back.

"Don't sneak away from me," I commanded gently.

"Never," Blake replied, pulling me in for another kiss. He reached up and pulled my shirt off over my head, tossing it across the room. "Being a firefighter has done wonderful things for your body."

"Thank you?" I said, laughing at the comment.

"What's this?" Blake asked as he traced a scar along the side of my chest.

"It was my second year as a firefighter. We were trying to put out a barn fire. I was young, stupid, and eager to make a name for myself. A part of the building collapsed, and a burning board flew right at me, slicing through my suit and cutting me," I admitted.

Blake gasped.

"Eh, it's fine. I was naïve," I said. "We all have to learn our lessons."

Blake leaned forward, kissing along my scar. It tickled, and I squirmed. Blake pulled me back toward him, pulling me down on top of him. I let my full weight sink into him, burying deep into the sofa. My kisses moved to his chin and down his throat, past his clavicle.

Further and further down, I kissed past his pecs, my tongue dancing in the hair of his treasure trail, down toward his navel. I paused briefly to kiss the soft skin around his navel before continuing my way down to his jeans. My fingers worked quickly at the button.

I unzipped his pants to find black, silky boxers. I pulled his jeans off and worked my kisses up his legs, then up his inner thighs. As I neared his center, his hands covered his crotch area.

"Thomas," he said, his voice serious. "We should talk…"

"About nothing. It doesn't matter to me what you have down here. I want all of you," I said.

I looked up to see a tear falling slowly down Blake's cheek. I quickly maneuvered back up to his face and wiped the tear away. I kissed him deeply.

I leaned in close, my voice a low whisper. "Now, are you ready to take this dick like the good boy you are?"

Blake shot me a devilish grin. "Fuck yes."

CHAPTER 9
BLAKE

THOMAS FLIPPED me over in an instant. I felt him remove his pants and underwear. He climbed on top of me and started kissing the nape of my neck. My body tingled with pleasure that shot through me like electricity.

His lips moved down my spine, stopping at my sides to give me gentle nibbles that made me squirm and snort. Thomas growled, and I could feel myself swell, arching my back into him.

"Yeah?" Thomas asked, his voice a low rumble. "Have you been a good boy?"

"Yessir," I cried out, barely able to speak.

"You want more?"

"Fuck yes," I gasped, desperate for him.

Thomas continued his journey down my back with kisses, his tongue teasing the waistband of my boxers, his fingers dipping just below. In a fit of passion, he grabbed the sides of my waistband and tore off my boxers in one swift motion.

He kissed the peaks of my cheeks, the touch tickling and sending bolts of passion through me. He arched my back up, dragging my legs beneath me, exposing my hole to him. He plunged his tongue in hastily, and I gasped, all the air escaping my lungs. I struggled to regain my breath as he worked his tongue deeper into my puckered hole.

Thomas used his hands to spread me open and lapped at my hole with the broadest part of his tongue, moving faster and more urgently. He pulled back and spat at my hole, then used his tongue to pick up the drop and shove it inside me. His finger followed, gently massaging the liquid into me.

Suddenly, he spanked me, rubbing in the impact. A feral groan escaped my lips, surprising even me.

"Oh, good boy," Thomas said, pleased with my reaction. He spanked me again, a little harder this time, and rubbed the heat into my ass.

"Oh... fuck," I screamed out, the intensity overwhelming.

He spanked me a third time, not quite as hard as the second, before returning his attention to my rosebud. His tongue moved with purpose, releasing more of his liquid and pushing it inside with his middle finger. I moaned with approval, my body responding to every touch.

My breath hitched as Thomas continued to work his magic, his movements slow and deliberate, drawing out every ounce of pleasure from me. His finger slid deeper, and I arched my back, pushing myself against him, craving more. The heat between us was electric, every touch sending shivers down my spine.

Thomas chuckled low in his throat, his breath hot against my skin. "You like that, don't you?" he murmured, his voice dripping with satisfaction. He added a second finger, twisting and stretching me, and I couldn't hold back the moan that escaped my lips.

"Yes," I gasped, the word barely a whisper as my body trembled under his touch. "Please... more."

He didn't need any more encouragement. His fingers moved with a practiced rhythm, pushing me closer and closer to the edge. I felt the pressure building, a tight coil deep inside me, ready to snap at any moment.

"Good boy," he whispered again, his voice filled with a mix of tenderness and command. The praise washed over me, making my heart race even faster. There was something intoxicating about the way he said it, like he was claiming me, making me his.

And I wanted it. I wanted all of it.

Thomas pulled his fingers out slowly, eliciting a groan of protest from me. But before I could complain, he was back, this time positioning himself at my entrance. I felt the tip of him press against me, teasing, testing.

"Are you ready for me?" he asked, his voice husky with desire.

"Yes," I breathed, my voice trembling with anticipation. "I need you… inside of me."

With a slow, deliberate push, he entered me, filling me completely. My body tensed at the sudden intrusion, but the discomfort quickly melted away, replaced by a deep, burning pleasure. I clung to him, my fingers digging into his skin as he moved, each thrust sending waves of ecstasy crashing over me.

Thomas picked up the pace, his movements becoming more urgent, more demanding. I matched his rhythm, our bodies moving together in perfect harmony. The room filled with the sounds of our breathing, the wet slaps of skin against skin, and the occasional grunt or moan as we lost ourselves in the moment.

It wasn't just sex. It was something deeper, something primal and all-consuming. I could feel it in the way he held me, the way he looked at me, the way he whispered my name like it was the most important word in the world. My name. My chosen name.

I was his, completely and utterly, and in this moment, nothing else mattered.

Thomas's thrusts grew more urgent, his breathing ragged as he drove deeper into me. I could feel every inch of him, the heat and pressure building to an unbearable peak. My body tensed, muscles clenching around him, pulling him in tighter as if I could fuse us together in that moment.

"Fuck, Blake," Thomas groaned, his voice thick with need. "You're so fucking perfect."

The praise sent another wave of pleasure crashing through me, and the tight coil inside of me started to unravel. My vision blurred as I lost myself in the sensation, everything else fading away until all that was left was him—Thomas, inside me, his hands gripping my hips as he moved faster, harder.

I was close, so close I could almost taste it. My breath hitched again, and I reached down, moving my fingers to my center in time with his thrusts. It was too much and, in the same breath, not enough. I needed more. I needed everything.

"Thomas, I..." I tried to speak, but the words caught in my throat, lost in a moan as the pleasure mounted, driving me closer to the edge.

He understood. His hand moved from my hip to

cover my hand, guiding me as he thrust into me with renewed vigor. "Let go," he whispered, his voice a low growl in my ear. "Come for me."

That was all it took. With a final, shuddering thrust, the tension inside me snapped, and I came hard, my body shaking with the force of it. My vision went white, my entire being consumed by the overwhelming rush of pleasure. I cried out his name, my voice hoarse and desperate as I rode the wave of ecstasy that crashed over me.

Thomas followed me over the edge, his grip on my hand tightening as he buried himself deep inside of me, his own climax ripping through him. He groaned loudly, his body stiffening before he slumped against me, both of us panting heavily in the aftermath.

We stayed like that for a few moments, tangled together, hearts pounding in sync. The intensity of it all left us both breathless. He collapsed awkwardly into the corner of the couch, pulling me into his arms. We lay there in silence, our bodies still intertwined, the warmth of him comforting in the quiet of the room.

"Blake," Thomas whispered, pressing a kiss to my temple. "That was…"

"Yeah," I breathed, turning my head to look at him. His face was flushed, his eyes half-lidded with satisfaction. I smiled, feeling a deep sense of contentment. "It was."

He smiled back, his hand moving to gently caress my cheek. "You're amazing."

I blushed, the compliment making my heart flutter. "So are you," I whispered, leaning in to kiss him softly, savoring the taste of his lips on mine.

As I lay there in his arms, I knew that this was where I was meant to be—right here, with him, in this perfect moment of bliss.

CHAPTER 10
THOMAS

I PULLED Blake off the couch and led him to the bedroom, our fingers still intertwined. Duke followed behind, his large paws thudding softly against the hardwood floor. The bedroom was dimly lit, the soft glow of the moon filtering through the curtains, casting gentle shadows across the room.

As we reached the bed, I turned to Blake, pulling him close for one more kiss, slow and lingering. The intensity from earlier had faded, replaced by a deep, quiet contentment. This moment felt right, like I was finally where I needed to be.

Duke circled his bed a few times before flopping down with a loud thud, finding his spot for the night. I smiled at the sight, feeling a warmth in my chest that had everything to do with the peace I felt in this moment.

Blake climbed into bed first, pulling the covers back and slipping under them with an ease that made my heart ache a little. I followed, sliding in beside him, and we naturally gravitated toward each other, our bodies fitting together as if they were made to.

I wrapped an arm around him, pulling him close so that his head rested on my chest. The rhythmic rise and fall of his breathing was soothing, grounding me in the present. I could feel his warmth against me, the steady beat of his heart, and it filled me with a sense of calm I hadn't felt in a long time.

As we lay there tangled in each other's arms, my thoughts drifted back to everything that had brought us here, to this exact moment. The years of separation, the uncertainty, the longing. And now, finally, we were together again, in a way that felt even more profound than before.

But with that realization came a pang of fear. I didn't want to lose this. I didn't want to lose him. The thought of Blake slipping away, of waking up to find him gone, was too much to bear. I held him a little tighter as if the strength of my embrace could keep him here with me forever.

Blake shifted slightly, nuzzling closer into my chest, and I pressed a kiss to the top of his head. "I'm not letting you go this time," I whispered, the words barely more than a breath but filled with all the emotion I couldn't quite say.

Blake murmured something in his sleep, his hand curling against my chest, and I felt a smile tug at my lips. I didn't know what the future held, but right now, in this moment, I had him. And that was enough.

The heaviness of sleep started to pull at me, and I let myself sink into it, my body relaxing against his. The last thing I felt was the warmth of Blake beside me. For the first time in a long time, I felt that everything was going to be okay.

The morning came gently, with the soft light filtering through the curtains. We took our time waking up, savoring the quiet moments of just being together. Blake was still curled up against me, his breathing slow and steady. I couldn't help but smile as I watched him, feeling contentment wash over me.

Eventually, Blake stirred, blinking up at me with a sleepy grin. "Morning," he murmured, his voice thick with sleep.

"Morning," I replied, leaning down to kiss his forehead. "How about some breakfast?"

Blake nodded, and we reluctantly pulled ourselves out of bed, the cool air making us both shiver slightly. I threw on some clothes and headed to the kitchen, Blake following close behind. Duke, sensing movement, stretched lazily and padded after us, his tail wagging in anticipation of the day.

I let Duke outside and busied myself making breakfast. I fried up some eggs and bacon while Blake set the table. The scent of coffee filled the air, and the sound of sizzling bacon joined in as we worked together in the kitchen.

We ate at the small kitchen table, chatting quietly about nothing in particular, just enjoying the simplicity of the morning. But as the sun climbed higher in the sky, I glanced at the clock and realized how late it actually was.

"We really slept in," I said with a laugh, glancing out the window at the daylight. "I called in sick to work while you were in the bathroom. They weren't thrilled on the busiest day of the year, but I don't care. Should we head down to the park for the fireworks show?"

Blake looked at me, a spark of excitement in his eyes. "We should go," he said smiling. "I need a redo."

I nodded, feeling a flutter of anticipation in my chest. "Yeah, let's do that."

We cleaned up the kitchen and got ready, heading out the door after making sure Duke was taken care of. The day was warm and bright, the sky a brilliant blue with just a few wisps of clouds. As we made our way downtown, the streets were buzzing with activity: kids running around with sparklers, people setting up chairs at the cliff's edge in preparation for the show, and the smell of barbecue wafting through the air.

But our destination was clear. We made our way down to the park, where the trees provided a trail into a clearing. The sound of the ocean grew louder as we approached the cliff, the scent of saltwater filling the air.

Blake and I walked side by side, our hands brushing occasionally, the anticipation building with each step. Finally, we reached the trail that led through the thick shrubbery and made our way to our secret ledge. It had been our place since we were kids, a sanctuary where we could escape the world and just be ourselves.

As we settled onto the ledge, the first few fireworks shot into the sky, exploding in bursts of color over the water. The reflections danced on the surface of the bay, creating a stunning mirror image that took my breath away.

Blake sat beside me, his eyes fixed on the sky, a look of awe on his face. I couldn't help but watch him, feeling a swell of emotions in my chest. This was it, the moment I had been waiting for.

"Blake," I said softly, turning to face him.

He looked at me, his expression curious, and I could see the love in his eyes, so clear and true that it made my heart ache.

"I've been thinking… about us, about everything we've been through," I began, my voice trembling slightly. "And I realized something. I don't want to waste any more time. I don't want to wait for the perfect moment or the perfect circumstances. I just want you."

Blake's eyes widened, his breath catching as he realized what was happening. I could see a question forming on his lips, but I didn't let him speak—not yet.

"I don't have a ring," I admitted, feeling a little self-conscious, "but I don't need one to know that I want to spend the rest of my life with you. Blake, will you marry me?"

The fireworks exploded in a brilliant display of light and color, the sound of the crowd cheering in the distance, but all I could focus on was Blake—his face, his expression, and the tears welling up in his eyes as he looked at me.

For a moment, he just stared at me, and I felt a

sting of anxiety in my chest. But then, slowly, a smile spread across his face, and he nodded, his voice choked with emotion.

"Yes," he whispered, barely audible above the fireworks. "Yes, Thomas, I will marry you."

Relief and joy surged through me, and I pulled him into a tight embrace, my heart racing with happiness. The fireworks continued to explode overhead, but they were nothing compared to the explosion of love I felt in that moment.

We stayed like that for what felt like an hour, just holding each other as the fireworks lit up the sky above us. Eventually, as the final bursts of colors faded into the night, I pulled back slightly to look at him, brushing another tear from his cheek.

"I love you," I said, my voice steady and sure.

"I love you too," Blake replied, his smile radiant.

And as we sat there on our secret ledge, with the smell of the fireworks still hanging in the air, I knew that this was just the start of something beautiful.

IF YOU ENJOYED *RED, White, and Ravished*, please consider reading some of my other books, like **Hanged Passions**, part of the Tarot Fantasies series.

A Tarot-Inspired Tale of MM Romance, Bondage, and Empowerment.

ANDREW:

I walked into The Arcane Room carrying the weight of my past. Then I met Julian. With every touch, he unraveled my fears, drawing me into a world where surrender wasn't a weakness but a pathway to strength. The tarot card promised a new perspective, and Julian showed me how to find it within myself. This is my story.

Andrew's life takes an unexpected turn when he draws The Hanged Man tarot card, symbolizing suspension, letting go, and gaining a new perspective. Julian, with his chiseled physique and magnetic presence, introduces Andrew to a world where the boundaries of control and submission blur, awakening desires Andrew never knew existed. As Julian expertly navigates the ropes of bondage, he helps Andrew confront his deepest fears and insecurities, teaching him to embrace his true self and the power of letting go. "Hanged Passions" weaves together the mystical elements of tarot, the raw intensity of bondage, and the tender growth of MM romance, creating a captivating story of love, trust, and spiritual awakening.

. . .

SIGN up for my newsletter and get a free book today!

https://mailchi.mp/158597581671/jax-wilder

HAUNTED BY HER

A SHORT, SMALL TOWN, MFF
BISEXUAL, LOVE TRIANGLE ROMANCE

CHAPTER 1
MOLLY

THE BRISK OCTOBER wind swept through the streets of Coral Cove, tugging at the hem of my coat as I hurried towards the office. The town always felt different in the weeks leading up to Halloween—darker, more alive, as if it, too, held secrets beneath the surface. I pulled my scarf tighter against the wind's icy fingers, my thoughts drifting from the morning briefing to the small, locked drawer in my desk where I kept my secret. A secret that gnawed at me, especially in moments like this, when the veil between my worlds felt so thin I feared it might tear.

As I pushed through the front door of the Law Offices of Lorenzo Moretti, the familiar hum of the heater in the old building greeted me. I flipped on the lights, made my way to my desk, and grabbed a cup of coffee from the Keurig. It was the same ritual every year: pretend everything was normal, go about my day, and wait.

My husband, Ethan, had kissed me goodbye that morning, his lips warm against my cool cheek. "Don't forget, we still need to pick up the pumpkins tonight," he reminded me with a playful grin. He knew how much I loved Halloween, how I threw myself into the decorations, the costumes, and the thrill of it all. To him, it was just one of my quirks, one of the many reasons he loved me. But he didn't know the half of it.

As I sat at my desk, the drawer seemed to pulse with its own heartbeat, a steady thud that matched the one in my chest. I forced myself to focus on the tasks in front of me—shuffling papers, drafting emails—but the weight of the secret was always there, pressing down, stirring guilt within me.

I glanced at the photo of Ethan on my desk, his easy smile captured in a moment of pure joy. We were standing by a lake on a sunny afternoon, his arm wrapped around my shoulders, pulling me close, his love for me evident in his eyes. I traced a finger over the frame, my heart twisting. How much of me did he truly know? He knew when he married me that I was a liberal, spiritual, free-spirited bisexual woman. But the secret I kept hidden away in a locked drawer at my office was a lie he had no idea existed. That felt wrong.

The chime above the door startled me, and I nearly dropped my coffee cup. "Morning, Molly," Lorenzo's voice rang out, his usual warm greeting.

"Morning," I replied, forcing a smile that didn't quite reach my eyes.

"Didn't mean to startle you," he teased, grabbing his pile of mail from my desk. "Do you know if we got the court date for the Stewart case yet?"

"We did. I forwarded you the email from the clerk just a moment ago," I said.

"Perfect. Thank you, Molly," he replied before retreating to his office.

As soon as Lorenzo's door clicked shut, I exhaled slowly, the tightness in my chest easing a fraction. My hand drifted to the drawer, my fingers grazing the cool metal of the lock. It felt as though the drawer was calling to me, urging me to open it and touch the things that tethered me.

With a quick glance around to make sure I was alone, I slipped the small key from my pocket and turned it in the lock. The drawer slid open with a soft, almost inaudible creak. Inside, nestled beneath a pile of files, lay a small velvet pouch, its contents hidden but all too familiar to me. I lifted it gently, feeling the familiar weight of the objects within—the tools of ritual, the artifacts that were crucial.

My heart pounded in my ears as I loosened the drawstrings and peered inside. The faint scent of lavender and something more ancient drifted up, stirring memories I kept buried deep. My fingers brushed over the smooth surface of a polished stone, a delicate vial of shimmering liquid, and the scrap of paper with her handwriting, the words etched into my mind as clearly as if they were tattooed on my skin.

The spell—no, the ritual—had been carefully crafted, its purpose singular and unavoidable. Every year, the same steps, the same incantations, the same longing that tugged at the corners of my heart.

I closed my eyes, the office fading away as the memories flooded back.

IT WAS DUSK. I stood in secluded spot deep in the woods, a place where trees grew thicker and the light barely penetrated the canopy. I had been drawn in years ago, the energy palpable in the air, buzzing against my skin. The small altar was already prepared, a simple arrangement of stones and herbs that seemed to vibrate with an otherworldly power.

Kneeling before the altar, I laid out the supplies

just as I had been taught, each item placed with reverence. The words of the ritual spilled from my lips, soft at first, then gaining strength as the air around me seemed to hum in response.

And then she appeared, as she always did, her silhouette emerging from behind a towering oak. The first thing I noticed was the way the shadows seemed to cling to her, reluctant to let her go, reluctant to give her form. Her dress wasn't just black; it was the black of a moonless night, absorbing all light and leaving only an impression of where she stood. It moved like liquid, rippling with each step, whispering against the leaves as though it had secrets of its own.

Her eyes were the most unsettling part—not dark in color, but in depth. They were the color of old amber, rich and deep, yet within them was a darkness that seemed to swirl, like a storm brewing just beneath the surface.

When she looked at me, it was as though she could see right through to the part of me I kept hidden from everyone else, the part that only existed for her.

She crossed the distance between us with a grace that made my breath catch, her steps silent, predatory. When she reached me, she didn't speak. She never had to. Her hand cupped my cheek, her touch cool and electric, sending shivers down my spine.

And then, without hesitation, her lips found mine, soft and insistent, stealing the breath from my lungs and the thoughts from my mind.

The kiss was intoxicating, a blend of hunger and tenderness that left me weak at the knees. I melted into her, the world spinning as her hands slipped around my waist, pulling me closer, grounding me even as she set me aflame.

I was hers, utterly and completely. In those moments, I was lost to the world, lost to Ethan, lost to everything but her.

THE MEMORY BURNED in my mind as I opened my eyes, my fingers trembling slightly as I tightened the drawstrings of the velvet pouch and placed it back in the drawer. I closed it with a firm push, the lock clicking into place, but the weight of what I was hiding only grew heavier.

I took a deep breath, trying to steady myself and focus on my job, but the ghost of her touch lingered on my lips. The guilt twisted in my gut like a living thing. Saturday night, I would see her again. And no matter how much I loved Ethan, no matter how perfect our life seemed, I knew I could never resist her call.

CHAPTER 2
ETHAN

I STOOD in the middle of the living room, staring at the array of decorations scattered across the floor. Plastic pumpkins, strings of orange lights, and a cardboard skeleton grinned up at me as if mocking my uncertainty. Halloween had never been my favorite holiday. I much preferred the calm warmth of Thanksgiving or the magic of Christmas, but Molly had a way of pulling me into the spirit of things.

I knelt down and picked up a garland of fake autumn leaves, feeling the stiff plastic between my fingers. "Where the hell do these even go?" I muttered to myself, glancing around the room. It was already decorated enough, in my opinion, but Molly always liked going all out. If it made her happy, I would gladly dive into the chaos.

Starting with the garland, I draped it over the mantle above the fireplace, adjusting it until it looked somewhat natural. Stepping back, I put my hands on my hips and tilted my head. "Not bad," I said to the empty room, though I knew Molly would find a way to make it even better.

The doorbell rang, startling me out of my thoughts. I wiped my hands on my jeans as I walked over to the door, half-expecting to see a trick-or-treater who had gotten the dates mixed up. Instead, a delivery man stood on the porch, holding a large box decorated with pumpkins and bats.

"Ethan Parker?" the man asked.

"That's me," I replied, signing for the package and taking it inside. I set it down on the kitchen table and tore open the top. Inside, nestled among layers of tissue paper, were more decorations—this time, the really creepy ones that Molly loved. A pair of animatronic spiders that would probably send me jumping out of my skin if I didn't know they were fake, some cobweb material, and a set of black candles shaped like skulls. They bled red wax when lit.

I chuckled, shaking my head. "She's going to love these," I said to myself. As much as I didn't get the appeal of the spooky stuff, I couldn't help but admire Molly's enthusiasm. It was one of the things that had drawn me to her in the first place—her boundless energy and ability to make the mundane feel magical.

I sifted through the last crumpled sheets of tissue paper, my fingers brushing against something smooth and delicate at the bottom of the box. With a slight tug, I pulled out the final gift and unfolded it carefully in my hands.

It was a stunning black negligee, intricately designed with sheer, netted fabric resembling delicate spiderwebs woven together. The material shimmered faintly under the light, each thread catching the glow as if spun from midnight itself. As I held it up, the fabric cascaded down, draping elegantly and promising to cling to every curve, like a dark web that would envelop Molly in mystery and allure.

The front of my pants tighten just thinking about it. I reached down and adjusted myself, trying to make things a bit more comfortable. Clearly, this gift was more for me than for Molly, but I sensed she would love it nonetheless.

I got back to decorating, arranging the new items, hanging the cobwebs in the corners of the room, and placing the candles strategically around the house. The spiders I saved for last, dreading the moment they'd inevitably spring to life and scare the daylights out of me.

As I worked, my mind drifted to Molly. She'd been working late a lot recently, something about a big case that everyone at the firm was pulling extra hours for. I missed her, even though she made a point of sending me texts throughout the day. I loved the little reminders that she was thinking of me, too. We'd been married for five years now, and though the honeymoon phase was long over, there was still a deep warmth between us—a comfort in the way we understood each other without having to say much.

I set the last spider in place and looked around the living room. It was starting to feel more like Halloween, and even though it wasn't really my thing, I found myself smiling. Molly would be home soon, and the house would be ready for her.

I was just about to grab a soda from the fridge when I heard the jingle of keys at the front door. My heart lifted at the sound. I walked over to the entry-way, ready to greet her with a kiss.

When the door swung open and Molly stepped inside, my smile widened. "Hey, you," I said, taking in the sight of her. She was a little disheveled from the long day, but still beautiful in that effortless way she always managed.

"Wow," Molly said, looking around the room. "You really went all out."

I shrugged, trying to play it cool. "Just getting into the spirit."

Molly laughed, the sound filling the room with warmth. "I love it," she said, pulling me into a hug. I wrapped my arms around her, breathing in the scent of her perfume.

"I got you something else," I said with a sheepish grin, dancing over to the box on the couch and pulling out the bag containing the negligee.

"You didn't have to do that," she said, smiling. She carefully pulled out the negligee. "Oh my gods, this is stunning. Where did you find this?"

"Never mind that. Try it on quickly to make sure it fits," I suggested, starting to tug at her shirt, eager for the reveal.

Molly laughed and shook her head. "I'm going to put it on in the bedroom and then come out to do a reveal. This looks complicated to get on, and I don't want you to see the struggle."

I pretended to pout, but I couldn't help the grin that spread across my face. "Fine, I'll wait. But don't take too long."

Molly playfully swatted my arm as she headed towards the bedroom, holding the negligee carefully as if it were made of spun glass. I watched her go, anticipation buzzing in my chest. She paused at the doorway, throwing me a teasing glance over her shoulder. "Patience, mister. It'll be worth it."

"I'm counting on it," I called after her, already imagining how the delicate fabric would hug her body.

As the door clicked shut, I found myself pacing in the living room, my mind racing with thoughts of Molly in that stunning piece of lingerie. The image of her wrapped in those black webs made my pulse quicken. I could feel the tension in my body, the anticipation nearly unbearable.

A few minutes passed, each one dragging slower than the last. I busied myself by picking up Molly's coat and bags by the door. I put her coat away in the closet and emptied her bag onto the table. I grabbed her lunch box, pulling out the trash and rinsing it before setting it on the drying rack.

I reached for a small brown paper bag I didn't recognize. It had "Arcane Room" stamped on the outside. "Of course," I laughed. The Arcane Room was a mystical shop downtown, dangerously close to Molly's office, that carried all sorts of crystals and gemstones, herbs and incense, magical tools, books, and grimoires. I'd once joked with Ms. Vesper, the owner, that I might as well direct deposit her half of my paycheck every week.

Finally, I heard the soft click of the bedroom door

opening, and I turned, my breath catching in my throat.

Molly stepped into the room, the light from the hallway casting a soft glow around her. The negligee clung to her in all the right places, the sheer fabric revealing just enough to leave little to the imagination while still maintaining an air of tantalizing mystery. The black spiderweb pattern wove across her skin, accentuating her curves and giving her an otherworldly allure that left me speechless.

She walked toward me with a shy smile, her cheeks flushed slightly as she did a slow twirl, letting the fabric dance around her legs. "So, what do you think?" she asked, her voice a mix of playfulness and uncertainty.

For a moment, I couldn't find the words. My mouth had gone dry, and all I could do was stare, completely captivated by her beauty. Finally, I managed to croak out, "You look… sexy as hell."

Molly's smile widened as she stepped closer, reaching out to take my hand. I led her in another spin to get a better view from behind.

"What do you think about it?" I asked.

She wrapped her arms around me, pulling me close. I felt the cool, delicate fabric against my skin. "I think it's absolutely perfect. I feel like a sexy witch."

"A sexy witch, huh?"

"Don't you think?" she asked, making a playful claw-like gesture with her hand.

"I love it," I said. "And I love you."

She tilted her head up, her eyes meeting mine with a mischievous glint. "Why don't you show me just how much?"

My heart raced as I leaned in, capturing her lips in a deep, slow kiss. The warmth of her body pressed against mine, and the softness of the negligee heightened the sensation. The anticipation that had been building began to unravel, and I knew we were both about to lose ourselves in each other.

In one swift motion, I lifted my shirt off, pulling her close again. The contrast of her smooth, warm skin draped in the silky fabric against my bare chest made the pressure in my jeans unbearable. My hands instinctively moved down to the small of her back, savoring the curve of her waist before traveling lower to cup her perfect ass. I tugged gently at the fabric, hiking up the skirt portion of the negligee until her bare cheeks were exposed to my eager hands. The heat of her skin under my palms sent a shiver down my spine. I tightened my grip, lifting her slightly as I pressed her harder into the kiss, our mouths colliding with an intensity that left us both breathless.

Our tongues danced together, exploring and tasting, as I felt the weight of her body melt into mine. She responded eagerly, her hands sliding up my back, nails grazing my skin and leaving a trail of tingling warmth in their wake. The soft fabric of the negligee brushed against my skin with every movement, heightening the sensation, making it feel like every nerve in my body was alive and on fire.

With a low growl, I lifted her higher, her legs automatically wrapping around my waist as I pressed her back against the wall. The pressure between us intensified, and I could feel the heat radiating from her as she moaned softly into my mouth—a sound that sent a surge of desire through me.

CHAPTER 3
MOLLY

BREAKING THE KISS FOR A MOMENT, Ethan looked into my eyes, dark and filled with the same hunger I felt, and whispered, "You're so damn beautiful."

My lips curled into a smile as his eyes stayed locked onto mine, the intensity between us growing. "Then show me," I said, and kissed him again.

Ethan needed no further invitation. He pulled me from the wall, my legs still wrapped around him, and carried me to the living room couch. He let me down with a thud, grabbing my thighs and pulling my hips over the edge of the seat. I could barely catch my breath before his face was at my center, kissing and teasing through the silky fabric.

I gasped and grabbed a handful of his hair as he worked, shaking his head quickly at my core. I stifled a giggle, letting out a moan to encourage him.

He pulled at the strings on either side of my panties, sliding the fabric aside to reveal my folds. He pressed his face against me, kissing and licking as if savoring every inch. Ethan trailed his tongue along my entrance, his movements gentle and exploratory.

I love this man, but he wasn't exactly skilled at oral. Still, I didn't want to discourage him, so when he asked, "You like that?" I replied with an enthusiastic, "Oh yeah. Now fuck me, baby."

Ethan stood up, unbuttoning his jeans. He quickly pulled them off, socks and all, leaving him standing in his tight red boxer briefs. The outline of his cock was evident, fully hard and eager. Thankfully, the gods blessed him with a well-endowed cock, and I couldn't help but admire the view.

He pulled off his boxers in one fluid motion, revealing his impressive length, hard and ready. I bit my lip, anticipation thrumming through my veins.

Ethan's eyes locked onto mine, dark with desire, as he positioned himself on his knees between my legs. The warmth of his body hovered just above mine, his erection grazing my inner thigh as he leaned in for another searing kiss. His hands roamed over my body, fingers exploring every curve, as if memorizing me.

Without breaking the kiss, Ethan reached down, guiding himself to my entrance. He paused, his breath hot against my neck, and I could feel the tension building.

"Ready?" he asked, his voice gritty with desire.

"More than ready," I breathed, wrapping my legs around his waist and pulling him closer, urging him on.

With a slow, deliberate thrust, Ethan entered me, filling me completely. The sensation was intense, a mix of pleasure and pressure that made me gasp. He began to move, his rhythm steady but deep, each stroke sending waves of heat coursing through me. I arched my back, meeting him with every thrust, the friction building with each movement.

Ethan's hands gripped my hips, pulling me closer as he picked up the pace, his breath ragged against my ear. I could feel the muscles in his back tense under my fingers, every movement perfectly synchronized with mine, driving us both closer to the edge.

"Gods, you feel so good," he groaned, his voice raw with need.

The intensity of his thrusts increased, and I felt the coil of pleasure tightening deep within me. I reached out, grabbing a handful of his chest hair, my nails digging into his skin as I held on, riding the wave of sensation that threatened to consume me.

"Ethan... I'm so close," I whispered, my voice barely audible over the sounds of our bodies moving together.

"Me too," he panted, his rhythm faltering as he neared his own release.

With one final, powerful thrust, he pushed us both over the edge. I cried out as the orgasm washed over me, every nerve alight with pleasure. Ethan followed moments later, his body tensing as he emptied himself inside me, his groan low and primal.

For a moment, we were both still, breathing heavily as the aftershocks of our release rippled through us. Then Ethan collapsed beside me, our backs resting on the couch, our legs tangled and our lower halves hanging awkwardly over the edge. We lay there, bodies slick with sweat and heat.

"I love you," he murmured against my hair, his voice soft as the passion of the moment gave way to tenderness.

"I love you too," I whispered back, snuggling into his embrace, feeling content and blissfully satiated. I was perfectly happy right there, wrapped in the warmth of Ethan, the scent of our lovemaking lingering in the air.

Yet, even as I basked in the afterglow, thoughts of

the witch slipped into my mind. I tried to shake them off, focusing on the man beside me, the man I loved. But the excitement, the anticipation of seeing her on Halloween night, was like an itch I couldn't scratch. It lingered at the back of my mind, a tantalizing thrill that I couldn't ignore.

I shook my head slightly, hoping to dislodge thoughts of her. I couldn't let her overshadow this moment, not when I was so happy with Ethan. But she had a way of seeping into my thoughts, especially as the day drew nearer.

With a sigh, I gently disentangled myself from Ethan's embrace and stood up, feeling the cool air against my skin. He looked up at me with a lazy, satisfied smile. "Where are you going?"

"I'm just going to change into something more comfortable," I replied, returning his smile. "And maybe start messing around with the Halloween decorations."

Ethan chuckled, his eyes half-closed with post-ejaculatory drowsiness. "That's my girl. You're insatiable when it comes to Halloween."

I smiled and made my way to the bathroom, carefully slipping out of the negligee and inspecting it for any staining before draping it on a hanger.

After freshening up, I went to the bedroom and pulled on a pair of soft leggings and an oversized sweatshirt—the kind of clothes that made me feel cozy and relaxed.

When I returned to the living room, Ethan had stretched out fully on the couch, still completely naked. He looked entirely too comfortable for someone who had just been thoroughly ravished. I smiled at the sight of him, a rush of affection warming my chest. He really was everything I could ask for in a husband. I walked over and lightly grabbed at the tip of his dick.

"Hey!" he shouted, curling up to protect himself. "You know you can't do that to me." He grinned, covering himself with his hands.

Ethan was incredibly sensitive after sex. Early on, I'd tried to go down on him after he came, and he'd jerked back so hard he'd hit the wall. Now I knew better. Even the slightest touch made him recoil, although it never hurt him, and it always made me laugh.

He gave me a playful slap on the butt as payback.

I turned my attention to the box of decorations that still needed unpacking. Ethan had made a good start, but I wanted more. I liked our house to look like an abandoned witch's cottage in the woods for the week of Halloween.

The task kept my hands busy, but my mind couldn't help but wander. As I adjusted a particularly stubborn garland, I glanced at Ethan, who had dozed off, his chest rising and falling in a steady rhythm. Thoughts of the witch returned, unbidden. Her dark presence, her velvety skin, the way she made me feel alive and reckless.

I felt a pang of guilt for thinking about her while Ethan slept nearby, so content and happy. But I couldn't deny the flutter of excitement at the thought of Halloween night.

I shook my head, focusing on the task at hand. For now, I would enjoy this quiet evening with Ethan, making our home ready for the holiday. The witch would come soon enough, and I'd deal with those feelings when the time came.

CHAPTER 4
ETHAN

I HAD no idea how long I'd been asleep on the couch, but when I finally stirred, I noticed that Molly had been sweet enough to cover me with a blanket. The soft fabric was draped over my bare body, a small but thoughtful gesture that brought a smile to my face.

I blinked a few times, trying to shake off the remnants of sleep, and looked around for her. The living room was quiet, and Molly was nowhere to be seen. A slight unease crept into my chest as I sat up, the blanket slipping off my shoulders.

My mind drifted back to the passionate moments we'd just shared. Our lovemaking had been intense, as always, but there was something I couldn't quite put my finger on. Something about Molly felt... off. It wasn't anything obvious, nothing I could easily describe, but it lingered at the back of my mind, gnawing at me.

Maybe it was the way she'd looked at me afterward, a little too distant, as if she were a thousand miles away even while wrapped in my arms. Or maybe it was just the weight of everything—her work, the holidays, and all the little stresses that had been piling up lately. I shook my head, trying to dismiss the thought. I was probably overthinking things. Molly had been working long hours, and we'd been caught up in the whirlwind of preparing for Halloween. It was natural to feel a little off-balance.

Still, the feeling nagged at me as I stood up, stretching out the stiffness in my muscles. I reached for my clothes, which were haphazardly tossed on the floor, and dressed. The house felt too quiet without her, and I felt an urge to find her, make sure everything was okay. I reminded myself: she gets weird every Halloween.

After pulling on my t-shirt, I padded around the living room, half-expecting to find her in the kitchen or maybe fiddling with the decorations I hadn't quite finished. But as I turned the corner into the hallway, I noticed a small note taped to the fridge. I plucked it off and read it:

Went to grab Halloween candy. Be back soon!

I smiled, though the unease in my chest didn't fully dissipate. I picked up my phone and dialed her number, listening to the ring as I walked to the front window and looked out at the street.

"Hey," Molly's voice came through the line, her softness always managing to calm me, even when my thoughts were running wild.

"Hey," I replied. "I got your note. Thought I'd catch up with you. Where are you?"

"Just made it to the store," she said, and I could hear the hum of the town in the background. "Why? Miss me already?"

I chuckled. "Always. How about I meet you at the pumpkin patch? We were planning to carve them tomorrow."

"Sounds good," she agreed, her voice lightening. "I'll see you there in a bit."

We hung up, and I grabbed my keys from the hook by the door, shrugging on a jacket as I headed out. The crisp autumn air greeted me as I stepped into the driveway, a welcome contrast to the warmth that still clung to me from our time on the couch.

As I made my way through town, I spotted a familiar Toyota up ahead. "Good timing," I muttered to myself. I picked up speed to get right behind her. I could see the top of her head barely peeking out above the seat.

She made a left onto Water Street.

"That's not the way to the pumpkin patch," I said, deciding to follow. I turned left behind her.

Molly continued down Water Street. She could, in theory, turn at the end and loop back around, but that would add several miles to the trip. Maybe she forgot something at the office? We passed by her office.

Nope.

She pulled into a parking spot a few blocks down. I continued past her and then pulled into a spot eight or nine spaces to the east.

I watched as Molly stepped out of the car and made her way into Spellbound Stories Bookstore. The shop was one of those eclectic little places that smelled of old paper and incense, with shelves stacked high with books on everything from world history and folklore to the occult. It was one of Molly's favorite haunts, but she hadn't mentioned anything about needing to stop by today.

Curiosity piqued, I decided to surprise her and slipped out of my car, crossing the street and into the shop. I pushed open the door as gently as I could, the bell tinkling softly above me. The cozy interior was dimly lit, with narrow aisles winding between towering bookshelves. I spotted Molly near the counter, talking to Lea, the shop's owner—a spunky, curvy thirty-something with a loud mane of orange hair.

I moved closer, staying just out of sight behind a shelf filled with old leather-bound grimoires. Molly leaned in slightly, speaking in a hushed tone, though the shop was empty except for the three of us.

"I'm here to pick up the order of sulfur powder," Molly said, her voice low and serious. I couldn't help but scrunch up my face. *Sulfur powder?* That was unusual.

Lea nodded, reaching under the counter and pulling out a small brown paper bag. "I've got it right here," she said, her tone casual. "Ms. Vesper called; you should have everything you need now."

Molly accepted the bag, slipping it into her purse, then fished out her wallet to pay. I stayed rooted to the spot, unsure of what to make of the exchange. *What could she possibly need sulfur powder for?* My mind raced, trying to come up with a plausible explanation, but nothing made sense.

As Lea rang her up, I took a deep breath and stepped out from behind the shelf, just in time to see Molly finish her transaction. She turned to leave, her purse slung over her shoulder, and nearly collided with me.

"Ethan!" she gasped, her eyes wide with surprise.

Her hand flew to her chest as she caught her breath. "What are you doing here?"

I raised an eyebrow, trying to keep my tone light even though my mind was buzzing with questions. "I could ask you the same thing. I was on my way to the pumpkin patch and saw you. I followed you here. I'm surprised you didn't see me behind you."

Molly blinked, clearly caught off guard. "I... I was just picking up a few things. I forgot I needed to stop by the bookstore."

"For sulfur powder?" I asked, unable to keep the curiosity out of my voice. I wasn't accusing her of anything, but I couldn't ignore the oddity of the situation.

Her eyes flickered with something I couldn't quite read. Nervousness, maybe? She quickly masked it with a smile. "Oh, that. It's for a little project I'm working on for Halloween."

I wanted to believe her, and maybe I was overreacting, but I couldn't shake the feeling that something more was going on. Now wasn't the time to press her on it, though.

I forced a smile and nodded. "Okay, just make sure you keep that stuff in the garage. It stinks."

She laughed, the sound a bit too forced for my liking, but it eased the tension. "I promise."

"Alright," I said, stepping back to give her some space. "Ready to head to the pumpkin patch?"

Molly nodded, her smile genuine this time. "Yeah, let's go."

As we left the shop together, I glanced back at Lea, who was watching us with a strange expression on her face. There was something unsettling about the whole encounter, but I pushed it aside. Molly was my wife, and I trusted her. Whatever she was up to was probably for some quirky Halloween project she'd seen on Pinterest.

Later at the pumpkin patch, as we walked hand in hand in the crisp autumn air, I couldn't completely shake the unease that had settled in the pit of my stomach. Whatever Molly was planning, I just hoped it wouldn't come back to haunt us.

CHAPTER 5
MOLLY

THE SCENT of hay and earth mixed with the faint aroma of hot apple cider wafting from a nearby stand as we made our way through the pumpkin patch. Families and couples meandered between rows of pumpkins, their laughter and chatter a distant hum. But between Ethan and me, there was a silence that felt heavier than the largest pumpkin in the field.

I glanced at him from the corner of my eye. He seemed absorbed in the task of finding the perfect pumpkins, his brow furrowed slightly as he examined one that was particularly lopsided. But I could tell his mind was elsewhere, probably still stuck on what he saw back at the bookstore.

The sulfur powder.

One of the necessary ingredients I needed for my ritual on Saturday. I mentally kicked myself for not coming up with a better excuse when he caught me off guard. The truth was, I hadn't expected him to follow me into Spellbound Books, and when he showed up behind me, my mind went blank. Now, the awkwardness between us was palpable, and I was sure he felt it too. If I'm being honest, I was slightly relieved—maybe it was time to tell him.

"Hey, what do you think about this one?" Ethan's voice broke through my thoughts. He held up a medium-sized pumpkin, its surface a smooth, deep orange.

"It's nice," I replied, forcing a smile that felt a little too tight on my face. "Perfect for carving."

He nodded, placing the pumpkin in the wagon we had borrowed from the patch's entrance. But instead of moving on, he hesitated, his gaze lingering on me longer than usual. I could see the questions in his eyes, the ones he hadn't asked yet, simmering just beneath the surface.

I pretended not to notice, crouching down to inspect a smaller pumpkin, running my fingers over its cool, bumpy skin. The silence stretched between us again, more strained this time. I knew I should say something, anything, to break the tension, but my words caught in my throat.

Ethan cleared his throat, shifting on his feet. He opened his mouth to say something but stopped.

I straightened up to meet his gaze, and for a moment, I considered telling him everything. But the words didn't come. Instead, I returned to the pumpkins. "What about this one?"

"I think it's a little too bumpy for carving. I mean, depends on what you want to do, I guess," he replied.

"Yeah, I thought this bumpy section could work for a witch's face, but I think you're right—it's easier to start with a flat surface," I said, offering a smile.

Ethan nodded slowly, but I could tell he wasn't entirely present. His eyes searched mine, and I had to resist the urge to look away. I hated lying to him, but how could I explain the real reason without opening a door I wasn't ready for him to walk through?

"Ethan," I said quietly.

"Yes?"

"I love you," I said without a smile.

"Okay," Ethan replied, stepping closer and wrapping an arm around me.

I leaned into him, pulling my sweater tighter around myself against the crisp autumn air. I breathed him in, catching the scent of sex mixed with his natural, masculine aroma.

"I kind of thought there was going to be a 'but' after that 'I love you,'" Ethan added a beat later.

"No but. I love you," I said.

"Aww, I love you too, Molly," he replied, leaning in to kiss the top of my head.

I smiled up at him, but it didn't quite reach his eyes. We continued walking through the patch, but the easy, lighthearted vibe that usually accompanied our trips to pick out pumpkins was gone. Instead, an awkward tension clung to the air between us, growing heavier with each step.

And it was all my fault.

I picked out another pumpkin, handing it to Ethan without meeting his eyes, and we continued this uncomfortable dance—both of us aware, but neither willing to confront it head-on.

Near the exit of the pumpkin patch, they had a beautiful fall display, something an artist developed every year. It was our tradition to take a picture there —a snapshot of each autumn we'd spent together, documenting the years in a growing series of photos that lined the hallway of our home. This year's theme was an unusual blend of Halloween and Valentine's Day. It was a mix of hay bales, cornstalks, and gigantic sunflowers adorned with bright red roses, green garlands, and delicate sprigs of baby's breath. It was an odd combination, but somehow it worked.

Ethan stopped and turned to me, a soft smile playing on his lips. "Ready for our annual picture?"

he asked, the tension in his voice easing as he gestured toward the photographer.

I looked at the scene, the vibrant colors contrasting sharply against the earth tones of the season, and felt a twinge of guilt in my chest. This was our tradition, a moment we always cherished, but the thought of capturing this memory this year, with this awkward tension, made my stomach churn.

I forced a smile and nodded. "Sure, let's take the picture," I said, trying to ignore the knot tightening in my stomach. Ethan's face lit up with relief, his smile widening as he reached for my hand and guided me toward the display.

We stood in front of the setup, the photographer giving us a cheerful wave as he adjusted his camera. I felt the familiar weight of tradition settling over us, but instead of comfort, it felt like a chain tightening around my chest. The roses and baby's breath entwined with the pumpkins and cornstalks were meant to symbolize a blend of love and the season's change, but all I could think about was Saturday night, when I would be with the witch.

Ethan wrapped his arm around my waist, pulling me close as we faced the camera. I tried to steady my breath, to focus on the moment, but the thought of taking this picture, capturing this memory, felt like a betrayal I couldn't shake.

The photographer lifted his camera, his finger hovering over the shutter button. "Alright, you two, say cheese!"

Just as he was about to snap the photo, a surge of panic rose in my chest. I couldn't do it—I couldn't pretend everything was fine. Without thinking, I turned to Ethan, grabbing his hand and pulling him away from the display.

"Molly, what…" Ethan began, confusion in his voice, but I didn't let him finish. I led him away from the photographer, from the scene that felt like it was mocking me, until we were out of earshot, near a quiet row of pumpkins.

Ethan looked at me, concern etched into his features. "What's going on?" he asked, his voice low, the earlier confusion now replaced with worry.

I took a deep breath, trying to calm the storm inside of me. "Ethan, I'm sorry," I began, my voice trembling. "I thought I could go through with it, but I just… can't."

He frowned, his grip on my hand tightening slightly. "Can't what? Take the picture?"

"No," I said, shaking my head. "It's not the picture. It's… everything. There's something I need to tell you, something I should have told you a long time ago."

Ethan's face grew more serious, his brow furrowing. "Molly, you're scaring me. What's going on?"

"I haven't been completely honest with you," I confessed, my heart racing. "Every year, on Halloween night… there's someone else. But it's not what you think. It's not a normal affair."

His hand dropped from mine as the words hit him. His face went pale. "What the hell are you talking about? Someone else?" His voice wavered between disbelief and hurt.

"It's a witch, Ethan," I said, forcing the words out. "I know it sounds crazy, but she's real. Every year on All Hallows' Eve, she comes to me, and I can't resist her. It's like I'm under her spell."

For a moment, Ethan just stared at me, like he couldn't comprehend what I was saying. Then he shook his head, taking a step back. "A witch? Molly, this doesn't make any sense." His voice rose, disbelief edging into anger now. "You're telling me you've been having an affair with—what, some kind of supernatural being? And you kept this from me?"

I could see the hurt in his eyes, a deep, growing pain. I tried to reach for him, but he stepped back again, his arms folding across his chest. "I didn't want to hurt you, Ethan. I'm telling you now because I can't keep hiding this. It's more than just… cheating. It's something else entirely."

His face hardened. "Cheating is cheating, Molly. Whether it's with a person or a damn witch!" His voice cracked slightly, the raw hurt bubbling to the surface. "How long has this been going on? How long have you been lying to me?"

I swallowed, my throat dry. "Years. Since before we got married."

Ethan looked like he'd been slapped. He ran a hand through his hair, his chest rising and falling with quick breaths as he tried to make sense of it. "You've been doing this behind my back for years? Jesus, Molly. What the hell am I supposed to do with that?"

Tears welled up in my eyes. "I didn't know how to tell you… I was scared of what it would mean."

"Scared of what it would mean?" he repeated, incredulous. "You didn't think it might mean you were betraying me?" His words cut deep, and I could see the pain in his eyes, raw and open. "You… you said you loved me. We built a life together, Molly. And now you're telling me you've been in love with someone else this whole time?"

"I do love you," I whispered, my voice shaking. "You give me everything—a love that's stable, real, something I couldn't live without. You're my best friend, my partner."

Ethan's jaw clenched, his eyes hardening as he

fought to hold back his emotions. "But that wasn't enough for you. You needed more." It wasn't a question. It was a bitter realization.

"I needed something different," I admitted, my voice breaking. "With her, it's... it's like I'm tapping into something darker, something I can't find anywhere else. It's not just desire—it's something deeper. She gives me a sense of power, of freedom."

Ethan let out a bitter laugh, rubbing his hands over his face. "So that's it? You're in love with both of us? You get something from her that I can't give you?"

"I don't know," I whispered. "I don't have all the answers. All I know is that I love you both, in different ways. And I didn't want to hurt you, but I can't deny what I feel for her."

Ethan stared at me, his face a mix of devastation and anger. "You lied to me for years, Molly. How am I supposed to just... be okay with that?"

"I don't expect you to be okay with it," I said, the tears flowing freely now. "I'm telling you because I can't keep lying. I want to figure this out with you. I don't want to lose you."

He turned away, his shoulders tense, his hands clenched into fists at his sides. "I can't... I can't even look at you right now." His voice was low, broken. "I need some space."

I reached out again, but he stepped further away, his back turned to me. "Ethan, please—"

"I need time, Molly," he said, his voice hard. "Time to figure out what the hell I'm supposed to do with this. With us."

The weight of his words sank deep into my chest, a sinking, suffocating feeling. I watched him walk away, the distance between us growing not just physically, but emotionally—an endless chasm that might never be bridged.

CHAPTER 6
ETHAN

I WAS RELIEVED, in a strange way, that Molly had finally told me what was going on with her. I'd been bracing myself for something entirely different —an affair with another man, a gut punch that would have left me reeling. But when she confessed her love for a witch, my mind struggled to process it.

A witch? Was that even real?

And if it was real, was that even technically cheating? It felt surreal, like something out of a story, not something that could actually happen in real life. Yet, here we were.

My thoughts churned as I tried to make sense of it. If she'd told me she was seeing another man, it would've been simpler, in a way. It would have hurt like hell, but it was something I could understand. It would have fit within the boundaries of what people typically go through. But this... this was different. This was something I hadn't ever imagined dealing with.

I found myself grappling with what she even meant by "witch." Was this some kind of metaphor? Or was she serious? And then a thought struck me— Calliope Vesper. No one ever called her anything but Ms. Vesper, yet Molly had always been on a first-name basis with her. I couldn't help but wonder if Molly was talking about *her*. Calliope was more than a little strange, always surrounded by mystery, and there were plenty of rumors about her and that *Arcane Room* of hers. Could it be her? Had Molly been involved with Calliope this whole time?

I shook my head, trying to focus. I'd always worried, deep down, that I wouldn't be able to give Molly everything she needed. I knew she was bisexual, and while that never bothered me, there was always a small, nagging fear that I wouldn't be enough for her. That she'd want something more, something I couldn't provide. Maybe this was part of that fear coming to life, but in a way I never expected.

Yet, despite how bizarre it all was, there was also a strange sense of relief. She hadn't lied about another man. Instead, this was... well, something entirely different. A witch. A woman. And somehow, that felt like something I could at least try to understand.

"Are you okay?" Molly's voice broke through my thoughts, pulling me back to the present. I'm not sure how long she had been standing there.

"I'm still just processing," I admitted honestly. "I have a lot of questions."

"I'd honestly be surprised if you didn't," she replied, her eyes watching me closely.

I wasn't sure how to feel about it all yet, but I knew one thing: I wasn't going to let this destroy us. I loved Molly, and if she needed this—if this was part of who she was—I was going to find a way to make peace with it. Because I loved her, and I'd do whatever it took to make our relationship work, even if it meant navigating this strange new reality.

I took a deep breath, feeling the weight of the situation settle on my shoulders. "We'll have to have a much longer conversation about this later," I said, my voice steady. "But for now, I want you to know that I love you. Nothing you've told me changes that. I love every part of you, Molly, even the parts that are complicated and messy. You are my everything, and we're going to figure this out together."

Molly's eyes shimmered with emotion, and she let out a deep breath. "I love you too, Ethan. So much."

I reached out, brushing a stray strand of hair from her face, my thumb gently caressing her cheek. "You've always been honest with me about who you are, and that's one of the things I love most about you. This might be new and unexpected, but it's part of you, and I'm here for all of it."

Her lips curled into a soft, relieved smile, and she leaned into my touch, closing her eyes for a moment as if soaking in my words. "Thank you," she whispered, her voice thick with emotion. "I didn't know how you'd react, but... this means everything to me."

I pulled her into a gentle embrace, holding her close. "You mean everything to me, Molly. We'll take this one step at a time, together."

She nodded against my chest, her arms tightening around me. For a moment, we stood there, wrapped in each other, letting the world around us fade away. I could feel the tension between us melting, replaced by a renewed sense of connection.

After a few moments, I pulled back slightly, tilting her chin up so I could look into her eyes. "How about we go take that picture now?" I suggested, my tone light.

Molly smiled, this time a genuine, radiant smile that reached her eyes. "I'd like that."

We walked back to the display, hand in hand, and stood in front of the setup once more. The photographer gave us a curious glance, as if sensing the shift in our energy, but said nothing as he lifted his camera again.

"Alright," the photographer said, his voice cheerful. "Let's try this one more time. Big smiles!"

I wrapped my arm around Molly's waist, pulling her close as we both smiled for the camera. The flash went off, capturing the moment in a burst of light.

After, I glanced at the screen on the photographer's camera as he showed us the shot. My breath caught when I saw Molly's smile—genuine, bright, and full of happiness. It was the kind of smile that lit up her whole face, the kind that made my heart swell with love.

In that moment, I knew we were going to be okay. We were a team, and this was just another part of our journey.

I looked at Molly, and she looked back at me, her eyes shining with love and gratitude. "Thank you, Ethan," she whispered, squeezing my hand.

I smiled, leaning down to press a soft kiss to her forehead. "Always," I whispered back.

We paid for the photo and the pumpkins, and soon after, we were heading to our car, the photo in hand.

When we arrived home, we unloaded the pumpkins and hung this year's photo next to the others in the hallway. It felt right, like adding another chapter to our story. We collapsed once again on the couch in the living room.

I sat there, still trying to process everything. My mind circled back to one specific question that had been nagging at me ever since she'd said the word "witch."

"Molly, is it... is it Calliope Vesper?" I asked, my voice tinged with uncertainty. "You're always on a first-name basis with her, and nobody else calls her that. Is she the witch you're talking about?"

Molly's eyes widened in surprise before she quickly shook her head. "No, no—it's not Ms. Vesper," she said, her voice firm but soft. "I mean, she's strange, sure, and the Arcane Room rumors don't help, but no. Elizabeth isn't her."

A wave of relief washed over me, though I still felt unsettled. "So, when did you meet this Elizabeth?"

Molly hesitated for a moment, her fingers nervously fiddling with the edge of her sleeve. "It's been six years now," she admitted, her voice quieter. "I met her the same year I met you."

I blinked, the weight of her words settling over me. "Six years," I repeated, trying to wrap my head around it. "So... you met her around the same time you met me?"

She nodded, her gaze shifting to the floor. "Yeah. It didn't seem like it mattered at first. I thought it was all a dream, honestly. After that first night, I wasn't sure if it had really happened. I didn't think it was real... but I had to follow through the second year to be sure."

"And that's when you realized it wasn't just some dream?"

Molly nodded again. "We talked all night that second year. And that was the first time I was... sexually intimate with a woman. I'd kissed a few girls before, but Elizabeth was the first—and the only—woman I've been with."

I could hear the vulnerability in her voice, the weight of what she was confessing. I stayed quiet, letting her continue.

"At first, it felt like this fun secret, like something separate from the rest of my life," she said, her voice trembling slightly. "But then... then you and I got engaged so fast. I went to see her the third year, planning to end it. I wanted to tell her that it couldn't continue, that I loved you, and I didn't want to risk what we had."

I could feel a lump forming in my throat as I listened to her. "What happened?"

Molly's lips twisted into a sad smile. "I couldn't do it. I love her, Ethan. I tried to tell her goodbye, but

I couldn't bring myself to walk away. I told her all about you, about us. About how happy I am with you. I told her I didn't want to risk what we have."

She paused, her voice growing softer. "Elizabeth encouraged me to tell you. She told me right there—call you, have you come meet us. But I was scared. I was so afraid of losing you, of ruining everything by keeping this secret. But I can't keep lying anymore. I want you to know all of me, and Elizabeth... she's part of that."

I let out a slow breath, absorbing everything she was telling me. Six years. For six years, she had been carrying this other relationship alongside ours. Part of me felt the weight of betrayal, but another part of me—maybe the bigger part—just wanted to understand. To make sense of it all.

"So, when do I get to meet this witch?" I asked, breaking the silence, my voice calm but filled with curiosity.

Molly's body tensed slightly. "Oh," she responded, startled by the question.

"I mean, I feel like I have to meet her," I said, my tone calm but firm. "If she's going to be a part of our lives, I need to understand it. I need to see her."

Molly shifted, sitting up slightly to face me. "Well, yeah... that makes sense, of course," she admitted, her eyes searching mine for understanding. "But she's only around for one night a year—on Halloween."

I nodded, encouraging her to continue. "Okay, so how does it work? What do I need to know?"

She took a deep breath, as if gathering her thoughts. "It's complicated," she began, her voice soft. "There's a ritual I perform every year at an altar in the middle of the woods. I've been doing it for years now. It's an ancient spell that brings her back from the beyond, just for that one night."

I listened intently as she explained, describing the steps of the ritual, the way she prepared the altar with candles and offerings, the words of the spell she recited to summon Elizabeth. There was a reverence in her voice as she spoke, a deep connection to the magic she wielded. I could tell this was more than just a ritual for her. It was something sacred, something that had become a part of who she was.

"And then she appears," Molly continued, her eyes distant as she recalled the moment. "It's like she steps out of the shadows, fully formed, as if she's always been there. We spend the night together. It's intense, Ethan. It's like nothing else."

I absorbed her words, trying to wrap my head around the reality of it. It was surreal, yes, but I could see how much it meant to her, how important this connection with Elizabeth was. And despite the strangeness of it all, I couldn't deny the feeling that was growing within me—a deep desire to understand and fully be a part of this aspect of her life.

"Okay, can I come for the ritual and meet her?" I asked, my voice steady. "I feel like I need to see this to believe it all."

Molly looked at me, her eyes a mixture of surprise and relief. "You really want to be there? For the ritual?"

I nodded. "If this is important to you, then it's important to me. I want to be there and see this part of your life."

She smiled, a hint of uncertainty in her eyes, but mostly gratitude. "Okay, I'll make sure you're there. It might be... strange, but if you're sure..."

"I'm sure," I said, cutting her off gently. "I need to see this. I want to understand what it means to you, and if that means I take off after she appears, then that's what I'll do."

Molly's smile grew, the tension between us easing as she leaned in, pressing her lips to mine in a soft, tender kiss. "Thank you, Ethan. It means more to me than you know."

I wrapped my arms around her, pulling her close again. "I never want you to feel like you have to hide anything from me. Even if it's something scary, we'll face it together, okay?"

"Absolutely," she said.

We sat there in silence for a while, the fire crackling softly beside us. There was still so much to process, so many questions left unanswered, but for now, we were together, and that was enough.

And come this Saturday, on Halloween night, I would meet Elizabeth—the other piece of Molly's heart.

CHAPTER 7
MOLLY

WE LAID THERE on the floor of the living room, in front of the fireplace, my head resting gently on Ethan's chest. I looked up at the man I married with such awe and adoration. He really saw me for who I was—every complicated piece of me—and still loved me with his whole heart. It was a love that made me feel safe, cherished, and understood in a way I never thought possible.

I reached up, tracing the line of his jaw with my fingertips, feeling the warmth of his skin beneath my touch. "You're an incredible man, Ethan," I whispered, my voice filled with emotion. "I don't think I tell you that enough."

He smiled down at me, his eyes soft and full of affection. "I just want you to be happy, Molly. That's all I've ever wanted."

A surge of love for him welled up inside me, so powerful it made my chest ache. I lifted myself slightly, pressing my lips to his in a tender kiss, pouring all my gratitude and affection into that simple gesture. He responded, his hand sliding into my hair, pulling me closer.

But tonight, I wanted to show him how much he meant to me, how much I appreciated his understanding, patience, and love. I wanted to give back to him, to make him feel the same pleasure and contentment he always gave me.

I broke the kiss, looking into his eyes with a soft smile. "I want to do something for you," I said, my voice gentle but firm.

He raised an eyebrow, his smile turning playful. "And what would that be?"

"Just let me take care of you tonight," I replied, my head resting on his chest, feeling the steady beat of his heart beneath my palm. "You've done so much for me, and I want to make you feel good. Just sit back and enjoy it. Let me do this for you."

Ethan looked at me for a moment, as if weighing his desire to participate against the sincerity in my voice. Finally, he nodded, a soft chuckle escaping his lips. "Alright," he said, his voice low and full of warmth. "I'll do whatever you want."

I smiled and kissed him again, but this time with

more intensity, more passion. My hands began to explore his body, massaging the tension from his shoulders, down his arms, and across his chest. I could feel him relax beneath my touch, his muscles loosening as I worked, my fingers kneading away the stress of the day.

I kissed along his neck, feeling the pulse beneath his skin, and continued down his chest, trailing my lips over every inch of him. My hands moved lower, finding all the spots that made him sigh in pleasure. It wasn't just about the physical pleasure; I wanted to show him how much I valued him, how deeply I loved him.

Ethan's breaths grew heavier. "Molly... you're amazing," he mumbled.

"Just relax," I whispered against his skin, my hands continuing their journey. "Let me take care of you."

He closed his eyes, surrendering to my touch, letting me guide him through this moment.

Tonight was about us—about our love—and I was determined to make him feel as cherished and adored as he made me feel every single day.

I pulled his t-shirt up, exposing his stomach, and gently kissed my way up his chest, pulling the shirt ahead of my kisses. He lifted his back slightly to help me remove the shirt completely before resting back down, all the while keeping his eyes shut tight.

I gently massaged his nipples between my index finger and thumb. He let out labored breaths, squirming underneath me. I ran my fingernails through his chest hair, pulling gently at several spots across his chest.

My tongue traced slow, deliberate circles down his chest, each soft kiss a promise of more to come. I could feel his heartbeat quickening beneath my lips, a steady rhythm that echoed the rising tension between us. His breaths came in short, uneven gasps as I continued, savoring him, watching carefully how he responded to every touch.

As I reached the center of his chest, I paused, letting my fingers trail lightly over his skin, feeling the way his muscles tensed and relaxed under my touch. I could sense his growing anticipation, the way his body instinctively leaned into my caresses, craving more yet content to let me set the pace.

I leaned in closer, my lips hovering above his skin, letting my warm breath wash over him. I could feel the slight tremble in his body, the way his chest rose and fell. He kept his eyes shut tight, surrendering completely to the sensations, trusting me to lead him through this moment.

Gently, I moved lower, kissing along the line of

his ribs. I could feel the heat radiating from his skin, the subtle shift of his muscles as he squirmed beneath me.

I let my fingers dance across his abdomen, my touch light and teasing, tracing the contours of his body.

My lips followed the path of my fingers, kissing lower just above the waistband of his sweatpants. I could see the tension in him, the way his body seemed to hum with energy, ready to burst but held in check by the fabric of his clothes.

I paused there, taking a moment to look up at him, to see the way his lips parted in quiet surrender, his eyes still closed, completely lost in the sensations. It was a beautiful sight, knowing that I was the one bringing him to this place of pure bliss.

I let my hands roam up and down his sides, feeling the contrast between the firm muscle beneath and the softness of his skin. Each touch was intentional, meant to heighten his awareness and draw out pleasure in a delicate way.

As I continued to explore his body, my touch growing more assured. But instead of rushing, I maintained my slow, deliberate pace, savoring each moment, each small reaction from him. This wasn't about raw, urgent need; it was about connection and showing him how deeply I adored and cherished every part of him.

I pressed another kiss below his navel, my hands gently kneading his hips, my fingers brushing the sensitive skin just above his sweatpants. He let out a soft moan, his body shuddering under my touch, and I smiled against his skin, knowing this was only the beginning.

He started to reach for me, but I gently placed my hand on his, guiding it back down to his side. He let out a deep sigh, his body relaxing back into the floor, his hands falling away as he surrendered. His trust in me, the way he let me lead, made my heart swell with affection.

I kissed lower, letting my hands wander freely, touching and caressing, bringing him closer and closer to the edge but always holding back just enough to keep him in that sweet, torturous state of anticipation. I kissed the space to the left of his center, letting my cheek brush against his swollen member. I could feel it pulse against my skin, but I moved back up to his navel.

My fingers danced around the front of his sweatpants, making gentle, teasing strokes over his bulge. He quivered beneath my touch, his breath hitching as I applied just enough pressure to keep him on edge.

I slipped my fingers under his waistband and

pulled down his pants and boxer briefs in one swoop. His cock sprang free with a quick thwap against his stomach.

Ethan cried out in surprise.

"Oh, I'm sorry, babe," I said, feeling terrible.

"It's okay," Ethan said with an exhale.

"Should I kiss it and make it all better?" I asked with a mischievous grin.

"Uh huh," Ethan nodded.

I wrapped my hand around his shaft, pulling it closer to my lips, and gave him a gentle kiss on the tip. "Like that?"

"Oh yeah," he said.

I started to kiss up and down the shaft, letting my tongue out to cover him in wetness. "Is that making it all better?"

"Definitely," he grinned.

I moved my lips back to the top and kissed the tip again, and when I pulled back, a sticky trail of precum came with me. I let him watch as I licked the salty drip off my lips.

Leaning back in, I released more wetness before taking him in, letting it drip down the sides of his shaft. I gripped him with my right hand, using the wetness to stroke him. Each stroke was deliberate, meant to remind him of my passion. I kept the pace slow, savoring the way he squirmed beneath me, his body begging for more.

His hands clenched the floor, grabbing a handful of the rug, his knuckles white as he tried to maintain composure. His tension was palpable, but I was determined to take my time, to make this moment last as long as possible.

I kept my rhythm, thrusting him deeper into my mouth, propping him up with my hand and applying gentle pressure with each stroke. I looked up at him. I could see the struggle in his expression, the way he fought to hold back, to let me lead. It made me love him all the more.

My hands and mouth picked up the pace, and I felt him shudder beneath my touch, his body trembling with pleasure. Slowly, I slid my free hand further down, brushing against the base of his length. I tickled my fingers down to his sack and scratched my nails gently over it.

I looked up at him again. His eyes were still closed, his chest rising and falling rapidly with each breath. I continued, picking up the pace with both my mouth and hand. His back arched off the floor and then slammed back down. Faster and faster, he arched again, his legs beginning to shake from the hips.

He let out a shaky breath, his body sinking deeper

onto the floor, and I knew he was about to release his tension. I could see the effort it took—the way he struggled to keep from reaching for me, to resist urging me to go faster. But he kept his arms at his side, letting me take him fully.

I focused on the head of his shaft, working faster and faster, applying more pressure with my hands.

"I'm going to come," he warned, trying to pull my head off of him.

I reached out with the hand on his sack, batting his hand away, and continued pumping.

"I'm gonna…" he gasped, cutting himself off with a loud moan.

His hot, salty load filled my mouth. I took it all in and swallowed it down, feeling its warmth slide down my throat. I stopped thrusting and pulled back but kept him in my hand. Another stream of white lava dripped from the tip, and I made eye contact with him as I leaned in and licked the creamy release into my mouth.

"Oooooh, fuck," he breathed, barely able to speak.

I swallowed the rest of him down and gulped.

"I love you," I said softly.

His chest hair glistened with sweat in the glow of the fireplace, his stomach rising and falling quickly as he caught his breath. His face was contorted in the exhaustion of his release—his brows furrowed, and his jaw clenched.

"I love you too, Molly," he managed to say between breaths.

I leaned in, pressing a kiss to his forehead before resting my head on his chest. His heart was racing beneath me, and I listened as it gradually slowed, both of us basking in the warmth and intimacy of the moment.

CHAPTER 8
ETHAN

THE DAYS FOLLOWING Molly's revelation were as blissful as our honeymoon. There was a renewed sense of connection between us, a deepened intimacy that colored every moment we spent together. We laughed more easily, touched more often, and shared our thoughts with a newfound openness that felt both exhilarating and reassuring. I was truly happy, but there was a shadow lingering at the edges of my mind.

Saturday evening was approaching, and with it, the ritual. The thought of meeting Elizabeth, this mysterious witch who had captured part of Molly's heart, was both intriguing and unsettling. I couldn't help but wonder what she'd be like and what this whole experience would mean for us.

We were cuddled up on the couch, the soft glow

of the television flickering in the background, when I decided to broach the subject. "So, what do you need to prepare for the ritual?" I asked.

Molly looked up at me, her eyes softening with affection as she shifted closer, resting her head on my shoulder. "Mostly things I've already gathered— candles, herbs, sulfur powder, and a few tokens I use to focus the energy. I'll need to collect a few fresh ingredients from the woods the day before, but nothing too complicated."

I nodded, trying to keep my expression neutral, though my mind was racing. "And the altar? It's already set up in the woods?"

"Yeah, it's in a clearing not far from here," she explained, her voice taking on a reverent tone. "I found it a long time ago. It's almost like the place found me. The energy there is special. It's the perfect spot."

Her words only added to the swirl of emotions inside me. The idea of Molly alone in the woods, summoning an ancient, powerful witch was a little unnerving. I mean, we were talking about summoning an actual witch. I still struggled with the concept.

I took a deep breath, trying to steady my growing unease. "And... what about Elizabeth? What's she like?"

Molly's eyes softened even more, a small smile tugging at the corners of her lips. "She's captivating. There's a strength about her, but also a vulnerability. She's powerful, yes, but there's a gentleness, too. It's hard to explain. You'll understand when you meet her."

I could hear the affection in Molly's voice, the warmth as she spoke about Elizabeth, and it made my stomach twist with a mix of jealousy and curiosity. "And what happens after she appears?"

Molly hesitated, choosing her words carefully. "We spend the night together, talking, reconnecting. It's like no time has passed since we last saw each other, but it's also like rediscovering each other all over again. It's intense."

I swallowed hard, trying to process what she was telling me. The reality of it all was sinking in, and I couldn't deny the nervousness building inside me. "And do you... have sex?"

Molly paused, looked down at the floor, and responded quietly. "Yes."

She must have sensed my unease because she reached up and cupped my cheek, her thumb brushing lightly over my skin. "Hey," she said softly, her voice full of reassurance. "I know this is a lot to take in, and I don't expect you to be completely comfortable with it right away. But I'm so grateful that you're willing to be there with me. It means more to me than you know."

I managed a small smile, leaning into her touch. "I just want to be there for you, Molly. I want to understand this part of your life, even if it's a little... intimidating."

"It's okay to be nervous," she said, her hand slipping down to rest on my chest, right over my heart. "I was, too, the first time I summoned her. But you'll see—it's not as odd as it seems."

Her words brought me comfort, but the nerves didn't entirely fade. I think they shifted into wondering: What would Elizabeth think of me? I was about to meet a being who defied everything I understood about the world, someone who shared a part of Molly's heart.

Saturday came quickly. We spent the day perfecting the house for the trick-or-treaters—dusting, rearranging decorations, filling candy dishes, and checking the outdoor lights. The house looked like something out of a Halloween storybook, with jack-o'-lanterns flickering on the porch and eerie shadows dancing across the lawn.

"What time does trick-or-treating start again?" I asked, placing the last decoration.

"According to the newspaper, 4:30 p.m.," she said, handing me the last bag of candy. The smell of chocolate and caramel wafted up as I opened the bag and poured its contents into the bowl.

"And it ends at seven?" I asked, double-checking.

"Yep!" she replied with a grin.

"Then, we head out to the woods?"

"Yes," she said. Molly's eyes sparkled.

The hours flew by as we handed out candy to excited children dressed as ghosts, witches, and superheroes. The sound of laughter and playful screams filled the air, and for a while, it felt like any other Halloween—joyful and carefree.

But tonight would be different.

As the last of the trick-or-treaters made their way down the street, I turned to Molly. "Ready?" I asked, trying to keep my voice steady.

She nodded, excitement clear in her expression. "Let's go."

We grabbed our coats, and Molly gathered a sack filled with items she'd need for the ritual. The sun had dipped below the horizon, casting the world in deep, dusky blue as we made our way out of the house and toward the edge of the woods.

The air was crisp and cool, carrying the scent of fallen leaves and damp earth. As we entered the forest, the sounds of the neighborhood faded away, replaced by the rustling of leaves underfoot and the occasional hoot of an owl. The trees loomed tall and dark around us, their branches intertwining to form a canopy that blocked out the faint light of the stars.

The deeper we ventured, the more the atmosphere seemed to change. The air grew thicker, more charged, as if the woods themselves were alive with an ancient energy. I could smell the earthy scent of moss and the sharp tang of pine, mingling with a faint, sweet floral aroma I couldn't quite place. The ground was soft beneath our feet, the leaves cushioning each step and muffling our movements.

I stayed close to Molly, my eyes adjusting to the dim light as we followed a narrow, winding path. I considered pulling out my cell phone light, but Molly was confident in our direction.

The trees seemed older here, their trunks gnarled and twisted, their roots snaking across the forest floor like the veins of the earth. The stillness was almost palpable; every sound—the snap of a twig, the crunch of leaves—was magnified, echoing through the darkness.

After what felt like an eternity, we reached a small clearing. The moon had risen higher, casting a silvery glow over the open space. In the center stood an ancient stone altar, weathered and worn by time. A thin layer of moss covered its surface, and vines curled around its base. It was as if nature itself had claimed the space.

Molly moved with purpose, setting down her bag and carefully removing the items she'd brought. I watched as she placed candles at each corner of the altar, their wicks catching the breeze and flickering to life as she lit them one by one. The soft glow cast eerie shadows across the stones, making the clearing feel even more otherworldly.

"Can I help with anything?" I offered.

"No, but could you stand outside the circle until she arrives? I just want to make sure everything is in order," she said, placing a stone in the middle of the clearing.

The scent of the candles mixed with the earthy aroma of the forest, creating a heavy, intoxicating blend. Molly's movements were deliberate as she arranged the herbs and crystals on the altar, each item placed with care.

As she worked, the forest seemed to grow quieter, as if the trees themselves were holding their breath, waiting. I could feel the energy building, a subtle hum beneath my skin, making the hairs on my arms stand on end.

Molly turned to me, her eyes reflecting the flickering candlelight. "Are you ready?" she asked softly.

I nodded, through my pounding heart. "Yes."

She smiled and turned back to the altar. She began to chant, her voice low and melodic, the words foreign but carrying a power I could sense deep in my bones. The air around us vibrated with each word, the energy in the clearing growing stronger, more intense.

The candles burned brighter, their flames dancing as if caught in an unseen wind. The shadows they cast grew longer and darker. I watched, mesmerized, as Molly's voice grew louder, more commanding. Her hands moved gracefully through the air as she called out to Elizabeth.

Then, suddenly, the wind picked up, swirling around the clearing with a force that took my breath away. The candles flickered wildly, their flames bending and twisting as the air crackled with life. Molly's chant reached a crescendo, her voice clear and strong, echoing through the trees.

And then, as if pulled from the very fabric of the night, a figure began to materialize before the altar. The air shimmered and rippled, and a rush of cold swept through the clearing. The figure took shape, solidifying into the form of a woman. She had dark hair and deep eyes.

She stood there before us, her presence awe-inspiring. Her gaze met mine, and I felt a shiver run down my spine. This was the witch who had captured Molly's heart. I realized right then and there that this moment would change everything for the rest of our lives.

She looked to Molly, a small, knowing smile playing on her lips, then turned her gaze back to me. The weight of it all was almost too much to bear, but I forced myself to meet her eyes, to stand my ground.

Elizabeth was here.

CHAPTER 9
MOLLY

I PULLED BACK SLIGHTLY, just enough to look into Elizabeth's eyes—those deep, endless pools of dark magic and mystery. "I want you to meet someone," I said, my voice softer now, but steady. I turned toward Ethan, who stood a few paces behind me, his expression carefully guarded, a mix of curiosity and uncertainty in his eyes.

"Elizabeth, this is Ethan," I introduced, taking his hand and squeezing it gently, offering him a reassuring smile. "My husband."

Elizabeth's gaze shifted to Ethan, and for a moment, the air between us seemed to still, the weight of the moment pressing in. Then, a warm, radiant smile spread across her face as she stepped toward him with a grace that seemed to command the space around her.

"Ethan," she greeted him, her voice soft but filled with strength. "I've waited so long to meet you. Molly has spoken of you with such love. I'm glad she's finally brave enough to introduce us."

Ethan swallowed hard, his hand tightening around mine, but he stood his ground, his eyes locked on Elizabeth. There was a tension in his body, a hesitation, but also a quiet resolve. "I've heard a lot about you," he said, his voice steady but guarded. "It's good to finally meet you, too."

Elizabeth took a step closer, reaching out to take his free hand in both of hers. Her touch was gentle but sure, as if she was searching for a connection in that simple gesture. She gazed into his eyes, her expression open and sincere, as if she were seeing right into the heart of him.

"I'm not sure what to say," Ethan admitted, his voice low, unsure. "This is… a lot to take in."

Elizabeth nodded, a soft smile playing at the corners of her lips. "I imagine it is," she said gently. "You're remarkable, Ethan. I can see how deeply you love Molly, how you protect her, and how you give her a life filled with warmth and care. That is something I admire greatly."

Ethan blinked, clearly taken aback by her words, his posture relaxing slightly. "Thank you," he said quietly, his cheeks flushing as he struggled to process her praise. "I love her more than anything."

Elizabeth's smile widened, and she released his hand, stepping back just enough to take us both in. "And she loves you," she said, her eyes soft as they shifted between us. "I see it in her eyes, in the way she speaks of you. You've given her a happiness that I cherish, even from afar."

A tension I hadn't realized I'd been holding eased, my heart swelling with emotion. I looked at Ethan, who still seemed to be grappling with everything, and I felt a pang of concern. "Are you okay?" I asked, my voice gentle.

Ethan glanced at me, his brow furrowing for a moment as he considered the weight of the situation. "I'm trying to be," he admitted, his voice thick with honesty. "It's a lot. But… I want to understand."

Elizabeth stepped back, giving him the space he needed, her expression tender. "I want you to understand, too," she said, her voice low but steady. "This—whatever this is between Molly and me—it's not meant to take anything away from what you share. It's simply… a different kind of connection. One that's been part of her life for years."

Ethan took a deep breath, his hand tightening around mine. "So, this has been going on for six years?"

Molly nodded, her voice soft as she responded. "Since the year we met."

Ethan let out a slow exhale, running a hand through his hair. "And you love her?"

Molly nodded again, her voice quieter now. "Yes. But I never wanted to hide this from you. I've just been scared—scared of what it might mean for us. I should have told you sooner."

Ethan's gaze flickered between the two of us, the weight of the years settling over him. "Six years," he muttered, shaking his head slightly. "I don't know how to wrap my head around it."

There was a long pause, the air thick with emotion. Finally, Ethan looked up at Elizabeth, his voice soft but firm. "I love her, you know. She's everything to me."

Elizabeth smiled, a gentle, understanding smile. "I know. And that's why I've wanted to meet you, Ethan. Because I see how much you mean to her."

He hesitated for a moment longer before nodding, his shoulders relaxing. "I don't know where this is going to go, but... I'm willing to try. For Molly. For us."

A wave of relief washed over me, and I squeezed his hand, gratitude welling up in my chest. "Thank you," I whispered.

Elizabeth stepped forward, her eyes locking onto

mine, and then back to Ethan. "This night is for all of us," she said, her voice soft but firm. "It's about understanding, about connection. I want you to stay, Ethan. I want you to see and be a part of this, because you're a part of Molly's heart, and that means you're part of mine, too."

Ethan took a deep breath, his gaze steady as he looked at her. "Alright," he said, his voice filled with quiet determination. "I'll stay."

Elizabeth's smile grew, warm and radiant. She turned to me, her hands finding mine again, her touch gentle but filled with a quiet strength. "Thank you," she whispered, her voice full of quiet joy. "For sharing this night with me. For allowing me to be part of your lives."

We stood there, the three of us, the air between us heavy with unspoken words but lightened by the shared understanding that had begun to form. It was a connection that bridged the gap between worlds, between relationships, something that went beyond the ordinary.

Elizabeth's radiant smile lingered as she took both my hands in hers, her touch firm but tender. Ethan stood beside me, the tension between them softening into something more open, more honest. The night air hummed with anticipation, but there was no rush. We were moving at our own pace, letting the

moment unfold naturally, slowly building the understanding we needed.

Elizabeth looked between us, her expression softening as if reading the silent agreement passing
between Ethan and me. "This night," she began, her
voice a quiet murmur, "is not just about me and
Molly. It's about you too, Ethan. We're all here, in this
moment, together."

Ethan nodded, his gaze meeting hers, and I could
feel the shift in him—something unspoken, but real.
He wasn't fully comfortable yet, but he was here, and
that mattered more than anything.

Elizabeth stepped forward again, her fingers
brushing lightly against Ethan's arm, as if testing the
waters. Ethan didn't pull away. Instead, he met her
touch, his breath hitching slightly but steady. They
held each other's gaze for a long, lingering moment,
a quiet understanding passing between them.

"I want this to be as much yours as it is ours," she
whispered, her voice low, almost reverent. "No rush,
no pressure. Just us. Together."

Ethan swallowed hard, his hand tightening in
mine before he let it go. "I'm... I'm still processing,"
he admitted, his voice low. "But I'm here. I'm with
you both."

Elizabeth smiled again, her gaze filled with
warmth, and she stepped back, creating space but

keeping the connection between us all alive. She reached for Ethan again, this time more confidently, her fingers trailing gently down his arm. He responded by stepping closer, his eyes flickering between us—between her and me.

Elizabeth's hand found his cheek, her thumb brushing over his skin in a slow, deliberate motion. "We'll take it as slow as we need to," she said softly. "There's no rush, Ethan."

He nodded, taking a deep breath as the tension between them seemed to melt away. Elizabeth looked back at me, her eyes dark and intense, and in that moment, something shifted. The air grew heavier, charged with something unspoken, something that ran deeper than the words we'd shared.

Elizabeth leaned in, her lips brushing mine softly at first, testing, tasting. I sighed into her touch, my body relaxing as she kissed me with a gentle urgency that made my heart race. The world narrowed to just the three of us—the weight of the moment sinking into every breath, every touch.

Ethan's hand found my waist, grounding me as Elizabeth deepened the kiss. My pulse quickened as the sensation of both of them so close, so intertwined with me, sent waves of heat through my body. I turned to Ethan, feeling the warmth of his gaze on me, and before I could think, I was kissing him too—

his lips eager, but tentative, as if still unsure, but needing this as much as I did.

Elizabeth pressed against my back, her lips trailing along my neck, her hands sliding down my sides. We moved together, our bodies intertwined, growing more urgent, more desperate. The heat between us was almost overwhelming—a potent mix of love, desire, and something deeper that connected us in a way I couldn't quite name.

Ethan's lips found mine next, and I kissed him with a hunger that surprised even me. My hands roamed over his chest, feeling the ruggedness of his skin beneath my fingertips. Elizabeth pressed against my back, her lips trailing along my neck, her hands sliding down my sides.

We moved together, our bodies intertwined, growing more urgent, more desperate. The heat between us was almost overwhelming—a potent mix of love, desire, and something deeper that connected us in a way I couldn't quite name.

Elizabeth's hands found their way under my shirt, exploring my body. I moaned into Ethan's mouth, my body arching toward them, craving more, needing more.

Ethan's hands joined hers, their touches blending together, creating a symphony of sensation that made me feel like I was floating. The three of us moved together, our breaths mingling, our bodies pressed so close that it was impossible to tell where one ended and the other began.

In that moment, surrounded by the two people I loved most in the world, I felt a sense of completeness, of utter fulfillment. The world outside the clearing ceased to exist, and all that mattered was this connection, this love, this shared moment of pure, unadulterated passion.

Elizabeth stepped back from the embrace, her movements deliberate and graceful. In one fluid motion, she let her dress fall to the ground, the silky fabric pooling around her feet. Her body, perfectly sculpted and glowing in the soft moonlight, was like an artwork come to life. Every curve, every line of her seemed crafted by some divine hand, and she moved with an otherworldly elegance that took my breath away.

She stepped out of her dress carefully, leaving it behind as she glided toward me, her eyes never leaving mine. The magnetic pull between us was undeniable, and I felt my heart pounding in my chest, my skin tingling with anticipation as she stopped inches from me, her gaze filled with intensity.

With slow, deliberate motions, Elizabeth reached out and brushed her fingers against the hem of my shirt. Her touch was feather-light as she began to lift the fabric, revealing inch by inch of my skin. The cool night air kissed my heated flesh, sending shivers through me. Her eyes followed the path of her hands, her lips curling into a satisfied smile as she exposed more of me.

Once my shirt was discarded, she wasted no time in finding the waistband of my pants. With practiced ease, she undid the button, her fingers brushing against my skin. Slowly, she slid the fabric down over my hips, her hands gliding along my legs as she helped me step out of them, leaving me bare before her.

Elizabeth stood once more, her hands roaming up my body, taking a moment to admire her work. The way she looked at me, as if I was something precious, made my heart swell with both lust and love. She leaned in, capturing my lips in a kiss that started soft but quickly grew more demanding. Her tongue teased mine, and her hands explored my now-exposed body with a sense of urgency.

I moaned into her mouth, responding to every touch. But even as the sensations overwhelmed me, I couldn't help but feel the tug of desire for the man standing just behind me. Ethan.

Elizabeth must have sensed it because she broke the kiss and turned her attention to Ethan, who was watching us intensely. She smiled—a slow, sultry curve of her lips—and reached out to him, beckoning him closer.

Ethan didn't hesitate. He stepped forward, his gaze shifting between the two of us. Elizabeth met him halfway, her hands sliding under his shirt as she pulled it up over his head in one fluid motion. She discarded it as easily as she had with mine, her hands already moving to his pants.

She undid the button with a flick of her fingers, her eyes locked on his as she slowly and deliberately slid the fabric down his legs. He stepped out of them, his breath catching as her hands skimmed over his thighs, teasing him just enough to make him groan with need.

Elizabeth's touch was as deliberate as it was gentle, savoring each moment as she built the excitement in both of us. Once Ethan was undressed, she stepped back, her eyes shifting between us, a look of pure satisfaction on her face.

"Perfect," she whispered, her voice like silk, before leaning in to kiss me again. This time, her hands roamed over my bare skin, exploring and teasing, while her other hand found Ethan's, guiding him closer.

Ethan pressed against my back, his chest warm and solid, his hands sliding around to rest on my hips as Elizabeth continued to kiss me, her tongue dancing with mine. The sensation of being with both of them, feeling both their hands on me, was nearly overwhelming in the most beautiful way. My knees buckled from the intensity of it all.

Elizabeth trailed kisses down my neck, nibbling gently at the sensitive skin as Ethan began kissing my back and shoulder. Their hands moved in unison— Elizabeth's fingers cupping my breasts, while Ethan's hands roamed lower, teasing the sensitive skin of my thighs.

I was lost in the sensation, my body responding to every kiss, every touch, every caress. Elizabeth's mouth found mine again, and this time, she pulled Ethan into the kiss as well, guiding his head toward mine until our lips met in a three-way kiss that was as hot as it was intimate.

Elizabeth left a trail of fire across my skin. Ethan followed her lead, his mouth finding my breast while Elizabeth's moved lower still, each kiss heightening the pleasure. My body was on fire.

"Shall we lay her down?" Elizabeth asked Ethan in a seductive whisper.

"Where?" he responded, his voice thick with desire.

They stood together, holding me between them, their movements synchronized as they carried me toward the altar. Behind the stone, the forest itself seemed to respond, and a bed began to take shape, as if conjured by the very magic of the woods. It was crafted from intertwining branches and twigs, woven together with an intricate elegance. Despite its delicate, stick-like appearance, the bed was impossibly soft when they laid me down upon it, cradling my body with a gentle embrace.

The forest had provided for us, shaping this bed from its own essence—a sanctuary woven from the earth and trees, as if it had been waiting for this very moment.

Elizabeth and Ethan stood over me, their eyes filled with desire, and I knew in that moment that what was about to happen would bind us together in ways that went beyond the physical, beyond the mundane world. This night, this love, would change everything.

And I was ready.

CHAPTER 10
ETHAN

ANY FEAR or trepidation I had felt melted away the instant I met Elizabeth. The moment our eyes locked, something deep within me shifted, like a puzzle piece snapping into place. It wasn't just that she was beautiful, though she was—in a way that defied description. It was the way she carried herself, how her presence filled the space around her, and the way she looked at me as if she already knew every corner of my soul.

As we laid Molly down on the bed the forest had created for us, I marveled at its delicate and perfect suitability for the moment. I could have questioned its magical appearance, but here I was, naked with a witch. Logic had already gone out the window. I felt a surge of emotion so powerful that it nearly took my breath away. I was in love with both of them, in love with the idea of sharing this night, and in love with the connection that had brought us all together.

Elizabeth turned to me, her eyes reflecting the flickering light of the candles surrounding us. There was warmth in her gaze, a shared understanding that this night was special—not just about the physical, but about the love that connected the three of us.

I leaned down and captured Elizabeth's lips in a kiss that was both tender and full of promise. Her response was immediate, her lips soft and yielding against mine, and I could feel the same excitement, the same anticipation building within her. My hand slid up her arms, feeling the smooth, cool skin beneath my fingertips.

Molly watched us with wide, expectant eyes. A flush colored her cheeks. Her chest rose and fell with each breath. I reached out, taking her hand in mine, and she squeezed it gently. Molly's touch grounded me, reminding me that this was real—that this was happening. "I love you," I whispered.

Molly smiled up at me, her eyes shining. "I love you too, Ethan." Then she turned her gaze to Elizabeth, who was watching us with a tender smile of her own. "And I love you," Molly added, her voice filled with the same warmth and affection.

Elizabeth leaned down, pressing a soft kiss to Molly's lips, her hand resting gently on her cheek.

The sight of them together filled me with a sense of peace and joy I hadn't known was possible. Every fear, every doubt, seemed to wash away.

I moved closer, my hands joining Elizabeth's as we began to explore Molly's body together. We were synchronized, each of us attuned to the other's needs and desires. The heat between us rose, Molly's body responding to every touch.

Elizabeth gently spread Molly's legs apart, exposing her wet hot center. "Look at that pussy," she said to me. "You want it, don't you?"

"Yes, I do," I said, and I did.

"Show me," Elizabeth said, a teasing edge to her voice. "Show me how much you want her pussy."

With urgency, I dove between Molly's legs, lapping at her folds. Her body retracted from me.

"Gently, Ethan," Elizabeth murmured. "I know you want her hard, but you have to treat her gently at first. Let me show you."

Elizabeth joined me, at Molly's center. She licked her thighs slowly and softly kissing her way to her center. Molly squeaked at the touch. Elizabeth stuck out her tongue, making gentle swirls up her leg toward her slit, only to veer away before reaching it. She made eye contact with me.

"You have to tease her a little," Elizabeth whispered, before returning to Molly. She licked her way back up to Molly's center, moving her mouth along Molly's folds. She found Molly's clit with her tongue. It swelled under her touch. Elizabeth moved her mouth over each side of Molly's lips, making her way to her clit with more intent. "Now you try," she said.

I mirrored Elizabeth's path up the opposite leg, swirling my tongue over Molly's folds, and then gently licking her clit with matching pressure.

"That's nice, isn't it, Molly?" Elizabeth asked.

"Oh gods, yes," Molly panted.

"How does she taste?" Elizabeth asked me.

"Like honey and vanilla bean," I replied.

Elizabeth rejoined me at Molly's center, and together we took turns lapping at her pussy, gradually increasing the intensity. Molly's gasps and moans filled the air, driving us to push her further, closer to the edge. Her body writhed beneath us, her hips bucking as she lost herself in the pleasure.

Elizabeth's hand tangled in Molly's hair as she leaned in to kiss her deeply, her tongue mirroring the motions we made below. I shifted, finding a rhythm that matched Elizabeth's perfectly. We alternated between teasing flicks and more intense strokes, Molly's moans growing louder with each moment. The taste of her, sweet and intoxicating, fueled my desire to give her everything.

Molly's body tensed as she neared her climax, her breath coming in ragged gasps. I glanced up, catching the look of pure bliss on her face, her eyes half-lidded as she surrendered to the sensation.

Elizabeth pulled back slightly, her lips brushing against Molly's skin. "Are you ready, my love? Ready to come for us?"

"Yes… oh gods, yes," Molly panted, her voice strained with the effort of holding back.

Elizabeth shot me a look, a wicked smile curving her lips. "Let's make her scream, shall we?"

Grinning, I adjusted myself and slid inside her. Elizabeth shifted, positioning herself above Molly's face, lowering her pussy onto Molly's mouth. As I began to move, Molly gasped from beneath Elizabeth.

I thrust my cock deeper. Molly's body arched beneath us, her cries growing louder and more desperate. We didn't let up, our movements more insistent, urging her toward release.

With a sharp cry, Molly's orgasm ripped through her, her body convulsing. We stayed with her, continuing our rhythmic movements as she rode out the waves of pleasure, her moans filling the night air.

Finally, when the last tremors had subsided, we both pulled back. Molly collapsed onto the bed, her chest heaving. She looked utterly spent, her skin flushed and covered in a sheen of sweat, but the smile on her face was one of pure satisfaction.

Elizabeth and I exchanged a look of shared triumph. I leaned in and pressed a soft kiss to Molly's lips, tasting Elizabeth on her mouth. "You're amazing," I whispered.

Molly opened her eyes, her face glowing with love and gratitude. "That was… incredible," she breathed, her voice barely audible.

I smiled and ran my fingers across her cheek. "And it's only the beginning, my love."

The heat between us began to rise again. I locked eyes with Molly and whispered, "Let's share her."

"Yes, please," Molly replied. Together, we maneuvered Elizabeth, spreading her legs. Molly took the lead, kissing and sucking at Elizabeth's body while Elizabeth let out a guttural almost primal moan that sent a surge of desire through me.

I positioned myself behind Molly, kissing her as she pleasured Elizabeth. My hand moved between Molly's legs, feeling the heat radiating from her.

"Can I fuck you?" I asked Molly, gently teasing her folds with my fingers.

"Yes, baby," she moaned, not stopping her attention on Elizabeth.

I slid my throbbing cock inside her. Thrusting into

Molly, I locked eyes with Elizabeth, who was on the brink of her own release.

Elizabeth moaned. The sensations consuming me. With one final thrust, I filled Molly with my seed, the release sending me over the edge. I howled, the sound echoing through the woods. A moment later, Elizabeth's cries joined mine as she climaxed.

The three of us collapsed onto the bed, our bodies tangled together, our breathing heavy as we came down from the high.

CHAPTER 11
MOLLY

THE FOREST SPARKLED with magic as I lay between my two loves. My head rested gently on Elizabeth's ample bosom, her heartbeat a soothing rhythm in my ear. My husband's chest supported my side, our legs intertwined in a perfect tangle of intimacy. The energy of the woods hummed softly around us, as if the very forest was alive with the aftermath of our ecstasy.

We lay in a cocoon of warmth and contentment, the world outside the clearing forgotten. Our breaths slowed as we basked in the afterglow. My body was heavy with the bliss of multiple orgasms. My skin still tingled with the memory of their touches, every kiss, every caress etched into my very soul.

"I could stay like this forever," I murmured, my voice a soft sigh as I nuzzled deeper into Elizabeth's chest, feeling the rise and fall of her breathing. "Here, in this place, with both of you."

Elizabeth's hand stroked my hair gently, her touch as tender as the love I felt radiating from her. "The love we share, the magic between us, amplifies everything, making the world more vivid and real. Remember this feeling, this moment, every day. Both of you. Until we meet again next year."

I sighed contentedly, closing my eyes as I soaked in the warmth of their bodies pressed against mine. "I've never felt so complete, so utterly fulfilled," I whispered, my heart swelling. "You both… are everything to me."

Elizabeth kissed the top of my head. "And you, my love, are everything to us. This night was a gift, a chance for us to be together in a way that transcends the ordinary."

I nodded, feeling the truth of her words deep in my bones. But even as I reveled in the bliss of the moment, a bittersweet awareness began to creep in— a reminder that this night, as perfect as it was, would pass too quickly. The candles around us flickered softly, their flames dancing in the gentle breeze that whispered through the trees, a silent countdown to the inevitable.

"This night always moves too quickly," I said, my voice laced with the melancholy that began to settle in my chest. "I wish we could make it last forever."

Elizabeth sighed, a sound filled with sadness. "I know, my love. I wish the same. But the magic that brings me here is tied to time, to the cycles of the seasons. Once the candles burn out, I shall return back to my reality too, where I will wait another year for you."

Ethan shifted beside me, his grip on my hand tightening slightly. "It's hard to imagine you not being here," he admitted. "After tonight, I can't imagine what it'll be like without you."

Elizabeth turned her head to look at him, her eyes soft but resolute. "I feel the same, Ethan. Being with both of you is everything I could ever want, but the forces that bind me are ancient and unyielding. When the time comes, I must return, no matter how much it pains me."

A tear slipped down my cheek, and Elizabeth brushed it away with the pad of her thumb, her touch gentle. "But we have this night," she continued. "This beautiful, magical night. And it's ours to cherish and hold onto when the year feels long."

Ethan pressed his lips to my temple. "We'll make the most of it," he whispered. "Every moment, every second."

We lay there in silence for a while. The forest

around us seemed to sense our quiet reflection, the rustling leaves and distant calls of nocturnal creatures providing a soothing backdrop to our thoughts. The cool night air tugged at my skin, but the shared warmth between us kept us comfortable.

"I'll carry this night with me," Elizabeth said finally, her words filled with resolve. "It will sustain me through the darkness, through the long wait until I can be with you *both* again."

I nodded, my heart aching at the thought of the time we'd have to spend apart. But I knew Elizabeth was right. This night was a gift, a moment to be savored and remembered.

The candles burned steadily, their flames gradually shrinking as the night wore on. I held onto both of them, my loves, feeling their warmth and presence, knowing this was where I belonged—here, between them, in this enchanted place. The stars twinkled above us, the forest humming with its quiet magic. And then, the candles burned out.

Elizabeth gradually dissolved into the night, her presence slipping away like a fading dream.

I rolled over, burying my face in Ethan's chest as tears began to flow. He responded by gently threading his fingers through my hair, offering what comfort he could. The pain of her departure was sharp, but this time, it felt a little more bearable because I had Ethan by my side.

Ethan, who had also fallen for the passionate and enigmatic Elizabeth, would be grappling with her absence just as much as I would. I knew he would miss her, perhaps as strongly as I did. I squeezed him tighter, and he responded in kind.

It would be our shared burden to bear, as we would both be haunted by her absence.

IF YOU ENJOYED *HAUNTED* by *Her* you might enjoy *Three of Swords* from my Tarot Fantasies series.

Heartbreak, betrayal, and a love that defies death.

LARISSA:

I thought a tarot reading would be harmless—a fun way to spend the afternoon.

But drawing the Three of Swords turned my life upside down.

Now, I'm caught between two irresistible vampires and facing a danger I never saw coming.

Love, heartbreak, and a battle for survival...

I didn't ask for this, but I can't turn back now.

All I can do is follow my heart, even if it leads me into the darkness.

. . .

IN THE ARCANE ROOM, *where every tarot card reveals a hidden truth, Larissa faces her deepest fears and desires.*

Larissa never imagined a tarot reading would change her life forever. But when the Three of Swords card emerges, it catapults her into a night filled with unexpected encounters and dangerous revelations. Drawn into the dark, seductive world of vampires, Larissa finds herself falling for Vlad, an enigmatic stranger, and Natasha, a powerful vampiress with secrets of her own.

But as ancient feuds resurface, Larissa is forced to confront the painful truths she's been running from. With hunters closing in, she must decide if she's willing to risk everything for a love that promises both salvation and heartbreak. In a world where nothing is as it seems, will she find the strength to choose love over fear?

Unveil the mysteries of the Tarot Fantasies series with *Three of Swords*, a story of passion, intrigue, and the courage to face your own darkness.

SIGN up for my newsletter and get a free book today!

JAX WILDER

https://mailchi.mp/158597581671/jax-wilder

ALSO BY JAX WILDER

Sleighed by Love

Harvesting Love

Dawning Desire

Knead You Now

Love Rewound

Perfect Lover Spell

Haunted by Her

TAROT FANTASIES SERIES

The Devil's Temptations

Strength of the Beast

Hanged Passions

Six of Cups

Death's Embrace

Queen of Pentacles

Seven of Pentacles

Ace of Wands

Three of Swords

Two of Swords

Lovers In The Veil

LORELAI HAMILTON

Encyclopedia of Divination

Encyclopedia of Cryptids

Tarot Tales and Magic Spells

Teenage Tarot

Arcane In Verse

The Eclectic Witch's Grimoire

Teenage Witch's Grimoire

Find Your Bliss

Tarot Reflection Journal

Tarot Refection Journal Coloring The Tarot

Dream Journal

MIRANDA LEVI

From A Youth A Fountain Did Flow

The Sea Withdrew

A Tear In Time

Mo(ther) Na(ture)

In Orion's Hands

JACKSON ANHALT

From The 911 Files

ISLA WATTS

A Fairy Bad Day

Surprise! You're a Vampire

Gorgeous, Gorgeous, Gorgons

Mork The Handsome Orc

Adopted By Werewolves

Bite Me If You Can

That's The Spirit!

ROSE DAWSON'S BOOK JOURNALS:

My Time With The Fairies

Enchanted Escapades

Enchanted Escapades

Dewey Decimal Diaries

Siren's Songbook

Pride and Prejudice

Bibliophile's Bounty

Book of Books Journal

Pages & Passages Reading Journal

Bookworm's Companion Reading Journal & Tracker

ABOUT THE AUTHOR

Jax Wilder is a passionate romance author hailing from a charming small town nestled in the picturesque Pacific Northwest. With a heart full of love and an unyielding belief in the power of happily ever afters, Jax weaves enchanting tales of love and connection that leave readers captivated.

Jax's novels are a reflection of her commitment to celebrating the magic of love, and her characters' journeys mirror the warmth and happiness she has found in her own life. Join her on the enchanting journey of love, passion, and enduring connection through her heartfelt romance novels.

www.ingramcontent.com/pod-product-compliance
Lightning Source LLC
Chambersburg PA
CBHW020418030726
47495CB00006B/1570